SIR,
YES
Sir

By: *Mike*
WARREN

Author of A Private Affair and Sweet Swagger

Life Changing Books in conjunction with Power Play Media
Published by Life Changing Books
P.O. Box 423 Brandywine, MD 20613

Library of Congress Cataloging-in-Publication Data;

www.lifechangingbooks.net
13 Digit: 978-1934230329
10 Digit: 1-934230324

DEDICATION

    I would like to dedicate this book to Mr. Kevin Whitley, for if it wasn't for him, I would not be a writer today. Rest in Peace my friend…

ACKNOWLEDGEMENTS

I'm not going to mention a whole lot of people in this acknowledgement because if I do, this section would be as long as the book itself! But there are a few I must give a shout out to.

Thanks to my Lord and Savior, Jesus Christ because through Him, all things are possible.

To my family who has been my biggest supporters thank you for your encouragement, love and patience.

To my friends, Gab, thank you for having my back and keeping a brotha grounded. To Andrew, thank you my brotha for what they call good ole southern hospitality. To Perry, thank you for the sightseeing tour of the south.

To Vodrey Miller, thank you…thank you…thank you. To all my friends and co-workers in Columbia, SC and Charlotte, NC, thank you for the support when I needed it the most.

To all the book stores, book clubs, radio shows and online shows, thank you for your love and support as well.

To all the writers out there that have become colleagues and friends of mine, hang in there, our time is now.

To my LCB family, thank you guys for allowing me to have creative freedom in my stories. You guys are awesome!!!!!!

To those of you who have read this manuscript before it came into print and said to me, "No, you didn't," I say to them, "YES, I DID!!!"

And last but not least, to my friend...partner...companion...confidant, Anthony L. Parker aka "Punkin" lol. What can I say about this muthafucka here? Lol. Thank you for your love and patience. While I sometimes bitch & complain, thank you for reminding me to write when I sometimes get side tracked. Even though it might not be written down, it's all up in my head. Now, let's go eat! Kekekekeke.

Mike Warren

becool031@yahoo.com
www.myspace.com/mikewarrentheblack1
mhill031@gmail.com
www.facebook.com/mikewarren
www.twitter.com/becool031
www.lifechangingbooks.net
www.mikewarren.yolasite.com

The First Epistle of
JOHN

John: 1:08 If we say that we have no sin, we deceive ourselves, and the truth is not in us.

The Holy Bible
In
The King James Version

Chapter ONE

Over the next thirty minutes or so, and drinking to the point of becoming drunk along with drowning my sorrow, I heard my name being paged over the speaker system. At that moment, I knew the person I was waiting for had finally arrived. I couldn't have been happier.

I stumbled a little getting out of my seat from the bar and thought, *Okay Sean, get it together.* I got my bearings, and straightened out my dress green Army uniform. My focus was to meet the brotha that was going to share his life with me while being on tour in Hawaii. Suddenly, I began to have second thoughts, *Was this really what I wanted to do? Did I really need to bring someone with me considering I had just buried my wife a few months ago? The man I fell in love with had gotten married and started a family of his own.* All these thoughts raced in and out of my head, but as soon as I approached him and saw him smiling from ear to ear, I knew I had made the right decision.

"I'm glad you made it on time," I said, helping him with his luggage.

"What, no hug, no kiss?" he asked pouting.

1

I honestly wanted to do more than that but considering where we were, I placed his luggage onto the floor and hugged him as tight as I could. At that moment, Southwest Airlines had just announced the boarding of flight 1271, destination Honolulu, Hawaii.

"Is that our flight?" he asked looking up at me lovingly.

"Yeah, come on, let's go!" I replied, picking up his bags.

We raced toward AB Pier where Southwest Airlines was located and fortunately, there were no lines and we made it through security without a hitch. We boarded our plane and I took the seat next to the window. There's something about looking out the window as the plane takes off the runway and leaving the ground that excites me. I'm not talking about becoming aroused; I'm just talking about the sudden drop the plane makes as it leaves the ground.

"You okay, Sean?"

"Yeah, I'll be okay," I replied while making myself comfortable for the ten hour flight.

"You sure? You seem troubled."

"Look Gabe, I don't know what the future has in store for us but I'm willing to find out. Why, are you having second thoughts?" I asked, looking into his eyes.

"Not at all, it's just that you've been through a lot and I don't want you to have any regrets. I mean, this is a big deal. Are you really ready for all this?"

"Do you love me?"

"You know I do, I wouldn't be here if I didn't. The question is, do you?" Gabe asked with a raised eyebrow.

It took me a minute or so to answer his question because I had to seriously think about it. I tried to compare the love I had for Cameron versus what I felt for him. And there was definitely a difference. I loved Gabe but I was in love with Cam.

"You must not be if it's taking you that long to answer the question, Sean."

"Will you stop worrying, I do love you and besides, it's

too late now because we're about to take off," I replied with a chuckle. Although, I could see that Gabe didn't find it funny in the least, I was only trying to lighten the mood.

After a few hours in flight, I had managed to reassure Gabe of the love I had for him as well as trying to get him to relax. I didn't know he had a problem with flying. He had informed me about his near death experience while flying a few years ago. He stated while flying to Chicago for a preaching engagement, the plane had to land suddenly because the aircraft was losing fuel. He'd seen so many movies where planes had to make sudden landings and in most cases, the plane never made it safely to the ground that he literally started peeing in his pants. Personally, I thought the shit was funny so I started laughing. Again, he didn't find that to be funny either.

I also informed Gabriel about the altercation I had with Mr. Lomax back at BWI Airport. He was already aware of the cards, pictures and texts that were sent to me. Mr. Lomax was a sick fuck because he'd now begun sending me the same crazy ass pictures of my now deceased wife, Venus, who'd died giving birth to my baby girl. Pictures of her as she lay dead in her coffin surfaced. Gabe just didn't know who had sent them, but once I told him that it was Mr. Lomax, for some reason he found that to be funny. I can see now that we have a difference of opinion as to what is funny and what ain't!

******

At 7:05 p.m. Pacific Standard Time we made our descent on the island of Oahu. Before coming here, I searched for as much information as I could about Hawaii and I learned that there were seven different islands; Kauai, Hawaii, Molokai, Lanai, Maui, Kahoolawe and the island of Oahu. Oahu was the island that most visitors enjoyed. It was the island that housed the city of Honolulu and Waikiki Beach. Sitting next to the window, I could see the island of Oahu as we approached and it was magnificent. I had never in my life seen aqua blue water other than on television but under me was the Pacific Ocean and it was as blue as the skies. We were so close to it as we were descending that I could actually see the coral reefs under the water.

"Gabe, can you see this?" I asked with excitement in my voice.

"I'd rather not," he replied with his eyes shut tight.

"Gabe, open your eyes. You have to see this, it's beautiful man."

"Just tell me once we've landed," he spat with his eyes still closed.

"Ah, this is your Captain speaking and we're finally making our descent on the island of Oahu. If you look out the left window, you'll be able to see the entire island and its beauty. It is currently 7:10 p.m. You may want to change the time on your watches and it's a beautiful 83 degrees with the winds coming from the south east at about five miles an hour. We'll be landing in just a few moments and we hope you enjoy your stay in Honolulu, Hawaii."

All I can say is that the scenery was breathtaking. The architecture of the buildings was out of this world, I thought, as I continued to stare in awe. What I found to be so different and strange was that the color of the buildings weren't your regular brownish-off-white color. The buildings were pastel colors. Some were painted powder-blue, mint-green, light-pink, and orange. I mean, these buildings were made up from the colors of the rainbow. I couldn't help but laugh to myself, thinking that since the rainbow symbol was symbolic for being gay, the architect had to be gay, there was no doubt in my mind.

Within minutes, our plane finally landed and people seemed to be in a hurry to get off the plane. *I guess people didn't want to waste a minute of their vacation time,* I thought as I informed Gabe that he could finally open his eyes.

As we made our way into the Honolulu International

Airport lobby, just like they have on the commercials, there was this Hawaiian dude playing his ukulele and this kid playing a serious beat on his bongo drum and four beautifully tanned Hawaiian honeys grinding their hips from side to side doing their welcoming hula dance. I placed my bags down beside me and watched these honeys do their thang. Hell, to be honest, I was getting a boner just standing there watching them. I knew right then and there before I left Hawaii for good, I was gonna fuck me a Hawaiian bitch, and that you can bet on! I even started to join in on their lil dance as one of them began to approach me and placed a lei around my neck. As for Gabe, he just stood there sucking his teeth like he was totally bored.

"Come on Gabe, join the party, man!" I yelled while grinding my shit up on one of the Hawaiian dancers.

My shit was so hard, I swear, I could have fucked her right then and there and she knew my shit was hard too, because she kept looking over her shoulder, smiling and shit, saying something in Hawaiian. For all I know, she could have been calling me all kinda niggas but I didn't give a shit. Shawty was phyne as hell. Olive-tanned skin, 5'2, couldn't have weighed no more than a buck, jet black hair that fell down to her round, shapely booty, slanted blue eyes and couldn't be a day over twenty-one, but legal, know what I mean?

After twenty minutes or so of getting my cheap thrill from this Hawaiian honey, who I found out that her name was Anela, I slipped her my number and asked her to call me when she was ready for the real thing. Now, I know I was wrong for doing that. Poor Gabe just stood there and watched the whole time while I got my mack on.

"Ah Sean, don't you think it's time for us to go check in the hotel?" Gabe asked with a slight attitude.

Of course I didn't blame him for that, I guess I deserved it but the more I thought about fucking one of these Hawaiian honeys, the more I realized the last time I even had some pussy was from Cat and that was more than a month or so ago. So, I wanted and needed some pussy, bad!

******

Gabe and I caught a taxi and were finally dropped off at The Royal Hawaiian Hotel, located on Kalakaua Avenue. What surprised me most about the hotel other than it being such a huge luxurious hotel was that the building was painted a bright ass pink. You couldn't miss it if you wanted to. The Royal Hawaiian Hotel stood directly across from Waikiki Beach. We exited the taxi and entered the hotel and just as we walked up to the check-in counter, we were greeted with, "Aloha and welcome to the Royal Hawaiian Hotel," some lil Asian guy stated.

"Ah yes, my name is Sean Mathews and I have a reservation here for the entire week," I replied giving him my driver's license and credit card.

After a minute or two, he found my reservation on the computer, swiped my credit card and gave me my room number and key.

"Here you go, Sir. Your room number is 313 and if you need anything, anything at all, please don't hesitate to call on me."

As I reached for the key, my license and credit card, I thought to myself, *Dayum, was shawty flirting or what?*

Gabe and I grabbed our bags and made our way to the elevator. We reached the third floor and found our room, which was the last one on the left hand side down this long hallway. I slid the card into the door and it opened and to my surprise, the room or should I say suite, was beautiful. The floor was covered with a wall to wall Asian style rug, a small chandelier hanging from the ceiling; there was a sitting area which had a plush, latte-colored sofa and two wingback latte and periwinkle chairs. There was also a small kitchen with a stove, refrigerator, and small granite top table with four chairs. The bedroom was on a platform where you walked up three steps and dead in the middle was a king size bed. Gabe placed his bags down on the floor, ran and jumped right up on the bed.

"Hey, Sean, let's have sex," he said, taking his clothes off while rolling around on the bed.

Well, needless to say, I was already horny as shit from humping on shawty earlier at the airport. But here comes a moment of truth for me.

I don't want to have sex with a brotha, when I know I'm feigning to be wit a bitch! I know some people might not understand that but I can't make that any clearer. Of course some brothas feel as though a nut is a nut, I'm not one of them. I want what I want when I want it. Also, as much as I enjoyed being wit Gabe, we've never had intercourse. Let me say that again, we've never had intercourse, and I'm in the mood to do some serious fucking. Gabe and I have bumped and grinded and have done a lot of oral sex but I have never penetrated him and truth be told, we really never discussed it. I know you're thinking, as much as I like to fuck, why would I bring someone six thousand miles and not at least be able to hit the booty?

"Sean, did you hear what I said?" Gabe asked while lying on his side totally nude.

"Oh, my bad," I replied holding onto my stomach while sitting on the side of the bed, acting like I wasn't feeling well.

Dayum shame, our first night in Paradise Island and here I was faking an illness. Now I guess I know how some women feel.

"You okay?" Gabe asked sounding concerned.

"Naw, not really," I replied while lying down on the bed.

Gabe, being the nurturer that he was, took my clothes off and took my temperature with the back of his hand. I gathered he thought I had a slight temperature, so he got me a cold wash cloth, placed it on my forehead and tucked me in for the evening. Deep down inside, I laid there feeling bad, not for me but for him. I tossed and turned most of the night thinking about my sexuality.

Was I truly gay? No, I don't think so. Am I homosexual?

7

Oh, Hell No! During these past couple of years, I have come to learn that being gay doesn't necessarily mean that you're homosexual and vice versa. I know most straight/gay people think that being one does mean being the other, but that's not true at all. In past years, brothas who are in the life argue that being gay is just that, a lifestyle. Meaning, hanging out in gay bars, living in gay areas, and having nothing but gay friends, that is not me. And according to Webster's Dictionary, a homosexual is having sex with the same sex, that's not me either. Besides, how could I be either one when it's not a lifestyle for me nor do I have sex with just dudes?

About an hour later of racking my brain about who and what I am, I looked over at Gabe who was sleeping like a baby. I know he didn't plan on spending his first night in Hawaii without us being intimate, so this should have been a warning sign for us both!

Chapter TWO

I woke up the next morning at 4:30 a.m. sharp. I took a shower, got into my fatigue uniform, and kissed Gabe on the forehead. I left one of my credit cards on the nightstand, since I didn't have much cash on me, grabbed my duffle bag and by six a.m., I was reporting to my new duty station, in Fort Shafter Hawaii. Fortunately, Ft. Shafter was only three blocks up the street from The Royal Hawaiian Hotel. That's why I made the reservations there even though they were a little more expensive, it was closer to the base and I wasn't about to carry my heavy ass duffle bag with all my military gear in it, but so far.

I walked inside 25th A.G. Head Quarters and informed the specialist at the desk who I was, along with giving him my orders.

"Okay, Specialist Mathews have a seat and I'll let Commander Hernandez know you're here," he said gesturing to a sitting area.

I took a seat in the sitting area as I was told and all I could think about is now a Puerto Rican or as we call them at home, Spain-u-Rican was going to be my new Commander. Don't get me wrong, I'm not prejudice or anything, I just like the name Spain-u-Rican betta because most times those that are

Puerto Rican ain't Puerto Rican at all. Besides, whether they were from Puerto Rico, Spain, Mexico or New York, the term Spain-u-Rican included all of them.

"Ah Specialist Mathews, Commander Hernandez will see you now," the specialist stated while snapping me outta my thoughts.

I got up from my seat and entered Commander Hernandez's office and stood at parade rest in front of his shiny cherry wood desk.

"Good morning, Specialist Mathews," he stated with an accent while looking closely at my orders.

"Good morning to you too, Sir," I replied while smiling to myself. Now, that I was a Sir too being in the Sirs & Boys Inc. SBI for short, maybe he should be calling me Sir as well!

"Ah, what is your MOS, Specialist Mathews?"

"75WD5, Sir," I answered proudly.

"And what is that again?"

My intuition told me something was gonna happen that I wouldn't like, considering Commander Hernandez didn't seem to know what my Military Operation Specialty, also known as MOS was.

"I'm an admin specialist Sir, who specializes in Sidpers. Meaning, I place all new recruits on an alpha roster Sir," I stated as intelligently as I could.

"Oh, I see. Well, Specialist Mathews, I don't think we have a position for one of those at the moment. Please, have a seat in the outer office and let me check on that and I'll get back with you as soon as I find out."

"Yes, Sir," I stated while doing an about face and returning to the outer office as instructed.

However, I wanted to punch Commander Hernandez right in his ugly ass face. As I took my seat, all I kept doing was praying that they find me a position right here at Ft. Shafter but word had it that when blacks came to Hawaii for their tour, they always got shipped off to Schofield Barracks. Why, you ask?

Being stationed in Ft. Shafter was pure heaven. The base sat right across from Waikiki Beach and was centered right downtown. You could take your one hour lunch, grab a quick bite and cruise the beach, all at the same time. Working at Ft. Shafter was like working a regular civilian nine to five type job with perks of phyne men and women tourists all around you.

Schofield Barracks, on the other hand, was an Infantry Unit! Need I say more? Well, perhaps I do. Schofield Barracks is a grunt unit that was located 15 miles or so out in the boon docks. Although it sat across from Wheeler Air force base, which had a serious Non Commissioners Officers Club, or so I heard and a small town called Wahiawa right outside the base but aside from that, there was nothing else there. Schofield Barracks, being an infantry unit was the first military base that was called upon during war-time. Since the war in Iraq, thousands of brothas have been called upon to do their civic duty. I for one, wasn't about to go to Iraq to fight a war I had nothing to do with!

Don't get me wrong, I wasn't scared, well maybe a lil but I still didn't want to go fight in some white mans' war! Not to mention that as an Infantry Unit, there was constant physical training, constant qualifying with your M-16 weapon, cleaning of your weapon, and field duty, which consisted of staying out in the field for days at a time and reenacted as though you were at war! Ah, I don't think so. I guess being at Ft. Meade for the past two years had spoiled me.

"Ah, Specialist Mathews, Commander Hernandez will see you now," the specialist at the counter stated while interrupting my thoughts once again.

I walked inside of Commander Hernandez's office and stood at parade rest. "Well Specialist Mathews, I made some calls and it appears that we don't have any positions available here in your field." At that moment I could have shitted bricks because I knew what was coming next. "However, we do have several positions for a Sidpers Analyst out in Schofield Barracks," he stated as though I didn't know that Schofield Barracks was a hell hole.

I had to think of something quick because Schofield Barracks was not for me. "Well, Sir, if you don't mind, I'm still an admin specialist as well. So if I can stay here and work under that MOS, I would appreciate that," I replied sounding desperate as though my life depended on it. And it did.

"Unfortunately, Specialist Mathews we don't have an opening for that either. As you can see, we aren't that big of a military unit," he replied while picking up the phone on his desk. "Ah, have Private Salgado bring the jeep around. I need him to take Specialist Mathews up to Schofield Barracks right away."

Dayum, my life seemed to flash before me in an instant. I thought to myself, *if I was white or Spain-u-Rican, my ass wouldn't be going up to no Schofield Barracks, racist muthafuckas.* For the third time this morning, I was asked to sit in the outer office and wait until my ride came for me. After waiting for fifteen minutes or so, I was approached by this phyne Spain-u-Rican asking if I was Specialist Mathews.

"Yes, I am," I replied while looking up at him.

"I'm PFC Salgado, and I'll be giving you a ride up to Schofield Barracks," he stated while reaching his hand out to shake mine.

"Cool and thanks," I replied while standing up and taking his smooth hand into mine.

The electricity that surged through my body was incredible. I looked into his eyes and noticed he too was staring into mine and I knew he felt it, too. I smiled to myself thinking about the "Ray" movie and how Ray Charles would determine whether he was interested in a woman by the feel of her wrist but with me; it was just a simple handshake. I could definitely tell whether a dude was down or not and PFC. Salgado was definitely down. I just had to find out while riding to tired ass Schofield Barracks.

"Is this your duffle bag?" he asked while picking it up to carry for me.

"Yes, it is and thanks."

We walked outside to his jeep and pulled off. With everything happening so fast, I forgot all about Gabe at the hotel. I definitely needed to call him once I got to my new duty station and report in.

"So, where you coming in from Specialist Mathews," the sexy, Spain-u-Rican asked, trying to make chit-chat conversation.

"You don't have to call me Specialist Mathews, my name is Sean and I'm coming from Ft. Meade, Maryland," I responded, slightly flirting while looking at him out of the corner of my eye.

"And I'm Edwin but peeps call me Eddie," he stated with a sexy accent while extending his hand once again.

"Eddie Salgado, hmmm, I like that," I replied while shaking his hand once again. And just like a few minutes before, I felt the same surge and by the look in his face, so did he.

"You gonna let my hand go, Sean?" he asked, smiling at me while trying to keep his eyes on the road.

"Oh, my bad," I replied, letting go of his hand.

Eddie was indeed one of the finest Puerto Ricans I had ever seen. Of course by now, I'm referring to him as a Puerto Rican. Eddie was truly in a class by himself. We of course had some at Ft. Meade, but most of them looked more like dirty-ass Mexicans than Puerto Ricans. Eddie couldn't be older than twenty-three. His lips were shaped perfectly as though a sculptor had molded them onto his olive smooth face. Deep, dark eyes with thick eyebrows and long eye lashes, he also had a small scar on the right side of his face that made me wonder how it got there.

Eddie stood about 5'6 and weighed about 140. "A *perfect lil shawty, just how I like 'em,*" I said to myself. The crazy thing is, the longer I looked at Eddie, the more he reminded me

13

of a mixture between Cameron and myself. In other words, if Cam and I could have had a child, Eddie would have been it. We had the same forehead, eyes, nose and swagger. I think Eddie noticed our similarities as well because he kept starring at me out of the corner of his eye. Oh, and let me not forget, when Eddie walked in front of me to get in the jeep, I noticed that he definitely had back. He would have gotten that from Cameron, along with Cameron's long, curly hair.

"So, what are you thinking about, Sean?"

Avoiding his question, I decided to ask, "So, where do you go to hang out?" See, this question is twofold; it tells me where the hot spots are as well as lets me know whether he will be honest enough to include any gay spots, hence letting me know what he's all about.

"Well, that depends on what you're looking for."

"Okay, well what do you look for when you go out?" I asked, throwing the question back at him.

"Sometimes just to party and other times to get my freak on, just depends."

"So, where do you go to party?"

"Well, there's club Zanzabar, which is a pretty nice spot. The music is hot and they love to party."

"Where do you go to get your freak on?" I noticed he seemed to hesitate in answering while looking around as though we were being monitored or something.

"Is something wrong?" I asked.

"No, but I don't know you like that. Besides you expect me to tell you all about who and what I do to get my freak on. For all I know, you could be working undercover and shit…"

I don't know what it was about this brotha that was turning me the fuck on so much. I suppose it was because he kept reminding me of Cam and me. What I also found interesting was that I could be turned on by someone that reminded me of myself. I know that might sound kinda strange but I believe that is something that you learn more and more about yourself dealing in this kinda lifestyle. I also noticed that Eddie had some feminine ways by the way he spoke, which definitely reminded me of Cam, but with an accent.

By this point, I had a hard-on just by watching and listening to Eddie go on and on about who the fuck I thought I was and for all he knew, I could be working undercover for the Commander. Therefore, already knowing what Eddie was all about and to prove to him that I wasn't working undercover, I did the only thing I could do to show I was definitely interested in getting my freak on.

"So, you still think I'm undercover?" I asked while unbuttoning my fatigue pants and pulling out my swollen ten inch dick.

I knew I caught Eddie off guard because he began to swerve a lil and started speaking in Spanish and laughing while watching me stroke myself. I didn't understand what he was saying but fortunately there were no other cars close by because we were on some highway heading towards the boon docks. But I could tell he was enjoying the view by the way his eyes seemed to glisten and the way he licked his lips. Needless to say, I'm proud of my shit and after jerking off during my Sir of the Year Contest a month or so ago, while in Baltimore, this was nothing.

"Damn, Poppy, you got it like that?" he asked smiling from ear to ear.

I couldn't help but laugh at his question because it really did make me think of Cameron, just by him calling me poppy. Poppy was Cameron's favorite name for me.

"Now you know, now what?" I asked putting my shit back in my pants.

"When you wanna hang out, Poppy?"

"I enjoy getting my freak on, so how about this weekend?"

Before I got a response, we were now turning into the base of Schofield Barracks. Dayum, this ride just wasn't long enough for me to find out a lil bit more about this Eddie Salgado person.

"Well, Sean, I guess this is your new home for a while," Eddie stated as he stopped right in front of the huge red, white, and blue sign that read: 25th A. G. Infantry, Home of the Brave.

"Again, how about this weekend?" I asked getting out of his jeep.

"Give me your number and I'll call you."

I grabbed my duffle bag out of the back seat and walked around to the driver side, "You have a cell phone on you?" I asked while looking around hoping no one was in ear shot of our conversation.

"Shoot," Eddie said while pulling out his cell phone.

"443-555-8277 and don't forget to use it," I whispered in my sexiest tone while smiling and showing off my dimples.

"I'll call you later, Poppy," he said backing up his jeep and then pulling off.

I stood on the sidewalk and watched as Eddie drove off, wishing that I too was going back to Ft. Shafter but instead, I was getting the shaft by being here at Schofield Barracks. I picked up my duffle bag and walked into Command Headquarters.

"Yes, my name is Specialist Mathews. I believe Commander Hernandez called up here to let someone know of my arrival," I said, informing the female private that stood behind the desk.

"Yes, Specialist Mathews, the Commander spoke to Captain Richardson and informed him that you were coming. However, Captain Richardson had to leave and go to an Officer's meeting but he told me that you could just take the day off and settle in. But, make sure you make the six a.m. formation right out front."

"So, where do I stay?"

"Oh, I'm sorry, you're in room 626 with Harrison," she said, pulling the information up from her computer.

"With who?" I asked making sure I heard her correctly.

Now, I know there are more people in this world with the last name Harrison, but I knew this couldn't be the same Harrison from Ft. Meade that Thomas and I had a threesome with, I thought to myself.

"Sp. Chuck Harrison, he just arrived here yesterday from Ft. Meade as well," she replied, looking his information up on her computer. "Do you know him?" she asked, looking at me smiling and shit as though we were going to have some kinda family reunion. I couldn't believe that fat ass Harrison was not only here at Schofield Barracks but was also gonna be my fucking roommate! As if this day couldn't get any worse!

"Ah, by chance, would there be any other space available?" I asked, hoping that I wouldn't have to deal with Harrison at all.

"No, I'm sorry. As a matter fact, that's the last bed available here in this entire quad."

"But Harrison is a MP, why would MP's be sharing a room with administrative personnel?"

"As I stated before Sp. Mathews, this entire quad is full. Why, you guys don't get along or something?" Nosey Nora asked.

"Forget it. Can I just get my key to the room please?" I asked becoming irritated.

Chapter THREE

The rooms were located alongside the Headquarters building, so I had no problem in finding my room 626. I didn't know if Harrison was in the room or not, so I decided to knock on the door. After knocking a few times and there was no answer, I used my key to open the door.

Fortunately, Harrison was not there. I looked around the room and I must admit, Harrison kept it quite clean and orderly. He had apparently taken the bed on the right side of the wall because there were a few of his personal belongings on them, such as a teddy bear and a red, heart-shaped pillow. The room itself was about 12x15 in size, very military and very basic with a bed on the left side of the wall with a small desk and a locker and the same thing on the right side of the wall, bed, desk and locker. Harrison also had a small TV as well as a small Bose sound system that sat on his desk. I knew he just bought the shit because the price tag was still stuck to both of the items. That's the one thing Harrison had going for himself. He wasn't much to look at being fat, black and ugly but the brotha had money all the time. Mainly because he came from money, his parents were what you called, well-to-do.

I remembered Thomas telling me once that the only reason Harrison joined the Army was because his parents told him they would cut him off if he didn't do something with his life. They gave him two choices, get a real job or join the Army. Since Harrison only had a high school diploma and really couldn't get a good job, other than working for McDonalds, he chose the latter.

I sat on the bed belonging to me, remembering the last time I saw Harrison at Thomas' funeral. I had moved on with the beef I had with him over Thomas and him stalking me but, I wasn't sure he had moved on even though he showed up at Thomas' funeral with a date. So, I definitely had to be ready for his fat ass, just in case he wanted to start some shit.

As I began unpacking my duffle bag, my cell phone began to vibrate. "Hello," I answered without looking at the caller I.D.

"Hey, Poppy," the caller stated.

The signal wasn't that clear and so I couldn't make out the voice. I looked at the caller I.D. and still didn't recognize the number. "Who is this?" I snapped.

"Damn, Poppy, don't bite my head off just yet, this is Eddie," he replied with a chuckle.

"Oh, hey you," I replied in a softer tone, knowing that I had this lil Puerto Rican brotha hooked already. Hell, it hadn't even been an hour and he calling me already.

"So, how is Schofield Barracks treating you?"

"It's hard to say, considering I just got here. But I've already been confronted with one surprise."

"And what's that?" he asked sounding concerned.

"It's not important. I'll tell you about it when we hook up," I replied in a nonchalant tone.

"Okay, so what time you get off from work?"

"I don't know. Captain Richardson gave me the day off so I can settle in, why?"

"You wanna go to the beach?" he asked, surprising me.

"The beach, aren't you at work?"

"I came back to the base and Commander Hernandez had to go to some officer's meeting that's going to be all day. And since I'm his personal driver that gives me the day off."

"Wow, must be nice. How can I get a job like you have?" I asked laughing and thinking what kinda meeting these officers were going to.

"So, do you want to go with me?"

"Sure, why not."

"Okay, I'll pick you up in say, forty-five minutes."

"I'll be ready."

I unpacked the rest of my belongings that were in my duffle bag and changed into a wife-beater, shorts and some sandals. I know I was wrong for doing what I was about to do considering poor Gabe was down at the hotel all alone but to be honest; I wanted to see and feel what Private Eddie Salgado had to offer. I flipped my phone open to call Gabe and let him know what happened. He picked up on the 3rd ring.

"Hello," he replied sounding like he was just waking up.

"Hey you," I replied in a sexy tone.

"Who's this," he stated as though he didn't know who I was.

"Stop playing Gabe, the shit ain't funny," I spat with attitude.

"I'm just playing, Sean," he chuckled.

"Are you still in bed?"

"Yeah, what time is it?"

"9:45."

I began explaining to Gabe what happened and since I was going to be stationed all the way up here at Schofield Barracks and didn't have any transportation to get back and forth, I had no other choice but to stay up here for the week. I couldn't help but smile to myself because this situation was somewhat similar to when I stayed down at Fort Meade and got my groove on while Venus stayed in Baltimore. I continued to ex-

21

plain, that in the mean time, I would find an apartment for us in this area. Now, of course, I could've rented a car, taken a taxi if need be, but hey, it sounded good to me. Besides, I was gonna be footing the bill for the hotel as well as finding and paying for an apartment, so what could he say? Uncle Sam calls and he takes precedence, right?

"So, I won't see you for a whole week?" Gabe asked sounding sad.

"The room there is paid for up until Sunday and I'll come down Saturday after finding us an apartment and then we'll spend the evening on the town Saturday night and come back up here on Sunday together, how's that sound?"

"Well, what am I suppose to do until then?"

"What you gonna do until then? What the fuck you mean, what you gonna do until then. You gonna check shit out, have a good time and find a job. That's what yo ass gonna do," I said yelling into the phone.

"Alright, Sean, I'm sorry, calm down."

"Calm down, what the fuck are you talking bout? I'm stressing out, they got me up here at this goddamn Schofield Barracks which I was not planning to be at and you're in a fucking ritzy hotel, downtown in Honolulu, Hawaii talking bout what you gonna do and you want me to calm down?" I yelled into the phone again.

"Alright Sean, I'm sorry, you're right. Please forgive me," he replied apologetically.

"Look Gabe, I know this is not what you expected but neither did I. Uncle Sam can be a bitch sometimes but there's really nothing I can do about it, if I could I would, you know that, right?" I said, combing my hair, getting ready for my date.

"I know, I know." He then hesitated and whispered, "I love you, Sean Mathews," forgiving me for all of my wrong.

"I love you, too. I'll call you later after I come from work." I hung up the phone before he could respond and I sat down on the bed with my head between the palms of my hands thinking, *that shit actually worked, I'm just too good. Sir, Yes Sir, muthafuckas.*

******

Eddie picked me up right where he dropped me off and we headed downtown to Waikiki beach or so I thought. After chit- chatting while riding for thirty minutes or so, he pulled up into a residential neighborhood and parked in this Tudor style house driveway.

"This is where I live, Sean, just in case you were wondering. I wanted to take a quick shower and put on something more comfortable. So, you can wait here in the car or come in and have a drink to wait for me," Eddie stated with a sexy Spanish accent while getting out of his car.

"I think I'll have that drink." Knowing this was just a ploy to get me in his house. *Hell, all he had to say was that he wanted to have sex with me, there was no need for game playing,* I thought to myself, while following him up to his crib.

Eddie lived in a three bedroom cottage right off of Kapahula Avenue. I'm still not sure how that's pronounced but on the drive down here, Eddie explained to me that Hawaii only uses seven consonants P, K, H, L, M, N, and W and five vowels, A, E, I, O, and U. So, I guess Kapahula would sound like it does phonetically. As I walked into Eddie's home I was surprised by its beauty. From the outside his home looked rather small but on the inside it was fairly large. As you walked in, there was a spacious living room on the right which no doubt appeared to have been decorated with a woman's touch. Several little whatnots were placed on the pine- colored coffee table with matching side tables. There was a stuffed bubble-gum-pink couch made out of wicker with matching chairs across each end of the coffee table and a huge pink and navy colored Persian rug that went from one side of the room to the other.

What I found to be funny was that instead of having throw pillows on his couch, he had African made dolls instead.

To top it off, Eddie had four large paintings on each side of the walls. The one that hung behind the couch was a painting of a black nude male and female that where embracing each other. The one opposite of the couch was a similar painting of just the man. The remaining two were pictures of two black nude men embracing and two black nude women embracing.

"Have a seat, Sean; what can I get you to drink?" Eddie asked as I looked around his living room.

"Ah, rum and coke if you got it," I responded while taking a seat on the couch. "You have some interesting artwork."

"Thanks, I guess that was a compliment, wasn't it?" he asked while handing me my drink.

"Yes, it was. Do you live here alone?"

"Yes Sir, I do. Why do you ask?" he replied while taking a seat next to me.

"Just wondering, besides I didn't want anybody coming in unannounced while I was raping you," I replied with a wicked grin.

"Sean, you're so bad. I'm going to go take my shower and change clothes, I'll be right back, okay?" he said getting up and walking out the room.

I sat there thinking, *this must be some kinda joke, was he serious? Didn't he invite me here to have sex or was he expecting me to come and join him in the shower?* At that moment, I heard water running so I knew he must be taking his shower so I placed my empty glass down on the coffee table, got up and followed the sound of running water.

The sound was coming from upstairs behind a closed door. I opened the door and saw Eddie in the tub, standing behind a glass door as the shower head sprayed water over his "come fuck me" body. Startled, Eddie wiped the water from his eyes and slid the shower door open and looked at me as though he was surprised.

"What are you doing, man?" he asked while continuing to lather his body with soap.

"I thought I would join you," I replied taking off my wife-beater and shorts.

I didn't give Eddie a chance to respond because by the time he could have said something, I was already butt naked and standing under the shower head with my eyes closed enjoying the hot water running down my hard body. As I opened up my eyes while looking into the water at Eddie, I could see he was becoming aroused. He wasn't looking straight at me, instead he seemed to be focused on my dick as he continued to lather himself up.

"Touch it," I said demandingly. Eddie reached out with his right hand and slightly squeezed my swollen tool. "You like that?" I questioned as he then began to lather it with soap and slid his hand up and down on me as though he was jerking me off at a slow pace.

"Yeah, I do," he whispered.

"Do you know what to do with it?"

"Definitely," he replied softly with a crooked smile.

"Then handle your business," I said once again in a demanding tone.

Eddie squatted down, opened his mouth and slowly began sucking and licking the tip of my penis. His mouth felt like a furnace, but for some reason, his touch shocked me. I mean literally, his touch shocked me as though there was an electrical current in his mouth. I pulled myself out of his mouth and looked down at him; he too seemed kinda shocked because he began gargling water that came down from the shower and spitting it out as though something wasn't right. I leaned my head back as the water continued to spray in my face and cascaded down my stiff body. I guess Eddie didn't know what to make out of it either and not to be out done; Eddie opened his mouth once again and swallowed me whole.

The water was hot and so was Eddie's tongue and after a couple of minutes of so much heat, I reached around and turned the hot water down to help cool me off. The contrast between the coolness of the water and Eddie's tongue had me going. I don't know where this little Puerto Rican dude learned how to give head but I knew if I didn't stop him soon, I was going to nut right in his mouth. I grabbed a hold of his head to push him up off me but he refused, saying some shit in Spanish that I didn't understand. All I knew was he kept going faster and faster as though he was ready for me to spit in his mouth. So, I let him do his thing. After a few minutes or so, my body flexed and I knew I was at that point. I placed one hand on the side of the wall and placed my other hand on top of the glass sliding door. I felt every pore in my body close as every sperm, secretion and fluid squirted out of me so fast, and with a vengeance my knees began to buckle. Eddie swallowed everything and continued to need more.

"Wait yo, hold up," I said trying to catch my breath and my balance.

"You POW?" he asked standing up and looking me straight in my eyes.

"Am I what?" I asked while lathering up my body.

"You POW, done, finish?" Again, he asked with that crooked, sexy ass smile of his.

"Well, give a brotha a minute or two and I'll be ready again," I replied while rinsing the suds off and stepping out of the shower.

Eddie followed suit and began to dry me off with a towel. I stood there as he dried off every inch of my body, "You have a nice body, poppy," he responded while giving special interest to my groin and buttocks area.

"Thanks and so do you shawty," I replied in a sexy tone and smiling while becoming aroused again.

Eddie then led me into his bed room. I watched him from behind as his ass cheeks seemed to bounce up and down like a slinky. The one thing I realized is that I had a thing for good skin. I don't mean just a blemish free type of skin but good skin, the kind that you just want to touch because it's so smooth, the kind that looks and feels naked, if you know what I mean? I couldn't wait to be inside of him.

"Lay down Poppy so I can give you a massage," he said, reaching onto his dresser for some lotion.

As if given an order, I laid down on my back with my hands folded under my head waiting for whatever pleasures I was about to feel from this Puerto Rican hottie.

The shades in his room were drawn making it appear as though it was dusk outside and with a switch of a button; I began to hear smooth sounds from the small stereo that sat on top of Eddie's dresser. As soon as I closed my eyes, I began to feel the coolness of the lotion as he pressed his hands down onto my chest and worked his way down to my six-pack. The circular motions of his hands from my sides to my groin made my body jerk but he continued as though he was sculpting a mold of my body. Each time his hands went near my dick, it jumped from his sensuous touch, which again felt like an electrical shock. Eddie's hands were smooth and soft, that of a woman's and the words he whispered in Spanish made me yearn for him that much more. Not that I understood what he was saying but whatever it was, made me hotter than a pan of frying grease.

For a second, I no longer felt Eddie's hands on my body so I opened my eyes and at that moment he'd raised my dick with his right hand and squatted himself directly over top of me. Inch by inch, I felt the warmth of his insides as he began to slowly take all of me. How can I possibly put into words the feeling I felt once our rhythm to the sounds of an old classic, "My Latest Greatest Inspiration" by Teddy Pendergrass began. I thought, *Thank God for Puerto Ricans having rhythm.*

Eddie matched me stroke for stroke as I looked up at his sensuous body moving up and down on top of mine. I grabbed onto his ass muscles and held them tight as I continued to go deeper and deeper inside him. I don't know whether Eddie had lubed himself up with the lotion or not but I do know we were fucking raw and his insides felt like pure hot silk. He then began to moan and groan and then said something in Spanish. Again, I didn't know what he was saying, so I continued to stroke even faster. A minute later, he said it again, as if wanting a response.

"You okay," I whispered through moans as I moved my hands from his ass to his waist.

"Poppy… you… going… ta… make… me… cum… soon," he answered while trying to slow down our pace.

"Hold that shit niggah, I ain't ready yet," I said, slapping him on his ass. I pulled out of him and placed him on all fours, doggy style, my favorite position. There must have been a mini concert being played on the radio because as soon as I entered Eddie from the back, another classic from Teddy Pendergrass, "Can't We Try" began to play. I slid in and out of him with ease, there's something about watching my dick go in and out a nice round, smooth, yet firm bubble butt that seems to make my dick harder.

"Wait, hold up Poppy," Eddie said, trying to catch his breath.

"Hold up, for what? Take that shit niggah," I demanded while continually pounding into him and slapping him on the ass.

Now, I know that might sound kinda harsh but dayum, I was on the verge of cuming and ain't nothing worst than a bottom saying, "Wait, hold up." That can turn a niggah off. After stroking for another five minutes or so, I was about to explode. I felt Eddie trying to move further and further away from me. I suspect that maybe it was hurting him a little but at this point, I really didn't care. I grabbed him by the waist and shoved my dick up as far as it would go. Just as I was about to release myself, I felt Eddie's ass muscles contract, pretty much the same way Thomas' would do. And then it happened. Both Eddie and I came at the same time, I don't know who yelled louder, me or him but I can truly say this is the best Puerto Rican ass I ever had. Well, for now, it's the only Puerto Rican ass I've ever had.

I pulled out as I collapsed on top of Eddie, I laid there trying to catch my breath and within minutes we were spooning. Eddie was exhausted just as much as I was but I laid there holding onto him for dear life. There were no words being said only another classic from Teddy Pendergrass, "It Don't Hurt Now," that filled the room. I don't know why but listening to the song and thinking about all of what I had been through, tears began to run down my face. Not because I was sad but because Teddy was right, it didn't hurt no mo! And for once in a long time, I was happy and felt at peace with Eddie in my arms.

As we laid there loving each others aura, Eddie educated me in more Hawaiian terms like, 'mahalo' meaning thank you, 'kuaua' meaning shower, 'ae' meaning yes, 'a'ole' meaning no. I wanted to know what the word was for fuck but unfortunately, there wasn't one but my favorite one is, 'aloha au la 'oe' meaning, I Love You.

Needless to say, Eddie and I didn't make it to the beach. But to be honest, I don't think he had intentions of taking me to the beach anyway, which was fine with me. Eddie and I eventually got up, took a shower and went to go get something to eat. We came back and fucked a couple more times and eventually fell off to sleep in each others arms. The next morning, we woke up just in time for Eddie to bring me back to Schofield Barracks so that I could shower, change in my fatigues and make my six a.m. formation.

There was something very different about Eddie. Every time I would touch him, kiss him or whatever, there would be that electric shock. Does this mean he must be the one?

SIR, Yes Sir

Chapter FOUR

I stood in the back of formation at parade rest looking at all the other soldiers in my squadron, when I noticed fat ass Harrison getting out of a new 2011 Lexus Si Series. *Dayum, the brotha just got here and already Mommy and Daddy done bought his fat ass a new car. Must be nice coming from a well-to-do family,* I thought feeling a bit jealous.

"Hey Sean, what's up?" Harrison asked, grinning all in my face as though we were the best of friends as he took his place beside me in formation.

"Nada," I replied nonchalantly.

"I was told we were going to be room mates when I got here a couple days ago. So when did you get in?"

"Yesterday morning," I said, trying to keep my answer brief.

"Hmmm, I was out, but I came back through around 1:00 a.m. this morning. I saw your things but you weren't there. Got lucky last night, huh, Sean?" he asked while nudging me.

Before I could reply, Captain Richardson made his presence known by yelling, "Atten-hut!"

As though we were all on one accord, we all slapped our heels together and stood at attention. I was surprised to see that

Captain Richardson was a brotha. He looked to be in his mid to late thirties, dark skin, bald and thin, kinda reminded me of Lou Gossett Jr. in the movie, "An Officer and a Gentleman." And if he was anything like that character, I knew he wasn't to be fucked with.

"At ease!" Captain Richardson yelled out. We all then came to a parade rest stance as he continued his morning spiel. "Everybody doing okay this morning," Captain said as he walked up and down our formation.

"Sir, Yes Sir!" We yelled in unison. For some reason, I felt like I was back in basic training.

"Before I let you guys head off to work and I'm sure you can't wait to put in a good eight hours worth of work." There were a few laughs from our squad as Captain stood in his tracks, smiled and continued to say, "I'd first like to make some introductions. Specialist Mathews, front and center!" he yelled.

I fell out of formation, ran as fast as I could and stood in front of Captain Richardson at attention and yelled, "Sir, yes Sir."

"At ease soldier," he replied as he walked around me. "This is Specialist Mathews everyone and he just arrived here from Fort Meade, Maryland yesterday. I hope that you guys will welcome him into our family and assist him if needed," the Captain spat introducing me to the squad.

"Sir, Yes Sir!" my new squad yelled.

"Back in formation, Specialist Mathews," Captain directed me.

I ran back into formation and stood at parade rest as the Captain then called Harrison and introduced him to the squad pretty much the same way he did me.

******

After formation I found my way to the administration building where I was to report for work. It wasn't hard to find considering it sat right across the street from our barracks. The administration building was four stories high and had different departments on each floor. The first floor was made up of offices for all the officers that worked in the building. The second floor was for administration clerks that specialized in data processing. The third floor was for just plain 'ole administrative clerks, clerks who maintain soldier's files. And the fourth floor, where I was going to work was for Sidpers Specialists.

A couple hours after filling out paperwork and being introduced to practically the whole building by my manager, who by the way was a queen and went by the name, Sergeant Graham, and stuttered profusely, I was given a desk, some files, office supplies, a few file cabinets and was told to get to work. Now, I'm not one to complain and I know I got an excellent duty station by being sent here on Paradise Island, however, at Ft. Meade; at least I had my own office. Here, I was in a huge room that took up the whole fourth floor where there were no partitions, cubicles or offices and I was supposed to work side by side with about forty other Sidpers Specialists? Give me a fucking break!

Setting up my area and organizing my file cabinets took up the whole day. I didn't even go to lunch. Although I did call my mom to let her know that I had made it here all in one piece and to hear Lil Man's voice. God, after hearing their voices, I didn't realize how much I missed them. I hadn't called Gabe, but I'm sure he was enjoying himself. I turned my phone off and continued to organize my area.

A co-worker of mine who sat behind me saw how busy I was and was nice enough to ask if I wanted her to bring me anything back for lunch but I declined. I couldn't pronounce her last name so she just told me to call her Kaliah. She was Samoan and was born on the big Island of Hawaii and had been in the military for almost ten years, she too was a specialist, the same rank as me. Unfortunately, there was nothing special about her, she wasn't attractive at all. She was very light-skinned, albino-like, frizzy red hair, at least twenty pounds over weight and very masculine. I knew she was a lesbian as soon as she said hello. Not that she had a deep voice or anything but just the way she carried herself. Nonetheless, this day was coming to a close and I couldn't wait to get back to my room to catch a few winks.

It took me all of five minutes to make it back to my room and lay across my bed. Thank God Harrison wasn't there. I hoped and prayed that he wouldn't come back and that somehow someway, being an MP, his fat ass got shot or some shit while on duty. Before I knew it, I was knocked out and dreaming about Eddie Salgado.

My dream was a repeat of last night. It took me back to his place and I was sitting in his living room as I heard the water running in his bathroom. I got up and went into his bathroom and saw Eddie through the sliding glass shower doors. I took my wife-beater and shorts off and got in the shower. Eddie began to pleasure me with his mouth, I leaned my head back and closed my eyes as the water from the shower head began to spray down on my face and cascade down my stiff body.

Then something felt strange, the head he was giving me still felt good but I opened my eyes and looked around and I was still in Eddie's shower but when I looked down, it wasn't Eddie I saw. Instead, it was fat ass Harrison. I thought I was just imagining shit so I leaned back hoping that the water would clear my vision. But after getting water in my eyes, I could not seem to open them. However, because of the pleasure I was receiving my body jerked. I began to nut once again in someone's mouth. Eventually after a minute or so, I opened my eyes and was still in Eddie's shower. He looked up at me and licked his lips and asked, "Are you POW?"

Suddenly, I heard loud music playing and it caused me to sit straight up. I looked around the room and Harrison was lying over on his bed watching me or the TV. I really couldn't tell considering it had gotten dark outside.

"Sleeping beauty finally wakes up, huh?" Harrison asked, smiling.

I didn't respond to his comment, instead I felt to see if my pants were undone and they weren't. However, my pants buckle was unfastened and I know I didn't do that myself and even though I just nutted, my shit was still hard as a rock. It felt like I had a wet dream and even though I came, I really wasn't conscience of it.

"Damn, Sean, why you over there feeling all over yourself, teasing a brotha and shit," Harrison stated while licking his tongue out at me.

"Man, fuck you," I spat while getting up to go to the bathroom.

I closed the bathroom door and unbuttoned my pants to see what the fuck was going on down there. I had pre-cum on my boxers but again, I don't know if indeed it was pre-cum or whether or not I was just still leaking by nutting so hard. I noticed on the left side of my inner thigh a small dried up cum stain which tells me I came but it's no where close to the amount of cum I usually nut, especially having a wet dream. So it doesn't take a Rocket Scientist to figure out where my shit went.

I couldn't help but laugh because how could I prove Harrison violated me and drank my nut? This shit was getting more fucked up by the day. What the fuck could I possibly say to Harrison, "Yo, you sucked my dick while I was sleep?"

As crazy as it sounds, I've always been a heavy sleeper. I remember when I was about sixteen years old and the house next door to where my mom and I lived caught on fire. That muthafucka practically burned to the ground and my mom tells me that it took her about five minutes or so to wake my ass up even though there were sirens coming from both police cars and ambulances right outside our front door. For precaution sake, my mom took me to the hospital because she thought that I might have slept so hard that I might have gotten smoke inhalation but according to the test the doctors gave me, it wasn't that at all. The doctors told my mom, I was one of those people that just slept hard.

But could it be possible that someone could take advantage of me while I slept and not know it, I thought as I turned the shower on and began to undress.

While in the shower, Harrison had the nerve to come in the bathroom and act like he had to take a leak. Of course if there was a lock on the door, I would have used it. Lawd knows, I've learned my lesson a long time ago but unfortunately, there are no locks on these doors. Just as I was washing the suds off my groin area, the water became sculling hot.

"What the fuck?" I yelled.

"Oh shit Sean, my bad, when someone flushes the toilet, the cold water turns off."

"Yo man, if you know that, why you decide to come in here to use the bathroom now?" I asked opening up the shower door.

"Hmmm, I can take care of that if you want me to?" he asked looking directly at my half limp dick and rubbing his hands together as though they were cold.

"Muthafucka, you probably already did. Now get the fuck out!" I spat closing the shower door.

After taking my shower, I realized I didn't bring a towel in the bathroom with me. I walked out into the room naked and grabbed one of my towels from my locker and began drying myself. Of course Harrison was playing possum when I knew dayum well he was staring at me the whole time, even though the TV was still on. I threw on a pair of clean boxers, pulled my laptop out of my locker and logged on. Fortunately, the barracks was wired for WiFi.

I signed on to check my email as well as send some out. As usual, nothing but junk and spam. But the first email I sent out was to Officer Sansbury, he was the officer that had arrested Mr. Lomax at BWI Airport. I forwarded him my address so that he could send me a notice letting me know the date of Mr. Lomaxs' trial because after all he had done to me, I was definitely pressing charges. I also sent an email to Ms. Ineedaman, giving her my address as well, so that she could send me some information as to my new found role of a "SIR" and any other information as to whether there were any SBI Organizations that may be located here in Oahu, Hawaii.

Several hours had passed and Harrison had finally turned off the TV as I continued to surf the net. For some reason I wasn't sleepy, I guess it was because of my nap earlier. I looked down at my laptop and noticed that it was almost midnight. I knew I was going to hate myself in the morning. However, I happened to stumble upon a website that seemed rather interesting.

It was a resort located over on the Big Island of Hawaii called, The Keiki Wahi and according to the definition, it meant, "The Boys' Place." There was a picture on its website of this mint green thirty story resort with men of all colors wearing different shades of G-strings and carrying waiter trays with tropical drinks on top with tiny umbrellas in them. I clicked on the icon that read, "Enter If You Dare." Of course not being that familiar with the site could have caused some kinda virus but truth be told, I wanted to find out what this resort was about that called themselves, "The Boys Place," and get a closer look at the dudes wearing G-strings. I immediately started thinking that this must be a part of the SIRS & BOYS Incorporated and since I was a SIR, I definitely wanted to check out what this site had to offer.

After a few minutes of scanning through their ad, it appeared as though this was a resort for those who wanted to get their freak on and for the cost of $2,500 dollars; you would receive three days and two nights of pure sexual satisfaction with any of the escorts listed in their ad. This also included a luxurious suite with an ocean view, complimentary breakfast and 24 hour room service.

I couldn't help but think, *People really must be hard up for sex, especially if they're willing to pay for it. Hell, I seem to get sex without even knowing it!*

There also was an icon that read, "Escorts," so I clicked on it and began to scan through the pictures of half naked men. I must admit, the dudes were hot, they had every flavor you could think of, but there was one escort that went by the name of, "Jose" that looked very familiar. I clicked on his picture to enlarge it and just as I thought, Jose was Eddie Salgado. He was standing under a palm tree, seductively eating a pineapple in his birthday suit. *Wow, no wonder his ass was so good at sucking and taking dick, he's a prostitute. That's how he could afford his own house as a Private,* I said to myself.

I really couldn't be mad at him. Besides, we just met and he didn't owe me shit. I had to admit, it was a dayum good picture of him and personally, I would pay the $2,500 dollars even if I didn't know him. As I continued to read about The Keiki Wahi Resort, they indicated that their clientele were very prestigious and in order to go there, you first had to pay your $2,500 dollars up front, a form of government I.D., driver's license etc… and a social security card for the purpose of a background check. Well, ain't that a bitch? I definitely had enough, so I bookmarked the website, shut down my laptop and carried my ass to sleep. Of course, all I could think about was Mr. Sexy ass, Eddie Salgado.

Chapter FIVE

The next morning, I barely made it to formation on time. Fat ass Harrison didn't even bother to wake me up as he left and slammed the door. I guess that was his way of waking me up. I picked up my cell phone to check the time but I had forgotten that I hadn't turned it back on from yesterday. I turned it on and the time read, 5:48 a.m. Oh shit, I had just twelve minutes to make formation on time. I jumped out of bed, threw some water on my face and got dressed.

"Atten-hut!" I heard Captain Richardson yell as I ran up to formation and stood at attention. "Everyone good this morning?" he yelled, pacing back and forth.

"Sir, Yes Sir," we yelled back in unison.

"This morning, I have a bit of bad news to deliver. I don't know if any of you guys noticed coming in this morning, but we have our flags flying at half mass." Captain then became silent and looked like he was actually about to cry. "I'm sorry to announce that last night, our Commander Lt. General Garrett passed away in his sleep and therefore our offices will be closed today and what that means people, is that you guys will be off today."

Personally, I wanted to shout for joy but I had to maintain. After all, someone's husband and father died but deep down inside, I felt like a kid who had just found out that school was closed because of snow. Hell, I couldn't wait to get back up in my room and carry my tired ass back to sleep. Just as we were directed to "fall out," Harrison grabbed me by the arm.

"Yo, Sean, let's go to Mickey D's and get some breakfast," Harrison said like we were the best of friends.

As much as I wanted to go back to sleep, I was feeling kinda hungry considering I couldn't remember the last time I ate, so I decided to go. Fortunately, Mickey D's was located just a few blocks outside the front gate heading north in a small town called Wahiawa. We ordered our food and decided to eat there.

"Sean, can I be honest with you about something?" Harrison asked out of the blue.

"What?" I responded while checking my cell. I had ten missed calls and three voice messages.

"I just wanted you to know that what I did at Ft. Meade was wrong. And I just wanted to apologize and hope that we can be friends," he stated in a genuine tone.

"Yeah right, whatever," I spat as I continued to listen to my voice messages and chow down on my big breakfast.

"I'm serious, Sean. I want us to be friends. I mean, we're going to be roommates for the time we're here so why shouldn't we at least try to be friends?"

"Naw bruh, I don't think so. I'm not staying in the barracks, I'm going to look for an apartment today," I stated as a matter of fact.

Dayum, Gabe had left two messages wondering where I was. I can't believe I forgot to call him and the third message was from Eddie, asking when we could hook up again.

"Oh really, so is it that bad that you don't even want to be my roommate?" he asked, sounding hurt and a little annoyed as I listened to my messages.

"Naw Harrison, it ain't that man."

At that point, I put my cell back in my pocket and thought seriously about what Harrison was talking about. He wanted to be friends and shit and I needed him to take me around so I could check out some of these apartments in the area. Since he had a car, I said, "Yo, Harrison, you cool, bruh. Besides, you're the only one I know here and we do go back a ways so hey, it's all good," I replied giving him some dap.

And just like that, Harrison and I became the best of friends or so he thought! A muthafucka ain't gonna suck my dick without me knowing about it and get away with it. But for now, I needed to use Harrison to my advantage; he had a car, gave a mean blow job and had money. I had my own but why should I use mine when I could use his. I remember Thomas telling me once that Harrison enjoyed spending money, not only on himself but on others as well, so why shouldn't it be me? Anyway, after eating he began to drive me around in the area and I really didn't see anything I liked in Wahiawa and he told me there was a really nice complex going south, down in an area called, Waipahu.

"Let's go check it out," I said, pulling the passenger seat back and getting comfortable.

I didn't tell Harrison the reason I was getting an apartment was because Gabe had come to Hawaii with me, besides it wasn't any of his dayum business. This is what you call your left hand not knowing what your right hand is doing, as my mother would often say. We finally pulled up to a high-rise apartment complex and it looked very nice on the outside, somewhere I could actually see myself living. It kinda reminded me of the apartment complex on the old sitcom, "The Jefferson's." Hell, I wanted to move on up too. Harrison parked his car right in front of the rental office. We both got out and entered and were greeted by an old Hawaiian female, who looked like she was about a hundred years old but had a very sweet demeanor.

"Aloha, how can I help you gentlemen today?" she

asked while sitting behind the counter.

"Aloha, to you as well," I replied with a chuckle considering this was the first time I actually used the word, 'aloha'. "I'm looking for a one bedroom apartment, do you have any available?"

"Yes, we do. We have one that rents for $1,100 a month and another that rents for $1,250 a month."

"What's the difference," I questioned out of curiosity.

"One has a dining room and the other does not."

"Can I see both of them?"

"You sure can," she said, reaching behind her for the apartment keys that hung on a wall. "This one is for apartment 207 and this one is for apartment 1012," she said, handing me the keys.

Harrison and I went to apartment 207 first and it wasn't bad, but it was a little too small even for a one bedroom apartment. It had very small rooms, and tiny closets. The bathroom was as small as a closet and the whole apartment had an ugly ass beige wall to wall carpet. It truly wasn't worth $1,100 a month. We then proceeded to check out apartment 1012. Now, this apartment definitely was for me. The kitchen sat over to the right as you walked in the door with an island in the center of it, the dining room was adjacent to the kitchen, the living room was huge and had a huge floor to ceiling glass sliding window. The bathroom was kinda small but bigger than the one in the other apartment and the bedroom was a nice size with a floor to ceiling glass sliding window door as well.

"This one's not bad, Sean," Harrison said as he opened and closed the bedroom glass sliding window door.

"Yeah, I like it," I replied looking around at me and Gabe's new home.

Harrison and I went back down to the rental office and I filled out all the necessary paperwork and wrote a check for first month's rent and security deposit. I was told that I would be notified by Friday to let me know if my application had been approved. Once we left, I was no longer feeling sleepy. As a matter of fact, I was feeling pretty good about moving into my own place soon and wanted to go shopping for some furniture. As for Harrison, he was more than happy in chauffeuring me around. After all, we were the best of friends. Besides, he was smiling and cheesing the whole time like I was his niggah and shit. But hey, that was his fantasy, not mine.

Anyway, we went back into the town of Wahiawa where they had several furniture stores. In one of the stores they had this 52 inch flat-screen Digital TV that I fell in love with but what shocked me was that shit almost cost $900 bucks. What surprised me even more was Harrison.

"Yo, Sean, you like that, huh?"

"How can you tell?" I asked in a sexy tone.

"Because you keep staring at it, niggah," Harrison replied while laughing.

"Yeah, I do. I'm gonna buy me one of those one day," I said playing it off as though I couldn't afford it. When in actuality, I was going to come back another day and pay cash for it. I just didn't want Harrison to know I had money especially after paying first month's rent and security deposit for an apartment.

"Then niggah get that shit if you want it?" he asked as though it was no big deal.

"And what am I suppose to pay it with, my looks?" I replied acting like I was broke.

"Niggah puh-lease, where's the sales person at? Ah, excuse me," Harrison said, getting the attention of one of the sales clerk.

"Yes, can I help you?" The young female sales clerk asked.

"Yes, we would like to purchase this TV here," Harrison said, pointing to the TV.

"Alright, will that be cash or will you be charging it?"

"Bitch does it…," At that point I looked at Harrison, letting him know that he didn't have to get black or act ghetto. He

43

then rephrased and said, "I'm sorry, here's my credit card." Harrison pulled out his Black Visa credit card and handed it to the sales clerk.

"Will you guys be taking this with you today?" the sales clerk asked after completing the sale.

"Well Sean, your call. You want to take it with us today?" Harrison asked as though we were a couple.

"Naw, we can come back and get it on Friday evening. That way we can just take it to my crib," I replied while being shocked at Harrison's gesture and making sure that once we get it, it would be in my own dayum apartment.

"Yeah, that sounds like a good idea," he said, handing me the receipt as we walked out the door.

Believe it or not, Harrison and I spent the whole dayum day together. We drove downtown and checked out all the sites, like tourists always do. Hawaii is a beautiful place and everywhere I turned, there were palm trees. Hell, a niggah like me being from the east coast ain't never seen a palm tree in person before. But Harrison being as sweet as he was, bought me everything I asked for, cotton candy, ice cream cone, a lei, a pair of blue and white Hang Ten tennis shoes, a couple of genuine Hawaiian shirts, some Hang Ten shorts and to top it off, a candle lit dinner at a restaurant alongside Waikiki beach. We sat there eating and gazing out at the beautiful sunset that seemed to lie on top of the Pacific Ocean.

"Sean, you know I like you, right?" Harrison whispered as he looked into my eyes.

"Yeah, I know but you still not getting any dick," I spat sarcastically.

"See Sean, why you got to be like that?" he asked sounding disappointed.

"Be like what?" I replied as if I didn't know what he was getting at.

"Look, Sean, I know I'm not what you would normally go for. I know I'm not that attractive and I know you can probably have any dude here and I also know that I'm a little on the heavy side…"

"A little?" I said smiling.

"See Sean, why you gotta go there? What I'm tryna say is, I got something these other dudes don't have."

"And what's that?" I asked out of curiosity and with a raised eyebrow.

"I got money and I can buy you anything you want!" he replied sounding cocky.

Before I had a chance to respond, I thought my eyes were playing tricks on me but I looked to my left and saw Gabriel coming towards our table and he didn't look happy at all. "Oh shit," is all I could say.

"What's wrong?" Harrison asked.

"So, this is why you can't return any of my phone calls?" Gabe asked as he looked down at Harrison.

"Who the fuck is you?" Harrison asked while looking up at Gabe and then looking at me for answers.

"Gabe, calm the fuck down, this is Harrison, Harrison this is Gabriel," I said trying to calm the situation before it got outta hand.

"Look Sean, don't play with me. I didn't come 3,000 miles and give up my life back in Baltimore so I could come here and watch you cheat on me with some fat, ugly queen," Gabe said with his arms folded and almost in tears.

"Who the fuck you calling a queen, you short, yella muthafucka!" Harrison spat while getting up out of his seat.

By this time, people began looking in our direction and I knew if I didn't do something quick, Harrison's big, fat ass was going to fuck Gabe up. But just before I could get up and pull Harrison's ass away, he threw a right hook so hard against the left side of Gabe's jaw that Gabe fell back onto one of the other patron's table. The next thing I knew, people began crowding around us and cheering Harrison on. I was so stunned that I just stood there; I couldn't believe what was happening. Gabriel actually had enough balls to get up and make a charge toward Harrison. I watched as they both fell on top of the table that Harrison and I were eating on. Gabe had fallen on top of Harrison and like a madman; Gabriel was throwing punches all in Harrison's face. I couldn't believe what I was seeing; Gabriel, being a man of the cloth was actually fucking Harrison's ass up. I thought that shit was funny; I stood there and laughed my ass off.

I suspected that by this time, management had called the police because I noticed the red and blue lights flashing outside as well as their loud ass siren. I pulled Gabriel off Harrison and rushed him out the back door of the restaurant so his ass wouldn't get locked up.

"Gabe, take yo ass back to the hotel and I'll meet you there. Just let me take care of this, a'ight?"

"You ain't got to come nowhere, Sean, I'm going back home tonight!" he yelled walking away from me.

"Don't play with me Gabe, you betta have yo ass there when I get there!" I yelled. Truth be told, Gabriel beating Harrison's ass kinda turned me on. I didn't know the little niggah had it in him. I couldn't wait to get back to the hotel and hold Gabe in my arms.

Once inside the restaurant, I saw Harrison talking to one of the officers. I walked over and explained to the officer that I really didn't know the guy who was there and that he had been stalking me. Fortunately, Harrison didn't say anything. He just stood there wiping the blood from the side of his mouth.

"Mr. Harrison, would you like to file charges?" the cop asked.

I looked over at Harrison and gestured no.

"Naw, it's cool. I don't know the guy who did this anyway, so there's no point in pressing charges," Harrison replied.

"Are you sure? We can have you come down to the precinct and look at some mug shots," the officer advised.

"Naw, I'm a'ight, thanks anyway."

The officer spoke briefly to the manager and left. Harrison paid for our meal and we both apologized profusely to the manager for the all the trouble we caused. Once outside, I tried to apologize to Harrison for what had happened but interestingly enough, Harrison said it was cool and told me not to worry about it, just as long as I seriously thought about what we had talked about earlier.

"Look, Harrison, I got to go handle some business. So, why don't you go back up to Schofield Barracks and I'll check you out tomorrow?" I said once we made it to Harrison's car.

"How are you going to make it back to the base?" he asked sounding concerned.

"I don't know, I'mma big boy, I'm sure I can find a ride."

"A ride, huh? How about I come pick you up in the morning?"

"That's cool. You can meet me back here in front of the restaurant."

"You know I wouldn't do this for nobody else but you. You know that right?" he asked starting up his car and giving me a pitiful look.

"That's what friends are for, right?" I chuckled.

"Whatever Sean, I'll meet you back here at five a.m."

"Cool," I replied walking toward The Royal Hawaiian Hotel.

******

Once I made it up to the room, I realized I didn't have a key. So after knocking a few times, Gabe finally answered the door.

"What's up," I stated walking through the door as though nothing had just happened.

"What's up is I can't get out of here until tomorrow," Gabe said angrily while slamming the door.

"Come on Gabe, you know you don't mean that," I

replied while taking my clothes off to take a shower.

"Sean, why would you do that to me?" Gabe asked while standing in front of me and holding a cold wash cloth against his jaw.

"Do what?"

"Cheat on me," he replied in a sad tone.

"I wasn't cheating on you, Gabe. Now let me take a look at that jaw," I said while holding onto his face.

"Ouch," he sounded with a grimace.

"Hold still," I said looking at his jaw. "Hmmm, it's not that bad. But, Yo Rev, you tore his ass up. Dayum boy, I didn't know you had it in you." I laughed, then tried to feel on his ass.

"Look, Sean, I'm not in the mood, okay?" Gabe said backing away from me.

"What's wrong with you?"

"Like I said, I'm not in the mood, Sean," he replied while lying down on the bed in a fetal position.

Chapter SIX

Several months had passed and learning my way around Hawaii had become quite interesting. I bought a brand new, silver Mazda 626 turbo so that Gabe and I could get around and also so Gabe could use the car while I was at work to find a job. But since moving into our apartment, we'd been arguing on a daily basis, mainly because he hadn't been able to find a job. But as much as I cared for Gabe, I understood that as a man, you want to be able to pay your own way. And he doesn't feel as though he has been able to do that. However, Gabe takes his frustrations out on me and I'm getting tired of trying to convince him that it's ok and that maybe tomorrow will be a better day. At this point, I'm ready for Gabe to go home.

Harrison on the other hand has been at my beck and call since day one. I ask Harrison to jump, he says, "How high?" My relationship with Harrison is kinda crazy. He does whatever I tell him to do, whenever I tell him to do it. I can understand why Thomas had gotten himself involved with him. Harrison is one of those people that you don't wanna like, but you can't help but like them anyway. Of course our friendship is sexual as well, but only when I want it to be. Harrison will drop to his knees in a heartbeat just to suck my dick. How can you not like someone who does that? Moreover, I've gotten to know Harrison a lot better and I have to admit, he's cool people. Although, I wouldn't admit to anyone openly that Harrison and I are indeed fucking. Mainly because Harrison is not the type of guy you would really wanna be seen out in public with. Being 5'10, 300 pounds, blacker than black and not attractive in the least. However, fat boy can suck a dick. Gotta give credit where credit is due.

Now, the lil niggah in my life is Eddie Salgado. It's funny when you get involved with someone emotionally that when you're not around them, you can still smell them on you. I can honestly say, I'm truly feeling this brotha or shall I say, Spain-u-rican. Up to this point, I hadn't mentioned to him about the ad that I saw on the website about him being an escort because as much as I was feeling him, I wanted him to do him. However, I have since received all the information I need from Ms. Ineedaman about being a SIR and my plan is to make Eddie my first BOY while in the land of paradise. What makes this interesting is that this will be the first time that I would be the one to send someone through a BOY initiation process and the thought alone is making my dick hard.

Eddie was actually in the process of cooking us dinner at his place tonight and I told him that there was something very important that I wanted to discuss with him. Personally, Eddie would make the perfect BOY. Fuck, I can't wait to get off work because I have done nothing but shuffled papers back and forth from one box to the other all day. *Thank God it's Friday,* I thought to myself.

The plan was for me to be at Eddie's house at 7:00 p.m. sharp. However, I was so excited about being with him, that I didn't bother to go home and shower or anything. Instead, I left work and headed over to Eddie's. I pulled up at his house around 5:30 or so, parked the car and sat there in disbelief. Right in front of me sat Harrison's car. I knew his car when I saw it, besides, he had personalized tags that read, "Big Boy".

"What the fuck is Harrison doing here?" I said to myself.

I approached Eddie's front door and turned the knob and to my surprise the door was unlocked. I entered as quietly as I could in hopes of finding out what was going on without them knowing I was there. The aroma of baked chicken hit my nostrils as I tiptoed from the living room to the kitchen with no one in sight. As I climbed the stairs, I began to hear the faint sounds of Eddie moaning. Once I reached the top, I stood there looking into Eddie's bedroom and watched Harrison in between Eddie's legs giving him head.

To be honest, I really didn't know what I expected but the weird thing was that I wasn't upset or angry. Truth be told, I was turned on like a muthafucka. My dick began to throb as I watched Eddie squirm and gyrate his torso as he shoved his dick in and out of Harrison's mouth. As I stood there in the doorway, I pulled my semi-erect boner out and began masturbating. Harrison's back was toward me and therefore had no idea I was standing there but after Eddie's eyes stopped whirling around in his head, he finally noticed me standing there.

"Oh shit, Sean," he said, scrambling and trying to pull his pants up. Harrison came up for air and turned around and noticed me standing there.

"Don't stop on account of me," I replied seductively while still playing with myself. I think they both were a little surprised at my presence as well as my don't give a shit attitude.

"Sean, what are you doing here?" Harrison asked looking baffled.

"Don't worry about me; you guys keep doing what y'all were doing."

Harrison looked at Eddie and Eddie looked back at Harrison. They both shrugged their shoulders and continued as if I wasn't even there. I continued to watch as Harrison drove Eddie crazy while slobbering up and down on his pole. I felt as though

I was watching a repeat performance of the threesome that me, Harrison and Thomas had.

"So, you gonna join us Sean, or what?" Eddie asked, knocking me out of my trance.

After a couple hours of sexual gratification had by all, Harrison got up and began dressing. Before leaving, he went in his pocket and pulled out three crisp hundred dollar bills and sat them on Eddie's nightstand. The next thing I heard was Harrison closing Eddie's front door. I laid there with Eddie in my arms thinking, *what the fuck just happened and will Eddie admit to me he was a prostitute?*

"Eddie," I whispered.

"Huh," he sounded exhausted.

"How do you know Harrison?" I asked sitting up in the bed.

"I don't."

"What do you mean you don't know him?" I asked becoming upset.

"Are you jealous?" he asked climbing out of the bed and heading towards the bathroom.

"Jealous, of that fat fuck, you gotta be kidding," I replied following him in the bathroom.

Eddie climbed in the tub and turned the shower on, "Wanna join me?" he asked while giving me that sexy crooked ass smile of his.

As much as I wanted to, I first and foremost wanted some answers. I knew Eddie sold his body because of what I found on the internet but I wanted him to come out and tell me. I wanted his honesty but instead he was being secretive and that was pissing me off. I'm not sure why I did what I did next but I guess it's because I can be somewhat controlling at times, especially if it's with someone I like. As a result, I yanked the shower door back and snatched Eddie by the throat and yelled, "How do you know him?"

"I don't know him, he hit me up on line," he responded

trying to catch his breath.

I looked at Eddie and for the first time, I saw a little fear penetrating through his eyes. I really don't know what's coming over me and I hate to admit it but I think I'm becoming more and more like Thomas. I released my grip from Eddie's throat and apologized profusely. Eddie just looked at me weird as I began to lather and wash his body from head to toe.

"Sean, what's gotten into you?"

"I'm sorry, I guess you were right, maybe I did get a little jealous. Please forgive me. Wow I'm hungry, how about you?" I asked softly looking into his eyes and trying to change the mood.

"Well, I did cook dinner for you. I'm sure it's cold now but I can warm it up Poppy," he said hugging me and whispering in my ear.

"Cool, why don't you go get it started and I'll be down in a few."

Minutes later, I sat at the kitchen nook watching Eddie prepare our dinner, wondering if he had put anything in my food to get back at me for doing what I did to him minutes before. My imagination was running wild. I really didn't know Eddie that well but there's something about having good sex with someone that you began to feel as though you know all there is to know about them but the truth is, you still don't know them at all. And I still seemed to get that electric shock when we touched one another.

"Is that what you charge brothas to have sex with you?" I asked breaking the ice.

"Damn, Sean, you almost made me drop this plate," he responded while sitting my plate in front of me.

"Answer my question."

Eddie grabbed his plate out of the microwave and sat across from me and began to tell me his story, for we all have one. He began telling me that his family was very poor; he was raised by a single mother on welfare. He never knew his father and as far as he knew his mom didn't have a family, so she did her best in trying to take care and feed him, his brother and his baby sister. He was born in Harlem, New York and while growing up, he had girlfriends but older dudes would constantly step to him and offer him money to have sex with them.

At sixteen, he pulled his first trick and that was because his mother had left home one night and they didn't know when she would return. Three days had gone by and she hadn't returned and there was no food in the house, so being the oldest, he felt it was his responsibility to feed his siblings. So one night he went on the "Ho Stroll" as it's called and this brotha named Spike, who was thirty-one years of age and a known drug dealer from the streets, offered him $100 dollars to bang his back out. Eddie stopped talking and looked as though he was actually remembering the incident and with a tear running down his right cheek, he looked at me and almost whispered, "He hurt me bad."

"What happened?" I asked feeling the anger boil inside of me.

Eddie wiped the tear from his cheek and continued his story. Saying that he informed Spike that he'd never done anything like that before but he was in desperate need of money and therefore would try it but asked him if he would be gentle since it was his first time. Instead, Spike did the complete opposite. Eddie said he got in Spike's car and they went to an abandoned building and Spike literally tore all of Eddie's clothes off, threw him against the wall and rammed his dick up in him raw and without any lubrication.

. Since that time and as time went on, Eddie stated that although his first time was very painful, he would periodically hook up with a brotha just to make some fast cash. At nineteen, he had been with several of the ladies from around the way, but that was just to make him still feel like a man. But he enjoyed having sex with dudes more. Besides, he had gone from being paid $100 to at least $300. He said that brothas loved his golden complexion and that his was the best fuck they'd ever had.

I have to admit, Eddie was an attractive Puerto Rican young cat, packing in the front and back. Hell, I know this might sound kinda sick, but my dick was at attention the whole time he was telling me his story. I guess that's because I understood what the other brothas saw in Eddie, he just reeked sex for any man or woman.

"So, why do you feel the need to prostitute yourself now? I mean, you have a decent job with Uncle Sam. I know it's not a lot but it's an honest living."

"Because I want more than what Uncle Sam can offer. How do you think I can afford this house? I wouldn't be able to pay for this house here in Hawaii for what Uncle Sam pays. Besides, a lot of dudes want the affection and I want their money, even trade, don't you think?"

"So, Harrison hit you up on line and was willing to pay you?"

"Yeah, hell all he wanted to do was suck my dick and for $300, you damn right," he said laughing and cleaning off the table. "By the way, how do you know him?"

"Before I answer that, I have a question for you?"

"And that would be?"

"You don't charge me, why?"

"Because."

"Because what?"

"Just because, now tell me your story," Eddie stated standing between my legs and placing small kisses on my face.

I began telling Eddie my story and how I got started in this life-style. He seemed to be fascinated and interested in all the details of my life. He then hugged me when I told him about losing Venus, he genuinely seemed sincere and that turned me on. However, he thought it was funny when I told him that he reminded me of Cameron although he nodded indicating that he could see the resemblance between us. I told him that I met Harrison through Thomas. I then began explaining my role as a

"SIR" and how I wanted him to be my "BOY" and if that was something he would be interested in?

"What's in it for me?"

"What do you want or need?" I replied looking into his eyes.

"I have everything I need and want…except."

"Except what?

"My family."

"What do you mean, your family?"

"My mom never returned home and I took care of my brother and sister the best I could for two years but Family Services came and put them in foster care. They didn't bother with me because I was already eighteen but I couldn't show them at the time that I could financially take care of them because I didn't have a real job. But that's why I do what I do because I plan to hire an investigator to find them," he said, holding his head down and sounding sad with a heavy Puerto Rican accent.

"I can provide that," I whispered, holding his chin up.

"Don't play Sean, I'm serious."

"So am I and I know you're serious because I've noticed that when you're emotional or serious, your accent gets heavier," I replied smiling and showing my dimples.

"Anyway Poppy, how would you do that?"

"Let me worry about that, a'ight? However, I will need their full names, ages and social security numbers if you have them." I looked at my watch and it was almost midnight. "But look, I gotta go, so hit me up tomorrow and give me the information, a'ight?" I said while getting ready to leave.

"Hey, Sean, if you're serious, what do you want from me in return?" he asked and again with a heavy accent.

"You!"

******

I finally pulled up to my apartment complex and noticed

that all the lights were on. I looked at the clock in the dash board and it read 12:48 a.m. It was strange that Gabe would have all the lights on considering he would normally be sleep by now.

"Gabe," I called out as I entered the apartment.

There was no response and no Gabe. I went from room to room and there was no sign of him anywhere. I opened the closet in our bedroom and saw that all of his things were gone as well and on the bed sat an envelope. I sat on the bed, picked up the letter and read it at least twenty times.

SIR, Yes Sir

Chapter SEVEN

When I got up the next morning, I still couldn't understand how I felt after reading Gabe's letter. I picked Gabe's letter up that laid beside me and read it once more and still wasn't sure whether I should be happy or sad but my emotions were outta control. I didn't know whether to laugh or cry, especially the part at the end when he said, "I'll see you next month and we will talk more when you come home."

I got up to take a leak and then headed in the kitchen to fix me some coffee. I turned the stereo system on while waiting for my coffee. As I stood there, I noticed on the dining room table a letter that appeared to have been lying on the table, open for anyone to read. I picked the letter up and it was from the Howard County District Court of Maryland. It was my summons to appear in court for the charges that I was pressing against Chauntel's father, Mr. Lomax and the hearing was scheduled for the 23rd of next month.

I got my phone that I left in my pants pocket in the bedroom to check the calendar to find out what day the 23rd fell on and just as I thought, it was on a Monday, which meant that I would have to leave here that Friday after work on the 20th. I fixed my coffee, turned the stereo off and went and sat on the couch. *This must be what Gabe was talking about seeing me next month,* I thought to myself. I turned the TV on and placed it on mute as I began dialing my mother's number.

"Hey, baby," she said answering the phone.

"Hey, Ma, how you doing and how's Lil Man?"

"We're okay, you taking care of yourself over there?"

"Yeah, I'm cool. I just called to let you know that I'll be coming home next month on the 20th."

"Oh really, what for?" she asked sounding surprise.

"Dang Ma, why you saying like that, you don't miss me or sumf'n?"

"I'm sorry, Sean; you know I didn't mean it like that. Of course I miss my baby and your son misses you, too."

"I miss all you guys. How's Lil V doing? Have you seen her? I know my baby girl is growing by the minute and are Venus's parents taking good care of her?"

"Yeah baby, your precious daughter is doing fine and she's being taken care of and being loved, okay?"

"Oh okay, I just needed to know Ma. Could you put Lil Man on the phone?"

"He's not here, Sean, you know my friend Ms. Betty up the street?"

"Yeah."

"Well, she took a group of the kids in the neighborhood to the circus; they just left about a half hour or so ago."

"That's cool. But anyway, I'm coming home because I received my summons to appear in court for the charges I was pressing against Mr. Lomax, it's schedule for next month on the 23rd and that's on a Monday, so I thought I would just come home that Friday before."

"Well baby, I definitely look forward to you coming home but are you sure you want to do that?" she asked sounding concern.

"Do what?"

"Press charges."

"Hell yeah," I said raising my voice.

"Who you yelling at? Don't think just cause you in Honolulu, Hawaii, Waikiki or whatever it's called that I won't come over der and beat yo but Mister!" she said only as a mother could.

"A'ight ma, calm down, my bad. I didn't mean to raise my voice, okay? I just don't understand why you don't think I should press charges?"

"Have you seriously thought about this, Sean?"

"What's there to think about, Ma? This man stalked me for months and tried to kill me."

"I know baby but…"

"But what, Ma?"

"Nothing baby, we'll talk more about it when you come home. I can't wait to see you, seems like years since I've seen my baby," she replied while becoming emotional.

"Okay Ma, well kiss Lil Man and Lil V for me and I'll talk to you lata a'ight?"

"Ah, Sean."

"Yeah, Ma."

"Ah never mind, we'll talk when you come home."

"Is something wrong, Ma?"

"Naw, everything is okay. We just need to talk when you come home, okay?"

"Look Ma, if something is wrong, I wanna know now!" I replied getting irritated.

"I said we can talk about it when you come home. Just take care of yourself and make sure you bring me and your son and daughter something nice from Hawaii."

"Okay Ma, talk to you lata."

My next call was to Justin. He had called me a few times and had left messages but I really didn't have a chance to call him back until now. Besides, I wanted him to know I was coming home and in a way, I had missed him.

"Well, I see you hadn't forgotten my number after all,

huh?" he answered with much sarcasm.

"Watch yo mouth, Justin. Now, how is my favorite BOY doing?"

"But Sean, I called you several..."

"Ah ah ah, what did I say Justin? Now, how is my favorite BOY doing?" I asked with authority.

"Missing you SIR," he replied calming down.

"I miss you too, man."

"Really?" he asked sounding unsure.

"Yeah really." Justin didn't reply but I could tell he was a little upset with me for not calling him back when he had been calling just to check on me. "Hey Justin?"

"Yes."

"Yo man, don't be upset a'ight besides; I have a surprise for you." I knew that would spike his interest, Justin lives for surprises.

"Oh yeah, what is it," he replied squealing into the phone.

"I'm coming home next month for a visit." Justin didn't have to respond because I could hear him smiling from ear to ear and jumping up a down like a big kid. "Did you hear what I said, Justin?"

"When, what day?"

"On the 20th," I heard movement in the background so I knew Justin was checking to see what day that was on.

"That's on a Friday, Sir."

"Yeah, I know."

"What time you coming in so I can pick you up?" he asked excitedly.

"I don't know yet but I'll let you know once I place my reservations." But as I continued to talk, I kept hearing Justin talking to someone in the back round. "Justin, whose there with you?" I asked becoming upset.

"Hold on, Sir." Justin said handing the phone to the other person he was talking to.

62

"Yo Sean, what's good with you bruh?"

"Mike, is this you?" I asked with a smile on my face.

"Yeah bruh, it's me. How's the fam over there in those parts of the woods?" Mike asked laughing into the phone.

"Wow Mike, its nice hearing your voice, man. I guess since I've been gone you've been keeping Justin occupied, huh?"

"Yeah, you know he likes black dick, so what can I say? So, I hear you coming home next month, huh?"

"Yeah, I am." I suddenly started thinking about the time Mike and I were in the shower. I can't even count how many times I've thought of him and being with him.

"Yo, Sean, you still there, bruh?"

"My bad Mike, I was just thinking about that time you and I were in the shower, you rememba?"

"Of course I do, I think about that from time to time, too. Maybe we can make that happen when you come home? I definitely will make it worth your while!"

"I'm sure you would, I don't doubt that for a minute, Yo."

"No doubt, so Sean, you find yourself a BOY over there yet?"

"Yo man, I'm working on this phyne ass Puerto Rican shawty. Yo Mike, you would love him man, he bad. Shawty got a tight little body and packed in the front and back."

"Damn, sounds hot. You need to bring Shawty home with you when you come, bruh."

"Trust me, I plan to."

"What's his name?"

"Eddie Salgado."

"Puerto Rican, hmmm, it's been a minute since I had a Spain-u-Rican." Mike stated while laughing into the phone.

"Look Mike, I gotta bounce in a few, tell Justin I'll call him back lata and that I need him to do me a favor, a'ight?"

"A'ight Sean, I'm sure he'll love that. He misses you,

you know that right?"

"So, he tells me and what about you?" I asked out of curiosity.

"He does, and as for me, I can show you betta than I can tell you."

"Damn, Mike, that sounds like a threat?"

"Yeah, it is but a good one!"

"Peace, my brotha," I replied smiling and hanging up the phone.

I really didn't have any plans so I thought I would chill and have some me time. I grabbed my laptop and went online and ordered two round trip tickets back to Baltimore, one for me and the other for Eddie. I thought this would be a nice surprise for Eddie as well as I wanted to introduce him to my family as well as my extended family. And even though I've only been in Hawaii for a few months, I had to admit to myself that I missed being back at home. The cheapest flights I could find were a little over five hundred bucks a piece, *dayum,* I thought to myself. But truth be told, being able to see my kids and my mom, I would have paid two grand.

While surfing the net, I decided to check out the gay website "Adam4now" to see what kinda brothas were in my area. I created a new profile using the name "WHIP_APPEAL" and I used a photo that Justin had taken of me at the "SIRS & BOYS" contest. It was a picture of me on stage with the off white suit I wore while answering the judges' questions. It was one of the best pictures that Justin took, although I did use the photo of me on stage masturbating as my private picture.

I chose my location and within minutes, dudes were hitting me up left and right. Before reading any of the messages, I viewed the pictures of the individuals that hit me up and I wasn't interested in any of them. So, I decided to change my location to the MD/DC/VA area to see if anyone was on that I knew. After chatting with a few brothas who just wanted to view my private picture and then wanted to hook up with me, I got a strange message from this one brotha who wrote:

Milbru4u: Hey Sean, how you been and how's Hawaii treating you?

WHIP_APPEAL: Who dis?

Milbru4u: An admirer

WHIP_APPEAL: What's your name and how do you know me?

Milbru4u: My name is not that important SIR.

This brotha was now spiking my curiosity, especially after calling me SIR. I checked his profile, he only had one picture and it wasn't very clear, rather dark and looked like it was taken from a distance. His stats indicated that he was 5'9 160 pounds, thirty-five years of age, versatile, and dark skin. The only message in his profile read: Made for Man. His location indicated that he lived Columbia, MD. This brotha was almost ten years older than me and I was intrigued, not just because he was physically fit but because of his message, *Made for Man.*

Milbru4u: Hey Sean, u still there?

WHIP_APPEAL: Yeah, w'sup?

Milbru4u: oh, I thought u left me.

WHIP_APPEAL: Naw, I'm here. So ur in the military, huh?

Milbru4u: Sumf'n like dat. So when are u coming home?

WHIP_APPEAL: Next month, y?

Milbru4u: I have sumf'n 4 u.

WHIP_APPEAL: and what's dat?

Milbru4u: I can't tell u, dat would ruin the surprise. After all, I know how much u like surprises. Lol

WHIP_APPEAL: u seem to know a lot about me and yet I know nuf'n about u?

Milbru4u: I do know a lot about u. I've been in love wit u for a long time.

WHIP_APPEAL: in love? Look bruh, what do u want from me?

Milbru4u: I just want 1 nite with u.

WHIP_APPEAL: to do what?

Milbru4u: anything u want. I'mma versatile brotha and I can please u anyway u want me to. Btw, how's yo boy Cameron?

WHIP_APPEAL: As far as I know, he's fine. Where are u stationed?

Milbru4u: Aberdeen Proving Ground. So what u coming home for?

WHIP_APPEAL: An overdue visit.

Milbru4u: lol, u only been gone a few months. U still pressing charges against Mr. Lomax?

This brotha shocked me with his last message, how did he know bout the charges I was pressing against Mr. Lomax. Who the fuck was he and why was he fucking with me? I looked at his picture again and still couldn't make out who he was. But yet, I was still intrigued and continued to chat with him.

WHIP_APPEAL: How do u know about Mr. Lomax?

Milbru4u: I know most of what there's to know about u Sean. I told u I was an admirer of urs.

WHIP_APPEAL: Why did u call me SIR?

Milbru4u: Because u are one. I was at the show and was thoroughly impressed wit yo style. I knew then and there that I had to have u.

WHIP_APPEAL: If u was at the show, why didn't u speak?

Milbru4u: I did, u must don't rememba. When u won, I was hoping that u would have chosen me as yo BOY but u didn't. I guess u didn't see me. So u chose Justin instead. ☹

WHIP_APPEAL: How do u know Justin?

Milbru4u: I've seen him around and hanging out at the club. But trust and believe, I can do more 4 u than he!

WHIP_APPEAL: Hmmm, is dat right? What makes u think that?

Milbru4u: Cause I know what u want and need, he doesn't nor does Cameron. But yo, I gotta run, I don't talk a lot but here's my numba. Text me
And I'll hit u back. 240-555-1234

WHIP_APPEAL: whoa, hol-lup, who do I ask fo? And here's mine, 443-555-8277

Milbru4u: don't worry; I'll know its u, PEACE!!!

The brotha just signed off and I knew this online crap is nothing but bullshit, but I wanted to get to know this brotha and find out how he knew so much about me. I stored his number in my phone under Milbru4u, since I still didn't know his real name.

I'll definitely hit him up in a few days or so, besides, that is the standard waiting time, isn't it? What I've come to learn is that brothas play the same game with other dudes as they do with females, no one wants to appear too anxious. Hey, I didn't make the rules; I just play the game and play it well.

Chapter EIGHT

At some point, I must have dozed off to sleep because I awoke drenched in sweat. I had that dream about Thomas and the little boy who turned out to be Jamaal. I hadn't dreamt about that in months, but what scared me was that Jamaal didn't have a gun, instead he had a butcher knife that was very similar to the one Mr. Lomax had. As Jamaal stabbed various parts of my body, I yelled out in agony as blood gushed out of my body. I fell to the floor, feeling as though I was dying. The only reason I woke up a few minutes later is because I actually thought I heard Thomas shouting, "Sean, wake up!"

I knew it was just a dream but it seemed and felt so real. The sweat pouring from my body felt just like the blood in my dream. I went to the bathroom to take a cool shower, so that my body temperature could cool down. Afterwards, I stood there drying myself off and looking into the mirror trying to figure out what the dream meant. What I did know was that Thomas was definitely trying to tell me something, but what? I smiled thinking about people who often talked about having a guardian angel and of all people, Thomas was obviously mine.

I quickly lotioned my body down and dressed in my jeans, wife beater, black boots and dog chain and headed downtown towards Honolulu to check out the clubs. I seriously needed to get out to clear my mind and be around other people. I thought about calling Eddie after getting several voice messages on my cell phone, but I wanted to check out Hawaii by myself and see what Paradise Island had to offer. Within minutes, I pulled up in front of this club called, "Hula's." I'd done a search online about all the clubs in the area and Hula's was supposed to be the hotspot to go to when those who were in the lifestyle wanted to, "Cum and Party." With cars everywhere, I had to park a few blocks away because the club appeared to be packed.

The nightlife in Hawaii is beautiful, I thought as I walked the few blocks towards the club. It was nice to breathe in the various exotic flowers that filled the Hawaiian air and listen to the sounds of music being played in people's cars as they drove by. With a perfect 75 degree temperature outside, I felt like a new man already. The thought of my dream had escaped my memory as I anxiously waited for what my evening would bring.

Moments later I approached the club's entrance, paid my admission and swaggered my way over to the bar. I didn't wanna act like this was my first time being here, but Hula's was amazing. I couldn't help but look at all the ethnic groups partying in one place. I smiled thinking about Michael Baisden's slogan, "One Station, One Nation." Back home, blacks partied with other blacks and whites partied with other whites, but of course you had those that were considered snow bunnies as well as those few whites who shall I say, liked darker meat.

"Aloha and welcome to Hula's, what can I get for you?" the female bartender asked snapping me outta of my thoughts.

"Ah my bad. Can I have a white wine, please?" I replied not really knowing what I wanted.

"Wet or dry?"

"Dry," I replied while looking around at the various patrons. I felt like a kid in a candy store eyeing all the different types of gay men. There were a few old heads trying to get their groove back but for the most part these men were of all nationalities and sexy as hell.

"Here you go, sir."

After paying for my drink, I began walking around to check out what the club had to offer. I noticed the DJ's booth back in the corner and decided to check out who he was because the way he was pumping the latest jams, I knew he had to be a brotha. The closer I approached the booth, I spotted this phyne ass brown tone brotha mixing and spinning his vinyl's like he was in another world. After standing against the wall and staring at him for ten minutes or so, he finally noticed me with a smile and waved his hand towards me as if to say, 'come here.'

Okay, here comes the game, I thought to myself as I approached his booth.

"Waddup bruh, I'm Obie and you are?" he shouted over the music while giving me dap.

"Just checking out the scene man, I'm Sean!" I shouted back.

"So, how long have you been here?" he asked starring me up and down.

"I just got here about twenty minutes ago."

"Naw bruh," he said laughing. "I mean how long have you been here on the island?"

"What makes you think I just got here?" I spat with one eyebrow raised.

"Trust me, I know. I know everybody who comes in and outta here and this is the first time I've seen your fine ass, so you gotta be new."

"So, I guess that's a compliment, huh?" I asked looking into the crowd as though I wasn't fazed. But truth be told...I was.

He stood about 5'8, short wavy hair, trimmed moustache and a pair of lips that I wanted to feel on every part of my body.

71

"I was just telling the truth but if you wanna take it as a compliment, that'll work, too," he answered while licking his lips.

"So, are you in the military?" I asked changing the subject and trying to keep my dick from rising.

"Naw, I'mma Army brat, my dad has been in since I was born."

'How old are you?" I asked in a curious tone.

"Twenty-two…why, am I too young for you?" he asked sounding a little disappointed.

"Naw, I'm only twenty-six. So, how could you be too young?" I asked pressing my body against his and realizing how funny it is that as men, we know when we're turned on. Mainly because our dicks forsake us and give us away whereas with females, they can hide their arousal state of mind.

"Yo man, what are you doing after the club?" he asked while looking up at me like a sick little puppy.

"Haven't decided yet," I said backing away from him. "I don't wanna take up too much of your time since you're working. Here's my numba, call me sometime."

I left Obie standing at the booth looking down at me as I began to mix into the crowd on the dance floor. That's one thing about brothas; you always gotta leave them wanting more. However, I was surprised when Obie took the mic and said, "Even though I just met you Sean, this one's for you, a'ight?"

Seconds later, the sounds of Jaheim's, "I Ain't Leaving Without You," filled the club as people raced to the dance floor to get their grove on. Looking up at Obie I winked, nodded my approval, then began to get my groove on as well. I had to give Obie credit, his spinning style was off the chain because I hadn't danced that much since being back at home.

By the time I finished dancing, I realized I had gathered a small crowd around me. Feeling a little embarrassed, I bowed before them and exited my way through the crowd heading towards the bar to quench my thirst. I took a seat at the bar and ordered another white wine. Obie thought he was being slick but I noticed him checking me out the whole time. *Dayum he sprung already,* I thought to myself as a smile creeped upon my face.

"Ah, 'scuse me bruh, would you like to dance?" this light skin brotha asked while standing over my shoulder.

"Naw, I'm cool man. I just got finished getting my groove on. Thanks anyway," I said looking up at his tall, slim frame.

"Oh okay, I'm Corey and you are?" he asked holding out his hand.

"I'm Sean, nice to meet you Corey," I replied shaking his hand.

"Okay Sean, well look, I'm not tryna come on to you or anything cause I'm not gay," he said with a straight face and a heavy New York accent.

"Oh, is that right?" Was the only response I could give. Always games with these brothas. Here this brotha is in a gay bar, asking me to dance but he's not gay. Ain't that a bitch?

"What's that suppose to mean?" Corey questioned looking baffled.

"What?"

"The oh, is that right, response you just gave."

"What am I supposed to say or think? Here you are in a gay bar, you ask me to dance but yet you say you're not gay."

"Dayum, my bad bruh, I guess that does look kinda strange, huh? Actually, I am straight, the reason why I asked you to dance is because my wife," he said pointing at this sexy, dark-skin sista sitting on the other side of the room. "She wanted to see you and I dance together. I know that might sound strange, but she likes to watch brothas dance together, especially if they dance well. You see, my wife and I were checking you out while you were dancing and looks like you can swing a little and since I swing a little as well, she wanted us to swing together."

73

"Wow, your wife is phyne."

"Thanks, I'll let her know you paid her a compliment. So, how about that dance?"

"Why don't you let me catch my breath and when I'm ready, I'll come get you, how's that?" I responded as I looked up at Obie and noticed the frown on his face.

"Okay, is that a promise?"

"I don't make promises to people I don't know. However, I will come get you."

Corey lowered his head as he strutted back over to his so-called wife. I sat there sipping on my fourth glass of white wine while checking the couple out. I wasn't sure what was going on between them, but he was very attentive towards her and couldn't seem to keep his hands off her. And the more I stared at them, the more I wanted to get to know this dark-skin sista. Shawty was perfect, long braids that hung down to her apple-shape booty, sexy dark bedroom eyes, and a small frame. The crazy thing about the whole situation was that the more I looked, the more I became jealous of Corey. I wanted to be with her, I wanted to be the one holding her hand and teasing her earlobes with my tongue. After gulping down the rest of my drink, I wanted to put an end to this show they were performing. I got up from my seat and headed in their direction.

"Well, Corey, are you ready?" I asked standing behind him.

"Sean, you scared the hell outta me," he spat turning around and being surprised.

"Sorry, I didn't mean to. Aren't you gonna introduce me to your beautiful wife?" I asked stepping in front of him and showing shawty my smile and dimples.

"Slow down playa playa, this is my wife, Peaches. Peaches, this is Sean."

"Nice to meet you, Mr. Sean," she stated with a smile

"Please, just call me Sean and the pleasure is definitely mine," I replied while visualizing her naked. "I hear you enjoy

74

watching your husband dance with other men?"

"Not just any man, he must be cute and be able to dance."

"So, you think I can dance?"

She nodded her head. "Yes."

"So, you think I'm phyne?"

"Yes," she responded in a sexy tone.

"Okay, okay…enough of this, I thought you came over to dance Sean, not hit on my wife," Corey spat sounding as though he was becoming angry.

"My bad, you're right. Let's do this," I responded leading him to the dance floor.

I was surprised to see that Corey could groove a little bit. The way he was gyrating his body was turning me on. It was a little strange at first because even though he said he was straight, it seemed as though he wanted our bodies to grind against one another. I looked over at Peaches and she seemed to be getting a cheap thrill while her husband and I danced. So I made the first move and I guess I caught Corey off guard because I began moving closer to him. I was only inches away and he looked at me as if to say, "What da fuck you doing?"

But I didn't care. I was curious as to how far this so called straight brotha would let me go. Taking things a bit further, I grabbed Corey around his waist as our torsos gyrated in sync. Although Corey looked at me like he could punch me in the face, his dick was telling another story. It was just as hard as mine. After that, we boogied as though we were the only two in the club. He humped and grinded on me as much as I did him. Peaches loved it; however, out the corner of my eye, I could see that Obie wasn't happy. His jaws were tight and he kept messing up on his mixing, personally, I thought it was cute.

Niggah don't know me from a can of paint and getting jealous already.

"You guys mind if I join in?" Peaches asked while sliding in between us.

"Not at all," I replied while grinding on her phat ass.

Over the next hour or so, Corey, Peaches and me grinded, gyrated and twisted our bodies as though we were having sex right there on the dance floor. Suddenly, the lights came on, letting us know that the night was coming to an end.

"Well, Sean, what are your plans for the rest of the night?" Corey asked as we walked off the dance floor.

"Nothing really, probably get something to eat and head on home. Why?" I questioned curiously.

Corey didn't respond, instead he turned around and whispered something in his wife's ear. I stood there waiting for a response while wiping the sweat that poured off my face with a napkin I'd grabbed from the bar.

"Sean if you like, I make a mean breakfast. So if you would like to come over and eat with us, you're more than welcome," Peaches stated with confidence.

Even though she was inviting me to eat breakfast with them, her body and the way she was looking me up and down was saying something else. I'm not sure whose idea it was to invite me, but I thought to myself, *naw, this married couple was not inviting me over to have a threesome or were they?*

"Sure, why not?" I heard myself say.

Chapter NINE

I got into my car and followed Corey and Peaches to their two story bungalow, no more than five minutes from the club. As I entered their house, I heard my cell phone buzzing. I took it out of my pocket and noticed that it was Harrison calling. I pressed the ignore button and placed it back in my pocket. *I'll hit him back on my way home,* I thought to myself.

"Yo Sean, welcome to our home. Have a seat," Corey stated while pointing to a couch that sat on the far left side of the wall.

I took a seat and watched as Corey and Peaches made their way upstairs. I suspected to change clothes and plot out what they were planning to do to me.

While waiting, I decided to check my message from Harrison, so I took my cell phone back out of my pocket. After dialing my voicemail, the automatic system informed me that I had four new messages.

The first message was a pleasant surprise from Justin, *"Hey Sir, when are you coming home? I'm missing the hell out of you and when you do get your phyne ass here, I have a surprise for you. Call me."*

Daymn, I'd just spoke to Justin, but it still brought a

smile to my face. My second message was from the brotha I'd met online. *"Hey Whip Appeal, this is Milbru4u. I had you on my mind and thought I would give you a shout out but I guess I caught you at a bad time. I'll hit you up lata. Peace."*

This was the first time I'd heard him speak and it sounded very familiar, but somewhat muffled. It also seemed as though like most gay brothas online do and that's trying to make their voice sound deeper than it really was. Most gay brothas do that to come off as being hard or a real dude as opposed to being thought of as a queen or punk. Fortunately, Mr. Milbru4u said he would call me back because not only had his number come up private, but he also didn't leave a call back number.

The third message was from the host of the SBI Show that I'd won several months ago. *"Hey Mr. Sweet Swagger, this is Ms. Ineedaman and I just wanted to know if you got your SBI packet that I sent out to you a few weeks ago. Give me a call cause I need to go over some things with you. Chow, kiss kiss."*

"Yeah, I have to remember to call her," I said to no one in particular.

The last message was from Harrison. *"Yo Sean, where you at? Tryna hook up wit you bruh for my protein drink, if you know what I mean,"* Harrison said as I heard his devilish laugh in the background before hanging up.

"You okay, Sean, would you like something to drink?" I heard Peaches ask as she entered the room with a long tank top on that clung to her body like paint.

"Some coffee would be nice," I replied while clearing my throat and trying to shift my manhood from one side to the other without it being noticeable.

"Sean, you're funny. Obviously you like what you like, so there's no shame in that. Why don't you come into the kitchen with me and keep me company while I make you some coffee and fix you guys something to eat."

Dayum, girl had busted me big time, but not to show any

embarrassment, I laughed it off, got up and followed this chocolate dark-skinned shawty out into the kitchen. I sat at the kitchen table and watched as Peaches prepared my coffee and a breakfast fit for a king. Peaches and I had basic conversation, but nothing too personal. I was too busy trying to look through her tank top because she didn't have a bra on or panties and the more I looked, the more I got excited. And she knew exactly what she was doing, as most women do. Now, if it wasn't for Corey, I would have had her ass up on this kitchen table by now fucking her brains out. And speaking of Corey, where was he? Was he giving me and his wife an opportunity to be alone? What kinda game were they playing?

And as if I was thinking out loud, I heard Corey coming down the steps saying, "Damn babe, da food smelling kinda good. Don't it Sean?" he asked entering the kitchen shirtless with just a pair of lounge pants on.

"Ah, yeah it does."

I was caught off guard as I watched Corey drop suddenly to his knees and start licking between her thighs. Now, don't misunderstand, I realized this was his wife, but the more I watched the more jealous I became. At that moment I came to the realization that I couldn't be just gay because both Corey and Peaches were arousing me. I sat there not knowing what to do. I didn't know whether to join in or get up and leave so they could have their privacy. How did I always get myself in these situations?

"Wow, I'm sorry about that Sean, but my baby taste as good as she cooks," Corey stated as he finally came up for air.

"No problem," is the only thing I could say while staring at Peaches as she tried to get herself together.

As I stated before, there was something about the look of ecstasy in a female's face that drove me insane. After shooting the breeze with Corey in the living room and looking through his work portfolio, since he was a photographer for Uncle Sam, Peaches finally announced that breakfast was ready.

We sat at the dining room table and ate until our hearts were content. Corey was right, Peaches had cooked omelets, hash browns, bacon strips, sausages, waffles and grits. One would never think that a phyne sista like Peaches could throw down in the kitchen, but the food was awesome. I did learn that both Corey and Peaches were from Harlem, New York and they were of Jamaican descent.

They'd been married for the past three years, but their families did not know they were married. Corey told me that three years ago just before going into the military, he asked Peaches on a whim to marry him and she agreed. Not believing that she would, they both went down to the Harlem City Court House and within minutes, they were pronounced man and wife.

However, after doing so, they both were scared and nervous as to what their families would say considering that Jamaicans believed in big weddings. So they both decided not to tell their families for fear of being cast out. And their families were actually planning a big wedding for them next summer. I told them as much as I wanted them to know about me. Basic things such as being from Baltimore and having been married, but my wife had passed away. I also told them that I was the proud father of two kids, a little boy and a baby girl. Corey and Peaches didn't have any children as of yet, but they were hoping to have a house full one day.

Time had passed by so fast that when I looked at my watch, it read 4:35 a.m. I then thanked both Corey and Peaches and stood up to leave.

"Well, Sean, I know it's late, but we have a guest room if you would like to stay," Corey said as I got up from the table.

"Of course, you're more than welcome to stay, Sean," I heard Peaches chime in as she got up to clear off the table.

It is kinda late and I am tired, I thought to myself. "Okay, I would like to take a shower, but I didn't bring anything with me."

"Don't worry about that, I have some lounge pants for you. Let me show you to our guest room," Corey replied while leading me up the stairs.

Corey loaned me a pair of his lounge pants, handed me a wash cloth and a towel. I stripped down to my birthday suit and took a nice hot shower. Afterwards, I climbed into bed and within minutes I heard moaning sounds coming from Corey and Peaches' room. It didn't take a rocket scientist to know what they were doing. I laid there tossing and turning until Corey finally walked in my room and sat down on the bed.

"Hey, Sean, you awake?"

"Yeah," I said groggily.

"I really wanna please my wife tonight and I know one of her fantasies is to have sex with two guys at the same time. So if you're down, feel free to come join us." As quickly as Corey appeared, he disappeared just as quickly.

I must admit, I really wasn't surprised by the invite. I was actually waiting to see who would come into my room first. However, now that I'd been invited, so many questions entered my mind at full speed. Questions like, *could I actually have sex with another man's wife while he watched? What was allowed and what wasn't? Isn't this sort of thing talked about before doing the act? And what would Corey and I do considering he was supposed to be straight?*

The moaning sounds coming from their bedroom motivated me enough to find out exactly what would go down. To show my boldness, I pulled off the lounge pants Corey gave me, swaggered my way to the entrance of their bedroom completely naked and aroused and watched as Corey fucked his wife in the doggy style position. Corey wasn't what you called built like me; however, his small light skin frame was tight.

He obviously worked out. Peaches was the first one who noticed me standing in the doorway and gestured me to come closer by the wave of her hand. I entered the room and stood in front of her with my manhood only inches from her mouth.

Corey looked up at me while still pounding his wife from behind and gave me that go ahead with a smile, nod and wink. I took another small step forward and watched as Peaches opened her mouth and engulfed my manhood. I looked down at her as my dick began to disappear, inch by inch. The warmth of her throat had me rock hard as I tilted my head back and my eyes rolled to the back of my head.

Peaches grabbed a hold of my ass cheeks and pulled me closer. I didn't know where I was going to go because all of my ten inches were down her throat. I then noticed Corey's pace had slowed down from pounding his wife as I noticed him looking right at me, eye to eye. I wasn't sure what he was thinking, *was I enjoying his wife sucking my dick too much or was his wife enjoying it too much*? But again, I couldn't read this look he was giving me. What surprised me even more is when Corey began leaning over his wife as though he was about to kiss me. Corey wasn't the best looking guy in the world, but he definitely had sex appeal. I stood there with my hands wrapped around Peaches' head as she continued swallowing me whole.

It seemed as though Corey was turning this staring match into an Alpha Male contest and I was not about to lose. I'd come too far at this point. So, if this was going to be another fuck or fight situation like it used to be with Thomas, so be it. Corey was only an inch or two from me, and then he closed his eyes and leaned in and tongue kissed me so sensuously I thought I was about to lose it. My knees began to buckle as he grabbed both of my nipples with his fingers and began to pinch them simultaneously. The sensation of this straight brotha, combined with the oral fixation I was receiving from Peaches had me at a point of no return.

Corey stopped kissing me for a second and looked dead in my eyes while licking my lips with his tongue. "Sean, you got some soft lips, bruh. You like that, don't you? Tell me you like it."

Before I could even utter a word, my nut squirted so

hard and fast that as I pulled away from Peaches and Corey's embrace, I literally fell back on the cold hard floor. Laying there and trying to catch my breath, I heard Corey and Peaches laughing as though someone had just told a funny joke. Corey was nice enough to stop doing what he was doing and actually gave me a hand up off the floor while Peaches had gone into the master bathroom and got me a warm wash cloth to clean myself up.

Not too many words were exchanged at this point. Next thing I know the three of us were back at it again. This time, I was instructed to suck Corey's dick since he'd never been sucked off by another guy before. Corey laid back on their king sized bed with dick in hand, waiting to see what the hype was all about. All I could think about was *the pressure of it all.* This could determine whether a brotha decided to continue with this kind of behavior or not. As Corey laid there, Peaches climbed over top of him and sat right in his face. Corey began to eat her out as he'd done earlier that night as I took my place between his legs and watched him stroke himself.

"Thank God he's circumcised," I said to myself.

Corey wasn't that big. If I had to estimate, I would guess he was about seven inches long but what he didn't have in length, he made up in thickness. I find it interesting that most slim dudes seem to have the thickest piece.

I began to lick his scrotum bag first so that he could get use to my touch so to speak. After a minute or so, I began to hear Corey moaning, thereby letting me know that he was enjoying what I was doing. I slowly lifted myself up from the bed and grabbed his manhood with my right hand and began to massage him. As I looked up, I noticed Peaches was staring at me as though she was taking notes. At first it bothered me, but when she smiled, whatever discomfort I felt had disappeared. At that point, I slowly began licking the head of Corey's manhood while masturbating him at the same time. Just to make things clear, I'm not that into sucking a brotha's dick. I can take it or leave it but there was something erotic about turning this straight brotha on as I continued to hear him moan, groan and squirm under me. It gave me a sense of power because as a man, I knew what he was feeling and what it would take to make him explode. That's called control, which in turn gives power.

I teased Corey long enough and therefore I opened my mouth, relaxed my throat muscles as I'd been taught and took all of him in...all in one swoop. I massaged his manhood as well as I did with my hand and from the sounds Corey continued to make, I knew that it was only a matter of time before he released. Peaches also seemed to be enjoying the action that I was giving to her husband because as in Murphy's Law, for every action there was a reaction and Peaches was definitely in an orgasmic state of mind based on Corey's thirst of her love canal.

Again, I knew it was just a matter of time and since I knew Peaches was in the process of having multiple orgasms; I wanted Corey to cum with his wife. So, I withdrew my mouth from Corey's dick and placed my right thumb in my mouth to moisten it and then I slowly began sliding my thumb up into his ass while going back down on him. I felt him tighten at first, but slowly he began to relax. And just as I suspected, he suddenly began to jerk and shiver and I knew he was cumin.

What surprised me was that I wanted to drink this so called straight man's protein drink. Corey even tried to pull me away from him but I wouldn't let him. He laid there shaking and gasping for air as Peaches stood and watched her husband in complete orgasmic state as though she had never seen him act that way before. And to my own credit, I laid there with Corey as he shook and quivered, giving me all he had to give.

"Shit, niggah," Corey managed to say while lying there, still trying to catch his breath.

All I could do is smile, not because of the cheap thrill he received, but because of the power it gave me.

"That was hot, Sean. My turn," Peaches squealed as she

lay down next to her husband with her legs spread open.

"Why not," I whispered while getting in between her legs. Peaches was such a beautiful black sista. Her body was smooth as silk but firm and soft all in the right places. I couldn't wait to stick my dick up in her.

Fortunately, Corey had gotten up and went into the master bathroom. When I heard the shower running, I assumed he would be in there for a minute, so for now, I was going to make Peaches mine, all mine. As I licked and kissed between Peaches' thighs, I found myself seriously desiring this woman. She was everything a woman should be phyne, sensuous, built like a brick house, smart and could cook her ass off. She had these small full lips begging to be kissed. I raised myself on top of her and then lowered my body weight on her and softly kissed her lips. At that moment, no one in the world existed, it was just me and her and we were free to do whatever we wanted to. As we kissed, I felt her nails digging into my back and the way she whispered my name caused a surge in me that God himself wouldn't and couldn't deny. And just as I was about to insert myself in her, I heard his voice.

"Yo, Sean, slow yo roll, bruh," Corey spat while standing over the bed watching us.

"My bad. I guess I was just getting carried away," I managed to say in disappointment as I rose up off of one of the phyness women I had ever met.

But deep down inside I wanted to tell his skinny ass to go back in the damn bathroom and let this man handle his business. As I stood there embarrassed, horny and thinking of what I should do next, she spoke.

"Sean, do you mind if I speak to Corey in private?"

"Naw, it's cool. Ah, I should be getting ready to go anyway, considering the sun is about to come up."

"Don't leave just yet, please."

She stated it in such a seductive way, how could I deny her?

Therefore, I made my exit into the guest room, turned on the portable radio that sat on the dresser just in case I needed to drown out any argument that was going to take place between them. I laid there thinking what was about to happen? Was she actually going to talk her husband into letting us fuck? I knew she was feeling me as much as I was feeling her, but would any man allow his wife to be fucked by another man who weren't considered swingers, or were they? Was this a game to them? Was I being played? What am I doing here? Just as I was about to say fuck it and put my clothes on, I heard someone tiptoe in the room. I naturally thought it was Corey wanting to thank me for our time together, but now it was time for me to leave. However, much to my surprise, it was Peaches.

"Do you mind if I lie down next to you?" she asked while sitting down on the bed.

"No, where's Corey?" I whispered curiously.

"Well, Corey and I have had a lot of experiences together with other women, and I've never complained because I will always satisfy him in any way I can. You are the first guy that we've ever had in our bed, whether you believe that or not and I want to be with you that way and I told him so. Besides, isn't marriage about communicating and being honest with your mate?"

"Well, I guess you got a point," I whispered while climbing on top of her. I didn't know where Corey was but at that point I really didn't care. What I did care about was how good of a fuck Peaches was and I was about to find out. In my mind, I wanted to bang her back out and place a permanent arch in her backside.

The black radio station in Hawaii was Power 98FM WKISS and they were playing some of the hottest slow jams. Being with Peaches, I felt like I was home in Baltimore and our fucking had turned into love making. I'm not sure whether it was because of all the familiar love songs that serenaded us in the background or if it was possible to make love to someone you weren't in love with. As I laid there in ecstasy as Peaches rode me like a jockey, I wondered if love making was an emotion or just simply a sensuous act. But whatever it was, Peaches was mine and I was hers, if only for one night.

SIR, Yes Sir

Chapter TEN

Mondays have always been the worst day of the week for me. Not only is it the beginning of the work week, but it's always been the busiest day since joining the military. Mainly because as a Sidpers Analyst, it was my job to slot all new recruits coming onto the base and after a full weekend, I had tons of paperwork from those recruits who had reported in over the weekend. There must have been at least eighty new recruits as I just sat there and looked over their paperwork.

Fortunately, everything seemed to be in order which allowed me to breeze through most of my work just before lunch. There was nothing worse than slotting a new recruit with missing or incomplete paperwork which would cause me to contact them personally and have them come into the office. Needless to say, this would often hold me up from getting my work done.

******

I left work just in time to make it to the gym in my complex and work out for an hour or two. I guess I was a little tired because after thirty minutes or so, I felt drained and decided to leave. There were so many thoughts going through my head, I just couldn't seem to concentrate. I kept thinking about what my mom wanted to talk to me about, Corey and Peaches from the weekend, and every time I thought of Eddie, my dick would get hard. I gathered my things and headed to my apartment. As I approached my front door, I noticed this brown package sitting on the ground. Bending down to pick it up, I noticed that it was the package I was expecting from Ms. Ineedaman. After opening the door and walking inside, I threw my stuff down on the couch and headed to the kitchen for something cold to drink.

I sat at my dining room table with my cold drink and opened up the package. The handbook Ms. Ineedaman sent was titled, "Sir, Yes Sir." There were also three dog chains with locks included along with a note that read;

This is your handbook Sean. Study it closely and show it to no one! Also I included three dog chains with locks to get you started, Enjoy!

With all my best,

Ms. Ineedaman

I immediately read the small handbook like it was a manual. I read it cover to cover and even though it was only eighty pages long, it took me up until midnight before I finished. Not that I was a slow reader, it's just that I wanted to get a full understanding as to what being a Sir was all about. In the back of the handbook was also a glossary section that gave definitions to the lingo used in this lifestyle. Included were different sections in the handbook which included chapters.

Chapter 1 The Beginning…

Chapter 2 The Responsibilities of Being a Sir

Chapter 3 The Initiation, Rules and Guidelines

Chapter 4 Finding the Right Boy

Chapter 5 Training your Boy

Chapter 6 Rewarding your Boy

Chapter 7 Punishing your Boy

Chapter 8 The Family

Chapter 9 Nationwide Organizations

Chapter 10 Contest, Rewards & Celebrations

Glossary

According to my new handbook, The Sirs & Boys Inc. was a subsidiary to the groups most widely known as the S&M (Sadism Masochism) Organizations. The first SBI began in 1971 and was formed by a brotha named Leroy Johnson. I know he was a brotha not only by his name, but there was a picture of him surrounded by several young white dudes wearing nothing but G-strings, dog chains and locks around their necks, obviously these were his Boys. I must admit there was something intriguing about this brotha being surrounded by these white dudes. In essence he was the HNIC (Head Nigga In Charge) and in this case, he was the only nigga, which gave him a certain amount of power that interested me. Mr. Johnson appeared to be in his mid to late 50's which meant he must have been around my age when he started the group. I had to salute any brotha who started any type of organization that still continues to grow after starting more than twenty-five years ago.

After reading Mr. Johnson's short bio, I learned that he started the SBI mainly because as a former member of an S&M group, he didn't agree with some of their rules and guidelines, but he enjoyed the brotherhood/family element that was missing from his own life. As I continued to read about his life, I learned that Mr. Johnson's father was a drug kingpin in Southside Chicago and his mom was a stay at home wife and mother. Mr. Johnson was an only child and at the age of six, he witnessed his mom and dad being murdered in their three bedroom home. Since that time, Mr. Johnson had been in one foster home after another. I guess that's why he craves so much in wanting a family.

I was also amazed that there was so much that went into being a Sir and how wide spread the "Sirs & Boys" organization had doubled in just the last ten years. This seemed to be some kind of underground fraternity that included females as well. And just as I expected, "The Keiki Wahi Palace" that stood for "The Boys Place," I had stumbled upon on the internet was located on the Big Island of Hawaii and was indeed owned by a Sir, at least according to the listing of Nationwide Organizations.

In reading the handbook I was surprised to learn that being a part of the "Sirs & Boys Inc." was not just about sex. Don't misunderstand, sex was definitely a part of it, but it focused more on what we as Sirs can provide to our Boys. There are people out here that seem to be missing something in their life. According to the handbook they give the example of a guy who wanted to learn how to cook like a chef. His Sir bought him several cook books and had him cook dinner every night for six months straight. Now, as simple as that might sound, there are people out here that need that extra encouragement and in some cases enforcement to complete their goal.

I began thinking about Eddie and his need for a family. This kinda reminded me of Mr. Johnson and his need for wanting a family. And I thought, not only could I provide an extended family for Eddie, but I could also have his brother and sister investigated and find out their locations. As I thought about Justin, I couldn't remember what his need for being a boy or even Rick's need, but I did remember Mike telling me that he joined mainly because he wanted to network his business as a consultant and not to mention that he also was a big freak; a smile crept upon my face.

Another interesting chapter was Chapter 3: Initiation, Rules and Guidelines. The manual clearly states that a Boy's initiation is one that is strictly unique and based on the Sir's judgment on what the Boy's needs might be. In other words, all initiations aren't the same, nor the time frame for initiations. And as a Sir, you may have as many Boys as needed and that you can have more than one initiation going on at any given time. Choosing the right Boy is based on the Sir's taste and desire and whether the Sir can indeed fulfill whatever need the Boy is missing in his or her life. The handbook also makes it clear that a Boy is not a gender nor is it an age factor, but a TITLE and therefore any gender of legal age may become a Boy.

Sexually, a Boy can be submissive as well as aggressive. He or she is responsible for making his or her Sir happy, including sex as long as the Sir is providing positive feedback and providing a path for the Boy to be successful in his or her overall goal. During a Boy's initiation, he or she may also be sexually active with Sir's other Boys. This is not mandatory however; it will be determined by both the Sir and the Boy. If it's determined that the Boy will be sexually active with his or her brothers and sisters, the Boy cannot be penetrated by anyone other than the Sir. Also during an initiation, a Boy cannot have other sexual partners, but once the Boy completes his initiation and becomes a full pledge Boy, he or she may have sex with others outside of the family.

The only requirement is that the Boy must ask permission from his Sir. Footnote: A Boy cannot and will not sleep with another Sir period. If he or she does, that Boy will no longer be a part of the family. The reason for this is considered disrespectful and can cause dissention between Sirs. A Boy may have a lover/wife/friend of their own only if that relationship does not hinder the Boys overall goal and that this other person understands that their extended family will come first.

Wow, this is some crazy shit, I thought to myself while laughing out loud.

The handbook continued to state that a Boy could resign or give up his position at any given time. For this position as a Boy is not a forced one and that anyone considering being a Boy must know that they can walk away anytime they chose not to want to partake in it any longer. Also, a Boy's position in the family is extremely important. A Sir can have as many Boys as desired and therefore, a Boy is placed in order, such as Boy 1, Boy 2, Boy 3 etc... And this is based on the Boys' initiation date. This is important because just like in the military, if anything were to happen, such as if Boy 1 decides to no longer be a part of the family, Boy 2 will then become Boy 1. Also Boy 1 will take on the responsibility of the Sir in his absence. The same will apply if both Sir and Boy 1 are absent; Boy 2 will then be in charge.

I found myself being so engrossed in my new handbook, I never bothered to stop to get something to eat as I laid there reading and hearing my stomach growl so loud that it startled me. I also began to wonder whether or not this was something that I could really do? And why would anyone want to be a Sir? Especially taking on the responsibilities of others? The more I thought about it I felt that some of the characteristics of a Sir would have to be confidence, aggressiveness, leadership skills, fairness, intelligence and more importantly a sense of authority. I knew I possessed all of the above but what could I gain from this other than Sex? Hell, I got sex anyway without having to deal with someone's issues and what was missing in their life.

As I pondered that thought, I continued reading about a Boy's reward and punishment. These chapters seemed to be somewhat vague mainly because the rewards and punishments were based on individual Boys and their likes and dislikes. As an example of a reward, if your Boy likes African American Art, as a Sir, you would spend a day and take him or her to an African American Art exhibit or African American Art museum. If your Boy enjoys going to the theater and watching live plays, then you take him.

An example of punishment can simply be just taking away your Boy's chain and lock for a period of time. Another form of punishment can simply be ignoring him/her. Meaning, no phone calls, no texts and no emails for a period of time. Again, these small examples are based on you as a Sir knowing what your Boy likes and doesn't like. However, no punishment will consist of anything life threatening. Knowledge of any Sir performing such acts will be dealt with accordingly.

I started wondering whether or not any Boy ever died in

the process. I knew that the SBI must have been very serious about this because Mr. Johnson signed his name next to the written statement. It's funny, I'd read books from time to time, but this little handbook was blowing my mind.

Chapter ELEVEN

I awoke early the next morning sprawled out on my couch still fully dressed in a cold sweat. After reading my new "Sir, Yes Sir" handbook all evening, I'd dreamt about my own initiation of being a Boy and how Jamaal had taken advantage of me. And even though it was just a dream, I was angry all over again and wanted to fuck Jamaal up. Fortunately, he was still in prison for murdering his own cousin Thomas. I stumbled as I sprung from the couch to prepare myself for work, took a shit, shaved and a quick shower, dressed and grabbed my briefcase and headed out the door.

Thank God most of the paperwork for the new recruits that came in over the weekend was completed before leaving work yesterday, so today was going to be more of a laid back kinda day. I pulled out my cell phone and noticed that I had several missed calls and two voicemails. The missed calls were from Justin, Corey from the club, Harrison, that dude from the internet, Cameron and Eddie. I called Eddie first without listening to my voicemails because I needed to get his brother's and sister's information so I could have Justin try to locate them. I also wanted to let Eddie know that I wanted him to come home with me and therefore he would have time to put his leave in.

Eddie picked up on the 2nd ring.

"Hey, Poppy," he answered sounding happy to hear from me.

"Hey you," I replied whispering.

"Why are you whispering?"

"Oh, I'm sorry, no particular reason. Is this better?" I asked raising my voice a little.

"Yeah, Poppy, and where were you yesterday? I called and left you a message."

"Let's just say I had some homework to do," I responded smiling into the phone.

"Homework, are you taking a class or something?"

"Somewhat, why you miss me?" I asked arrogantly. Eddie didn't respond and it sounded as though he was actually thinking about my question. "Hey you, you still there?"

"Yeah, Poppy, I'm here and to answer your question, yes I do. Why you ask?"

"I asked because I have to go home in a couple of weeks and I wanted you to come with me."

"Really?" he asked sounding surprise.

"Yeah, really," I responded confidently.

"How long are you going to stay and how much are the tickets?"

"I'm leaving on the 20th and will be coming back on the 31st."

"Well, I do have the leave time." He hesitated and then asked, "How much is a roundtrip ticket to Baltimore?"

"Don't worry about the ticket, I already got it for you."

"Oh, so you just knew I would say yes, huh?" he replied with a chuckle.

"Yes," I replied again with confidence. "And by the way, I need to get your brother's and sister's full name, place of birth, birth dates and social security numbers."

"Are you serious, Sean? What are you going to do with that?"

"I thought I might be able to help find them for you." There was a pause and it sounded as though Eddie was crying. "You okay?"

"Yeah, I'm okay."

"Are you sure?"

"Yeah, I'm sure." Eddie took a deep breath and asked, "Why would you wanna do that for me and what do you want in return?"

I wanted Eddie to be one of my Boys. But I didn't want to go into the details of that over the phone so I asked, "What are you doing lata when you get off?"

"Nothing really," he responded sounding a little sad.

"Okay cool. Well look, go ahead and put your leave in and I'll be over after work so I can get that information about your family."

"Okay, Poppy."

After hanging up, I couldn't help but smile at the thought of seeing Eddie again later tonight. I didn't know what it was, but I was really beginning to feel this little Puerto Rican dude. I then listened to my voicemail messages.

The first one was from Cam, *"Hey Sean, it's me. I just wanted to let you know that I was thinking about you and wanted to hear your voice. I also wanted to tell you something but I guess I'll talk to you once you get this message a'ight, bye."*

Damn, everybody seemed to have something to tell me. First, it was my mom, then Harrison wanted to tell me something and now Cam wanted to tell me something.

"What is this, tell Sean day?" I asked myself, feeling irritated.

I began calling Cam but closed my cell phone and I decided not to. Since I was going home, I thought I would just surprise him instead. The next message was from Corey, *"Hey Sean, this is Corey. I wanted to let you know that Peaches and I were going back home to New York in a couple weeks because our families' are throwing a wedding for us and I wanted you to come and possibly be my best man. I know we just met but considering the circumstances, Peaches or I can't think of a better best man. Hope you can make it, holla."*

I was flattered by the offer, not to mention that they were going to be in New York around the same time I would be in Baltimore. I picked up the phone and called Corey.

"Wassup?" Corey responded.

"Hey, Corey, this is Sean. I got your message but, hey, I thought you guys were already married?"

"Yo, Sean, I'm glad you called me back. Yeah man, Peaches and I are already married but our families don't know that, rememba I told you. Our families' are Jamaican and they believe in big weddings but Peaches and I didn't wanna have to wait so we just went to the Justice of the Peace and had it done more than three years ago."

"Oh yeah, I remember now. So, what's the date of the wedding?"

"It's going to be on the 22nd which is on a Sunday and it's at 2 p.m. So Peaches and I were hoping you might be able to make it?" Corey asked sounding excited.

"Well, interestingly enough, I'll be in Baltimore on the 20th. I have some business back home I have to take care of." I thought about it for a minute, considering all the things I had to take care of once I got home but then thought, *I could probably sneak away for a day and be a part of their special day.* So, I replied, "Yo Corey, I'll be more than happy to be your best man. Just tell me where and when." I knew deep down I was looking forward to seeing Peaches again and possibly be able to hit that one last time.

Corey gave me all the information such as location, address, date and time. Of course before hanging up Corey stated that Peaches would be thrilled that I decided to be his best man and that she had been talking about me since that night we met. I guess that was to make me feel good and it worked. What seemed crazy was that while thinking about the night I spent with Peaches and how much she turned me on, didn't negate the feelings and lust I had for Eddie, Cam, Justin or Mike. One would probably consider me a male whore and at this point, I really couldn't disagree with them. And as much as it hurts to admit that, I have to first and foremost be honest with myself. My only defense is that I'm still young, I have a decent career, I'm single or shall I say widower, I have a lot to offer and I'm phyne as hell. Hell, let's face it, if I can call myself a male whore, I can say I'm phyne as hell, right?

I didn't think my day was ever going to end but thank God it did and not a minute too soon. Just as I was about to leave, there were about thirty or more new recruits that had just signed in. I informed one of the privates in the outer office to gather the new recruits information and paperwork and I would input their information first thing in the morning.

******

The closer I got to Eddie's place, the more nervous I became. Mainly because this would be the first time I would have to explain what it meant to be a BOY and whether I could confidently entice him in being one, as well as explain the whole SBI organization. Even though I chose Justin as my Boy back home, he was already Jamaal's BOY and in a sense I just inherited him. But Eddie would be my first Boy as well as me being a SIR and having to initiate him. I checked my briefcase to make sure I brought one of the dog chains with lock that Ms. Ineedaman sent me. I grabbed the chain and placed it in my pocket while pulling up in Eddie's driveway.

I rung Eddie's doorbell and within seconds he opened the door wearing only a camouflage G-string and black army boots.

"Well, looks like you were expecting company, I see," I replied standing in the doorway smiling and looking him up and down while licking my lips.

"Oh Sean, I forgot you said you were going to be stopping by after work," he stated in a serious tone.

"Are you serious," I spat becoming agitated.

"Come on in, Poppy, I was just fucking with you," he responded while laughing.

"That ain't funny, Eddie," I said while pointing my finger at him.

Just as Eddie closed the door, he grabbed me and began kissing me as if he had seriously missed me. And as always his body and touch always sent an electrical shock through me. I wanted nothing more but to sex him right in his foyer area but this visit was not about getting a nut, this visit was about business. And obviously, Eddie knew something was wrong because he stopped kissing me.

"What's wrong, Poppy? You don't like what I have on?" he asked while standing back so I can see him from head to toe.

"Naw, it's not that. As a matter of fact, I love what you have on," I stated while trying to clear my throat.

"Then what's wrong?" he asked while looking me right in my eyes as though he would find the answer there.

Eddie was making it hard for me to concentrate. The way he looked at me, made me want to grab him tight and never let him go. His puppy dog eyes and his crooked smile made me weak in the knees, literally. It's funny how the simplest characteristics that people have can be so powerful against you that they can also blur your judgment. My body was calling and begging to be touched.

"Poppy, you're scaring me, what's wrong?" he asked again as his facial expression changed from being sexy to being concerned.

"Naw, I'm good shawty. I just need you…now," I replied in my sexiest tone and taking him in my arms.

******

Hours later while holding Eddie in my arms and lying in his bed, I began to have second thoughts about asking him to be my Boy. Not because I no longer wanted him, it was the complete opposite. I wanted Eddie all to myself and I didn't want to share him with anyone. We both just laid there not saying a word as though we were thinking the same thing but were afraid to say anything. The intimacy between us was electrical, no pun intended. We didn't just have sex and I couldn't say that it was making love either. To be honest, it felt as though it was on a higher plane. The kinda intimacy you have that just leaves you speechless. And if there was just one word to describe what you felt, that word would be, wow!

"So, what do you want from me, Poppy?" Eddie whispered while squirming around in the bed to get more comfortable.

"What do you have to offer," I replied giving him a devilish look.

"Don't start anything you can't finish."

"What makes you think I can't finish?"

"Come on, Poppy seriously, what do you want from me?"

"I want you to be my Boy," I blurted out not thinking.

"Boy? What do you mean, Boy?" he asked now sitting up in the bed.

I knew this was going to be a long and drawn out conversation so I got up to use the bathroom to stall for time. As I stood over the toilet handling my business, I still wasn't certain whether I wanted Eddie to be my Boy but the cat was out of the bag. I had opened my big mouth and it was a little too late to take it back.

"You remember the other day that you asked me what I wanted from you and I stated, I wanted you?" I reminded him as I sat on his bed facing him.

"Yes."

"Well," I said taking a deep breath. "There is something I want to tell you about myself and a question I want to ask you once I'm done. So before you respond, I want you to let me finish what I have to say, cool?"

"Okay, Poppy."

Damn every time he calls me Poppy reminds me of Cameron, I thought.

It's not a bad thing and I understand that's what Puerto Ricans use as slang but preferably that will change to Sir if he decides to be a part of my family. I took another deep breath and for the next 45 minutes or so, I explained how I had gotten involved in The SBI Organization and the reason, which was to help Cameron clear his name for murder. I went into detail about Jamaal and how he was trying to get Cameron and me out of the military and as a result in clearing Cameron, I agreed to become Jamaal's Boy. As Jamaal's Boy, he asked if I would compete in a Sir competition and to make a long story short, I had won which now made me a Sir.

As I continued to explain my story, I tried to figure out what Eddie must have been thinking based on his facial expression. However, I couldn't because he just laid there with a blank look on his face. I told Eddie about how Jamaal was found guilty in the death of his own cousin Thomas and when I won the Sir competition, I had chose Justin as my first Boy.

"Why didn't you choose Cameron, since you guys were so in love?"

"Cameron had just gotten married and knew nothing about the SBI Organization and I didn't want to involve him," I replied as honestly as I could.

"Why?"

"Because I don't think Cameron would be strong enough to handle the title of being a Boy and I've always felt the need to protect him."

"Wow, Poppy, you make him sound so weak."

"I don't mean to but I couldn't be his Sir and protect him

at the same time."

"You keep talking about protecting him, protect him from what?"

"Everything, the SBI as well as this lifestyle," I replied lowering my head.

"You must love him a lot," he responded while lifting my chin up with his hand. "Wow, someone once felt that way about me."

"How do you know if someone else doesn't feel that way towards you now?" I asked in a serious tone.

"Because I know the only reason why you are telling me all this is because you obviously want me to be one of your Boys and if you felt for me the way you felt for Cameron, is that his name?"

"Yes."

"You wouldn't be asking me to be one of them, right?"

I had to give Eddie credit, he was smarter than I thought but little did he know I was falling for him and if he had never brought up what I wanted from him, tonight may have gone a different way. Hell, I had known Cameron for over a year before I began to have feelings for him and I have only known Eddie for a few months, so this couldn't be love, could it? Before I could respond to Eddie's question he surprised me with this statement.

"Look, Poppy, I do know you care for me but I don't know whether you love me or not but I am falling in love with you and if you want me as your Boy, I would be honored, only on the conditions that once you do fall in love with me, and you will, I stop being your Boy and start being your lover."

"And what if that never happens?"

"It will, I promise you," he replied with his sexy ass crooked smile.

"Before you commit, there is an initiation for being a Boy," I responded while climbing on top of him.

"Trust and believe, I can handle myself Poppy."

"Well, in that case," I said getting up and searching my fatigues pockets for Eddie's dog chain with lock. "Stop calling me Poppy and call me Sir," I replied demandingly while placing the dog chain around his neck.

"Sir, Yes Sir," he replied laughing while giving me a fake salute.

Chapter TWELVE

Friday the 20th had finally arrived and I was on my way back to Baltimore. I seriously had butterflies in my stomach as I sat on the plane looking out the window knowing that within the next couple of hours, I would get a chance to see my children, my mom, Cameron, Justin and Mike again. It had only been six months or so but it had seemed like a lifetime since I left Baltimore. The thoughts that came in and out of my head were giving me a headache with such speed that my thoughts had consumed me.

"Excuse me sir, would you like something to drink?"

The beauty of being up in the sky and flying over the clouds was breathtaking. How could anybody deny there was God with such beauty?

"Ah, excuse me sir, would you like something to drink?" The attendant asked interrupting my thoughts.

"Oh, I'm sorry. Yes, can I have a rum and coke, please?"

"Not a problem and how about your friend, would he like something to drink as well?

I looked over at Eddie who was fast asleep and rightfully so considering that for the past couple of weeks, I have been running him ragged as a part of his initiation. "Naw, that's okay," I replied while the flight attendant handed me my drink.

Since that night at Eddie's house, I have been on him like white on rice. In training my Boy, the first thing I did was shave Eddie from head to toe as though he was a brand new baby and in a sense, he was. Eddie was completely bald. Around me, his wardrobe consisted only of a wife beater and faded jeans without pockets. Eddie was in training and that was his uniform. He had to ask permission to eat or even go to the bathroom. And when he did eat, I fed him like a baby and when he used the bathroom, I stood behind him, unzipped his pants and held his penis with my hand and when I said it was okay for him to pee, he peed. As a man, we should all know what our secretions look like and taste like. Therefore, once Eddie would urinate, I would take my forefinger and wipe his head and then place it in his mouth so that he knew what he tasted like.

Eddie bitched and complained at first but I gave him a mantra which was, "Sean is my Sir, he is my friend, he loves me and I trust him wholeheartedly." Eddie would have to repeat this every time he called me out of my name or tried to antici-pate my next move, whether it was for good or not. During his training Eddie and I did not engage in any kind of sex, whatso-ever. Reason being, Boys have a tendency to use sex as a weapon and try to get their way through sex. In most cases, Sirs need to abstain from sex with their Boys while in training be-cause it will take the power away. So, don't be fooled, sex has a lot of power!

Of course, these were just the basics when we were alone. But in public, Eddie knew his place. He wore his uni-form, dog chain with lock, wife beater, jeans with no pockets and tennis shoes without strings. He had to walk two steps be-hind me with his head down. He could not speak to anyone without asking for permission and when he wanted to speak, even to me, his mantra was, "Sir, may I speak?" Sometimes I granted it and sometimes I didn't. There were many times peo-ple would look at me and then at Eddie and probably wondered what the hell was going on but I didn't care and nor did Eddie. Most times when people stared, I would catch Eddie smiling which caused me to smile as well.

Eddie now calls me Sir consistently and has been a trooper and has done everything I've asked of him including not being sexual with anyone. He has passed with flying colors so far and has been wearing his dog chain and lock 24/7 and seems to take great pride in doing so. I've yet to tell him how much I appreciate that but I will. However, his final test will be based upon how he reacts and handles himself while in Baltimore. And in a sense, it's going to be a test for me as well. Meaning, how will he react while watching me having sex with my Boy Justin and possibly Mike and how I'll react watching him do the same. Eddie was right; I was indeed falling and falling hard.

Eddie doesn't know it yet but I've given the information about his brother and sister to Justin and a couple days ago, Justin called to let me know he'd found them. I had the information packed in my bags to bring with me so I wouldn't forget. I'm not sure why I hadn't told Eddie about finding his family, I don't know if it's because after reuniting with his family, he would no longer feel the need to be a part of my family? I guess time will tell as my mom would always say. Besides, if things worked out the way I expected in Baltimore, that information would be a wonderful graduation present for him.

"Sir, may I speak?" Eddie asked waking up.

"Sure. I see you finally woke up, huh?"

"My bad, but you should give me a break. You've been on my case for the past couple of weeks."

"So, you complaining, I thought you said you could handle yourself?" I asked laughing at him.

"I can and have, wouldn't you agree?"

"Yeah, you have," I replied conceding.

"Hmmm, I gotta piss like a muthafucka. May I use the bathroom, Sir?"

SIR, Yes Sir

"Yeah, you think you can handle it alone?" I replied smiling.

"Sean is my Sir, he is my friend, he loves me and I trust him wholeheartedly," he answered with his sexy crooked smile.

I sat and watched Eddie stumble and catch his balance while heading to the John. Damn, I was really feeling this dude, but how would I explain that to Cam or Justin? I knew they would be able to tell how I felt toward Eddie once they saw us together. Not that I cared, but sometimes I have a tendency to over think things and make things more complicated than they really are. Besides, I'm Sir; I shouldn't have to explain shit, right?

******

Once the plane landed, Eddie and I gathered our things and headed towards the baggage claim area. While waiting for our bags, I looked around searching for Justin who was to pick us up but he was nowhere to be found. Just as our bags were coming around on the conveyer belt, I heard the intercom paging me to let me know that my party was waiting for me out in front of concourse B. Suddenly, the butterflies returned. I led Eddie out in front of concourse B and standing there in front of his car was Justin looking good as ever.

"Hey, you," I said giving Justin a big hug.

"Hey, Sir, I've missed you so much," Justin said whispering in my ear.

"Justin, let me introduce you to Eddie, Eddie this is Justin," I said while putting our bags in Justin's trunk.

"So, this is the fellow that's been trying to take my place?" Justin spat.

"Sir, may I speak?" Eddie asked looking up.

"Ooo Sir, I see you got him trained pretty good," Justin replied while laughing.

"Justin, you went through it, so don't tease your brother," I replied while giving Justin a stern look. "Yes Boy,

110

you may speak."

"Well, you don't think very highly of yourself if you think someone can take your place. Maybe you didn't have a place to begin with." Eddie spat in return.

"Oh my, he's a feisty little one, ain't he?" Justin stated with sarcasm.

"Okay, that's enough from the both of you. I didn't come all the way here for no bullshit, a'ight?" I stated demandingly.

"Sir, Yes Sir," they both responded in unison.

I sat up front with Justin as Eddie sat in the back. I couldn't help but smile to myself about the comment Eddie made to Justin. It was funny and kinda reminded me of the spat that Thomas and Cameron once had. I know how catty Justin can be sometimes and was glad to hear that Eddie can indeed handle his own and can definitely handle Justin with no problem.

As Justin drove, I noticed that he was wearing his dog chain which brought a smile to my face. As we headed down 295 South BWI Pkwy, I began to realize just how much I missed being home. Justin talked a mile a minute the whole way but I also noticed that he kept looking in his rearview mirror checking Eddie out. I knew Eddie knew he was being checked out because one of the things I discovered about Eddie was that he was very observant, if nothing else.

"Sir, are you listening to me?" Justin asked interrupting my thoughts.

"Huh, what did you say?"

"I asked if you guys were going to stay with me, Mike or your mom."

"We're gonna stay with you as long as you treat Eddie with some respect, he is family."

"Sir, why you got to…"

"Justin, what did I say," I stated interrupting him.

"Okay, Sir." Justin repositioned his rearview mirror and stated, "I'm sorry Eddie, no harm meant."

"May I speak, Sir?"

"Granted."

"None taken; so don't worry about it," Eddie replied with attitude.

"Anyway, Sir, Mike told me to tell you, he would meet you in the shower," Justin said smiling at Eddie.

"Is that right," I replied smiling, "His place or yours?"

"I don't know, he didn't say but knowing him he'll probably be at my house by the time we get there."

"He still comes and goes as he pleases, huh?" I replied quickly knowing that Justin was just saying that to see if he could make Eddie jealous. I will definitely have to pull Justin to the side and get on him about his mouth. I could put him in his place now but unlike Jamaal, I wouldn't try to downgrade one of my Boys in front of another. And the thought of seeing Mike again was making me a little anxious. I guess that's because of the time we shared together when I went through my initiation. But first and foremost, I wanted to see my mom and children before fucking around with any of them.

"So, Edward, where are you from?" Justin asked sarcastically, knowing Eddie's name wasn't Edward.

"Sir, may I speak?"

"While we are here, you may speak to me or your brothers without permission, a'ight?

"Thank you, Sir," Eddie replied and then looked dead in the back of Justin's head and said with a heavy Spanish accent, "Now, if you're referring to me, my name is Eddie, not Edward and I'm from Harlem, New York."

"Oh my bad, I thought Eddie was short for Edward."

"It is, but not in my case. Is that a'ight with you?" Eddie replied angrily.

"Yo Justin, chill that noise. Eddie is your brotha, treat him as such."

"Alright, again no harm meant, I just thought I would mess with him a little bit. Considering he was still going through his initiation," Justin replied laughing and then whispered, "But he is phyne and seems like he can handle himself, too."

"He can, so watch yourself," I replied, warning Justin.

"Naw, we cool, right, Eddie?" Justin said while looking in his rearview mirror back at Eddie.

"Whatever man," Eddie responded

"But seriously, we're going to be the best of friends, you'll see Eddie," Justin confessed as we pulled up into his driveway.

As we got out of the car, I didn't notice Mike's car and that was a good thing because I wanted to drop Eddie over Mike's crib while I spent time with my family. At this point, I didn't think I could leave Eddie and Justin alone without somebody getting their ass beat by the other and I knew that someone would be Eddie.

We gathered our bags and took them in Justin's house and no sooner than we could get settled, Justin was all over me, kissing me as though he was some war bride and I was his soldier coming home on leave. I guess in some way, one could take it that way but I really didn't mind because I had missed Justin as well and also, I wanted to see how Eddie would handle me being with my other Boy.

I pulled Justin away and led him into the living room and took a seat on his couch. Both Justin and Eddie looked at me trying to figure out what to do next.

"Eddie, have a seat right there," I commanded as I pointed to a chair across from where I sat. "And Justin, you come here." I pulled Justin on top on me so that he could straddle me. Justin continued to kiss my neck, face, chest and any and every place he could.

"Would Sir like a blowjob?" Justin whispered in my ear and feeling how hard my dick was getting.

"Yes," I replied looking directly at Eddie.

Justin didn't waste any time; he stood up and stripped

from head to toe. I watched the expression on Eddie's face, but once again I couldn't read it and for some reason that made me angry. A Sir should be able to read his Boy; it's crucial in knowing what they're thinking. Most of the time, I could read Justin but Eddie wasn't going to be as easy. My thoughts were suddenly interrupted as Justin unbuttoned my pants and I felt him deep throat all of me at one time.

My eyes rolled to the back of my head as I thought about the first time Justin and I had sex in his home. One thing about Justin is that when he sucks dick, he makes more noise slobbering and licking than anybody I know and the louder he was, the harder I became. I opened my eyes and looked over at Eddie and once again, he was stoic. However, I noticed that he was obviously aroused because he had to reposition himself. I smiled at him as I felt myself about to bust my nut in Justin's mouth.

"Dayum Boy, I'm bout to bust this nut," I replied breathing deeply.

"Do your thing, Sir," I heard Eddie say as I saw him pull out his dick and begin to masturbate. I was so aroused by Justin handling his business and watching Eddie masturbate that I nutted so hard, Justin gagged as he swallowed every drop.

As I sat there trying to catch my breath and watched Justin wiping his mouth, I saw Eddie still masturbating trying to bust his own nut. "Justin," I whispered still trying to catch my breath, "Go help your brother out." Justin looked at me and then looked over at Eddie as though he wasn't sure as to what to do. "I said go help your brother," I replied demandingly.

Justin crawled over between Eddie's legs and took him in his mouth. Eddie looked at me and for the first time I noticed a surprised expression on his face. I couldn't help but smile at Eddie as he seemed to enjoy the head Justin was giving him. I left them alone as I got up to use Justin's bathroom to clean myself off. As I stood there running the hot water in the sink and lathering a washcloth, I thought maybe Justin and Eddie just might get along after all, which was definitely a good thing because that meant I could leave Eddie here with Justin while I go see my family. I couldn't wait to see my mom, Lil Man and my baby girl again. I felt like I had been gone for years. After cleaning myself, I looked at my reflection in the mirror above the sink and thought to myself how much my life had changed within the past couple of years.

I couldn't have been gone for more than ten minutes or so but when I came back into the room, Eddie had Justin leaned up against the wall as he pounded the shit out of Justin like he stole something. There was something erotic about watching Eddie standing behind Justin with his pants and underwear down to his ankles and watching his ass muscles flex with each pound into Justin's ass, not to mention that this was the first time I had seen Eddie fuck anybody. I stood less than twenty feet away gathering my thoughts and trying to figure out how it made me feel. I knew Justin was all bottom and Eddie was a versatile bottom, meaning he preferred to be a bottom but if need be, he could and would fuck like a pro. Eddie noticed me watching him and gave me a wink and a smile, which told me that he was fucking Justin not just for the enjoyment but also to take his frustration out on him because of the smart comments that Justin had made earlier.

I walked up and stood behind Eddie, kissed him on the neck and whispered in his ear, "I'll be right back. You guys play nice, a'ight?" as I felt his booty back up against me as he continued to pound Justin.

"I won't hurt him too bad, Sir," Eddie replied with his crooked grin.

"You betta not," I stated as I smacked him on the ass and headed to the front door.

SIR, Yes Sir

Chapter THIRTEEN

I pulled up outside my mom's apartment complex within minutes of leaving Justin's house, got out of the car and grabbed the bag of gifts in the trunk. I stood outside my mom's front door listening to my mom fuss with Lil Man. I smiled thinking how things have changed and yet how some things remained the same. It sounded as though my mom was trying to get him to eat his vegetables but Lil Man wasn't having it. I could have used my key but decided to knock on the door instead.

"Who is it?" I heard my mom yell.

I didn't respond, I just wanted her to open the door so I could surprise her, so I knocked on the door a second time.

"Lawd Jesus, I can't seem to get anything done," I heard my mom say as I heard footsteps move towards the door. I covered the peep hole in the door with my hand, knowing that my mom would look out to see who it was. "I said, who is it?"

"It's me, Ma," I responded knowing that she obviously wasn't going to open the door until I said something.

"Oh, my baby," my mom squealed as she opened the door and hugged me as tight as she could.

"Hey, Ma," I replied hugging her just as tight.

"Daddy, Daddy!" Lil Man yelled running up to me and grabbing me around my leg.

"Hey, Lil Man, I've missed you so much," I replied picking him up and hugging him.

"Well, Sean, come on in here, we don't need to let the world know our business."

I laughed and shook my head as I entered the apartment thinking how funny my mom could be sometimes. Here I was coming home for a visit but yet my mom thought we were letting out family business.

"Daddy, is you home for good?" my son asked sounding so grown up.

"Naw, Lil Man, but I will be home for a couple of weeks and we gonna have a good time, okay?" I replied sitting on my mom's couch with Lil Man on my lap.

"What did you bring me, daddy," he asked as he noticed the bag filled with wrapped gifts.

"How you know they're for you?" I asked playing with him.

"Now Sean, stop teasing," my mom replied as she began looking through the bag.

"Okay okay," I responded with laughter. I sat my son next to me on the couch, pulled out one of the boxes from the bag and handed my son his gift first. I watched him trying to unwrap the box and couldn't help but laugh because it was almost as big as he was.

"Sean, why don't you help him," my mom stated trying not to laugh.

"I can do it, Granny, I can do it," Lil Man squealed as he excitedly continued trying to open the package.

I reached in the bag and pulled out the gift I bought for my mom and handed it to her.

"Well, it's not as big as your son's but I guess good things come in little packages, huh?" she asked playfully.

"Awe Ma, you gonna love it," I said smiling from ear to ear.

"Lawd, what in the world is this?" my mom asked pulling her gift out of the box

"It's a muu muu, Ma. It's what the Hawaiian women wear in Hawaii."

"It's beautiful, Sean, I like this," she stated while holding it up against her frame.

"I thought you would, that's why I bought it for you," I stated proudly

"Oooo, Daddy Daddy, you got me an Xbox. Thank you thank you thank you Daddy," Lil Man squealed while jumping up and hugging me.

"You're more than welcome son," I replied hugging him back. I thought about buying him a WII console, but I thought it might be a little too advanced for him considering he's only three, even though he'll be four in a couple of months.

"Daddy, can you hook it up for me so I can play with it?" he begged.

"Sure, let's go and hook it up in your room, okay?"

My son placed his little hand in mine and dragged me into his room to hook up his Xbox. I didn't mind, considering this would give me and my mom some time to talk, while he played with his new toy. I couldn't stop thinking about what she had to talk to me about that was so important. As I stood there hooking up the Xbox, I noticed my baby girl asleep on Lil Man's bed. All I could say was, "wow".

She seemed to have gotten so big and my mom hadn't even mentioned that she was even here. I finished hooking up the console and my son immediately started playing one of the games that I also bought for him. I tiptoed over to the bed, picked my daughter up and held her in my arms. I looked down at her while she continued to sleep and I felt a tear run down my left eye. God she was so beautiful, coal black curly hair, reddish brown complexion, chubby cheeks and had the face of an angel.

I couldn't figure out whether she looked more like Venus or me.

I walked back out into the living room with my daughter still in my arms and noticed that my mom had begun cleaning up the dishes and dining room table.

"Ma, why didn't you tell me Lil Venus was here?" I asked taking a seat at the dining room table.

"You ain't the only one with surprises, Sean," my mom said smiling. "You hungry baby, you want me to warm you something up, we got plenty leftover."

"Naw Ma, I'm good. But wow Ma, she has gotten so big," I replied still looking down at her.

"Well baby, she's almost seven months old. What, you expected her to still be an infant?"

"No, well maybe. When did you get her?"

"I spoke to Venus' father last night and I told him you would be coming home today. So, he brought her over this morning."

"Thanks for everything, Ma. I don't know what I would have done without you."

"You don't have to thank me baby, just don't have any-more kids for a while," she replied somewhat jokingly.

"Oh trust me; you don't have to worry about that any time soon."

My mom finished cleaning up and joined me at the dining room table just to shoot the breeze about everything going on in Hawaii and that Gabriel left and decided to come back to Baltimore.

"Yeah, I know, he called me when he got back here. He mentioned that he had a hard time in finding a job over there. I guess it's as bad there as it is here, huh?"

"Pretty much."

My mom informed me that Gabe had been calling her at least once or twice a week to make sure she was doing okay and as a result they had started a friendship. She told me that she didn't realize how funny he was. Sometimes he was so funny that through laughter, she sometimes peed in her pants. I knew how funny Gabe could be and began wondering what he was up to.

Lil Venus began to wake up and started crying. I tried placing her on my chest and patting her back, but that didn't seem to help. Obviously my parenting and nurturing skills had disappeared because she continued to cry even louder. At that point, my mom took her from me and suddenly she stopped and dozed back off to sleep.

"Dang Ma, she must don't like me, huh?" I stated disappointedly.

"It's not that baby, she just doesn't know you because you've been away," she responded while rocking her back and forth. "The only reason she knows who I am is because I've been getting her on the weekend to give Venus' parents a break."

"How does Lil Man act towards his baby sister?"

"It was a little rough at the beginning because he was jealous of her, but now he is so protective. He won't let anybody touch her," my mom laughed.

"That's good. I'm glad to hear that," I stated feeling proud of Lil Man for acting like an older brother.

There was an awkward silence between us for a minute and I figured my mom wanted to talk to me about something but didn't know how to bring it up, so I thought I would help her out.

"So, Ma, what was so important you wanted to talk to me about?"

"A couple of things actually, the first thing is, are you sure you want to press these charges against Mr. Lomax?"

"Why shouldn't I, Ma? What kinda sick fuck takes pictures of a man's dead wife and sends them to him?" I spat angrily with flared nostrils.

"Okay, baby, calm down. I do understand your anger, but watch your mouth," she responded with a frown.

"I'm sorry Ma but every time I think about what he did, it pisses me off, you know?"

"I know, Sean, but have you thought about what would happen if he tells the court about your sexual lifestyle? I mean, I know the Army has that don't ask don't tell thing, but what if it gets back to your commander, then what? Wouldn't they try to kick you out of the military?" my mom asked in a concerned tone.

"I don't know Ma, but President Obama has signed the repeal on that policy, it just hasn't gone into effect yet. But I'm not gonna just sit back and do nothing. This man tried to jack me up with a knife out at the airport. If I hadn't kicked his ass, he probably would have tried to kill me," I spat still angry.

"I know Sean. I'm just trying to think rationally because I know how you are. You get angry and want to hurt someone before you think what it would cost you in the long run. Humph, just like your father." My mom looked at me as though she just said something she wish she hadn't but I wasn't going to let her say that just out of the blue and not give a reason.

"Excuse me, like my father, what are you talking about?"

"Sean, forget I even brought it up, okay?" she replied while getting up to lay my baby girl back down on Lil Man's bed.

While I waited for my mom to return, I sat and thought about why she would bring up my father considering that I really never knew him. And after her telling me how he used to beat on her while they were together, he was the last person I wanted to know. Now as an adult, I knew that if I ever met him, I would kick his ass all over Baltimore. Suddenly, my phone began to vibrate; I looked at it and saw there was a message from Justin. I put the phone back in my pocket and thought I would listen to it before I left but right now; I needed some answers from my mom.

I sat there for the next few minutes, but my mom never

returned, So I got up and walked to her room and there she lay across the bed reading a book.

"Ma, what's going on?" I asked while sitting on the side of her bed.

"Sean, I know you're upset about Mr. Lomax and going to court on Monday so maybe now is not a good time to talk about it."

"Look Ma, I'm sorry I got upset. It wasn't at you. I just want to do what's right and I don't think what he did to me was cool."

"No it wasn't and it angers me too, but I don't want to see you lose everything and get a dishonorable discharge just because of this, baby."

"I know you're only thinking of me but don't worry, I got everything under control, a'ight? Besides, like I said, that 'don't ask don't tell' policy has been repealed," I said, trying to assure her. "Now, what's this about my father?"

My mom took a deep breath and began telling me that my father had called her a couple of weeks ago and asked if he could meet me.

"Meet me for what?" I spat angrily.

"Well, I told him you were your own man and serving in the military and that that decision would be up to you."

"What does he want?" I asked with raised eyebrows.

"I don't think he wants anything. I guess he just wants to see how you've grown up."

"He wants to see how I've grown up, hell, where he been for the last twenty-six years or so?" Again I replied angrily.

"See, there you go being angry. So maybe this is not the right time."

"The way I see it, there is no right time and no, I don't wanna meet the niggah. Hell, I ain't got nothing to say to him, other than 'Hi Dad, where the fuck you been all this time'?"

"He's been living in New York, but he's been here in

Baltimore for his job or something he said. He's been staying downtown at the Hyatt Regency Hotel and left his number for you to call him," my mom said while handing me a piece of paper with his name and number on it.

I looked at the piece of paper and noticed the name which was Edward Salgado. I was stunned at the name for two reasons. One, I never knew my fathers full name. I knew his name was Edward, but I didn't know his last name was Salgado. When I was younger my mom never told me his last name but said that he was Puerto Rican and lived somewhere in New York. Since that time, we really never talked about him much other than the fact that he used to beat on her when he got drunk. So my mom always expressed the best she could that there was never a reason to hit a woman and I've tried to live by that.

However, I remember the day Venus had called my mother a bitch and I slapped the shit out of her. And as much as I hated to do it, she had it coming. Secondly, the last name Salgado jumped out at me and I suddenly became nauseous.

"You okay, baby?" my mom asked as I leaned over holding my stomach.

"I'm okay. I'm just feeling a little sick," I replied running to the bathroom.

I kneeled in front of the toilet expecting to throw up but nothing would come out. I stood up and grabbed a washcloth out of the cabinet to wash my face in cold water. I couldn't believe my father's last name was Salgado the same as Eddie's and that he too was also from New York.

"Sean, are you okay?" I heard my mom ask again through the bathroom door.

"Yeah, Ma, I'll be out in a minute, a'ight?"

As I stood over the sink looking into the mirror, I couldn't believe the coincidence in the fact that Eddie and my father had the same last name and both were from New York. What if Eddie was my brother, I kept saying to myself over and over and was that really possible? What were the chances of that really happening? I felt as though I was truly falling for this little dude, and now this. I remember every time Eddie and I would touched one another, there was an electrical shock and I thought it was because he might be "The One" and to think he was the complete opposite, "The Wrong One," my blood brother. Was God playing some kinda sick joke or what? The more I thought about it, the angrier I became at my father. My anger got the best of me and the next thing I knew, I threw a punch into the wall. The punch was so loud that I heard my mother yelling, "Boy, what are you doing in there?"

"I'm sorry, Ma; I'll get that fixed for you before I leave to go back to Hawaii, a'ight?" I replied as I opened the door and my mom saw the damage I made to her bathroom wall.

"Sean, what's going on with you? Are you that upset about your father?" she asked grabbing me by the arm.

"Answer this...does he have any other children?" I asked hoping the answer would be no.

"To be honest Sean, I don't know. Why do you ask, what's wrong?" she asked looking me in the eyes knowing I couldn't lie to her face.

"Ma, I have to leave, I'll try to explain every thing lata, a'ight?" I said as I brushed past her to go into my son's room. "Hey Lil Man, how's it going?" I asked then bent down on one knee next to him as he continued to play his game.

"Dad, this game is so much fun. You see that car right there? That's me and I have scored all these points. You see how many points I have?" he squealed, asking one question after another.

"Yeah, Lil Man, I see, you're pretty good at that," I replied while watching him enjoying his game. "Well son, I have to get going but I'll be back over on Sunday, okay?" I informed him while patting him on the head, but he was so into the game, he never responded.

Chapter FOURTEEN

I left my mom's house and sat in my car trying to gather my thoughts. *Should I meet my father if no more than just to find out the truth? Was Eddie Salgado my brother?* My anger was still getting the best of me as I felt my blood actually boiling inside of me.

"Fuck," I yelled as loud as I could as I banged my fist on the steering wheel.

I needed to talk to someone, but who? And in the back of my mind, I kept thinking to my self, *that's incest Sean, incest niggah, you foul, you foul.*

Suddenly I decided to pull my cell phone out of my pocket and call the only person I thought I could talk to. I noticed there were three voice messages but I ignored them and made my call. The phone rang several times and then went to voice mail. I didn't leave a message, what would I say? Maybe I could just let things go as they are, besides, who has to know and who's to say that Eddie is my brother?

"Fuck, fuck, fuck!" I kept yelling to no one in particular.

As I eventually calmed down, I grabbed my phone just to check my messages. The first one was from Eddie, the second was from Justin and the last call was from Mike, all telling me to meet them at the club, "Hippo," on Eager Street by 11:00 p.m. I checked my watch and it was already close to midnight.

******

Before walking into the club I ran into a couple of brothas that I knew just standing outside talking and smoking a blunt. As I stood there shooting the breeze with them, this black limo pulled up right in front of the club.

"Somebody living large, huh," I said to the brothas as I stood there to see who was getting out.

The first one to exit was this drag queen who was tall as hell. I knew it was a drag queen because her makeup was flawless, she wore a huge, fluffed up blonde wig and wore a blue sequin gown. And one of the brothas I was talking with told me her name was Akasha Casidine and the bitch was bad. The other drag queen that exited the limo surprised the shit out of me. She had long, straight black hair that hung down to her backside, a black sequin gown which was open in the back and her face was one that I would never forget, regardless how much makeup she wore.

I walked over to her just to see what she would do and she suddenly began screaming and hollering, "Sean, please go away! I don't want you to see me like this," as she tried to hide herself up against the wall.

"What the fuck you doing, what's this shit about, Cam?"

"Ah, excuse me honey, I don't know who you are but you need to leave my sista girl alone. Now, just because I'm in this dress and heels, don't mean I can't throw down. Don't get it twisted," I heard this tall drag queen say while standing behind me and taking off her heels as though she wanted to fight me.

"Look, bitch, you betta step off before I fuck you up," I spat while pointing my finger in her face. Cam continued to scream and holla so loud that a small group gathered around to see what was going on.

128

"Yo, my brotha, come on man, let's chill this out. What's the problem here?" One of the club's security guard asked me while trying to pull me to the side.

I stood there trying to explain to the security brotha that Cam is a friend of mine and I just wanted to talk to him but he started screaming and yelling and this big Amazon bitch stepped to me like she wanted to fight me and shit. By the time I finished talking with security and he realized I wasn't there to hurt anybody, Cam and the Amazon bitch got back in the limo and left. I guess it was for the best that they left considering what I was going through, I wanted to fuck somebody up anyway. I decided that I wasn't going to let it get to me so I went into the club to have a few drinks, see my Boys and have a good time.

The club was packed, standing room only. As I entered and made my way over to the bar, I ordered a rum and coke. I looked behind the bar and saw this huge banner that read, "Welcome Home Sir," I almost choked on my drink while reading the sign. I turned around to see if I could locate Eddie, Justin or Mike but they were nowhere in sight. Suddenly, the lights began to blink on and off and the DJ announced that the show was about to begin and to clear the dance floor.

The lights went out and the club was in complete darkness. The DJ blasted Christina Aguilera's "Show Me How You Burlesque," and the next thing I knew, Ms. Ineedaman came out in the spotlight and began doing her thing. Bumping and grinding, doing splits, and gyrating her big ass. The crowd roared as she tried her best to perform as Christina did in the movie, "Burlesque." Of course Ms. Ineedaman expected people to laugh because deep down, she's a funny bitch and no one can take that from her. Once she was done, people actually gave her a standing ovation and rightfully so. I too had to stand, clap and give the bitch her props.

After the applause, Ms. Ineedaman took center stage and breathing hard, she announced, "Welcome boys and girls.

Whew, Chile I'm tired. But anyway, whew, we're so glad you guys decided to come out and join us tonight. You see, tonight is a special night and we have a very special guest in the house that we want to celebrate his return back home from playing Uncle Sam's Army." People began laughing at Ms. Ineedamans' comment.

I couldn't help but smile from ear to ear at the thought of them wanting to celebrate my return back home. As Ms. Ineedaman continued to talk, I still didn't see my Boy's anywhere. And just then, my thoughts were interrupted as I heard Ms. Ineedaman call my name.

"Ah Sean sweetie, we have a seat right here up front for you so come on darling, and have a seat," she stated, pointing to a seat down front. I shook my head no because I really didn't want that kind of attention and besides, I could see clearly where I was. "Now, Sean, don't be bashful and don't have me come all the way over there and get you, so get your phyne ass down here, okay?" I felt like a child being scorned for being unruly as I made my way towards the front with my head hung low.

"That's betta, Sir," Ms. Ineedaman stated while winking at me. She continued to say, "For those of you who don't know who Sean is, he's the brotha that won the SIR competition we had several months ago and like I said earlier, he's been away on tour for Uncle Sam in Hawaii and he's come home to visit his family. And his family wanted to do something special for him. So are you ready, Mr. Sweet Swagger?" The lights shined in my direction that blinded me for a second and all I could do was nod my head, 'yes'.

The lights went out and it was pitch black and the only thing you could hear was Eric Benet's "Sometimes I Cry" booming through the speakers. As the lights began to come up slowly but surely, center stage was Justin wearing a black mask, a silk black shirt and black dress pants bumping and grinding slowly to the music. I must admit, I was becoming excited as he slowly began to strip down wearing only his mask, a G-string and his Dog Chain and lock. He came over to where I sat and began giving me a lap dance. I seriously wanted to fuck him right then and there but that wasn't the right time or place and I knew I was going to tap that ass later because that white boy had it going on.

As the song began to fade, the next person to come out on stage was Eddie, performing to a fast jam I wasn't familiar with. Eddie simply wore his Dog Chain with lock, a wife beater, jeans and tennis shoes. Once he came out of his clothes, the beat of the music changed to a slow jam by Fatty Koo called, "Chills". I couldn't take my eyes off of him; Eddie was truly an entertainer or just maybe an exhibitionist because even though people cheered for Justin, the room was cheering and on their feet watching everything Eddie did.

He did so many stunts and flips that he surprised me and when he straddled me, I thought I was gonna lose it. It had been weeks since Eddie and I had been intimate with one another and without thinking, I pulled Eddie's G-string off and began licking him all over. I believe we were going a little too far and the DJ stopped the music suddenly and Ms. Ineedaman had to remind me where I was and if I wasn't going to do the same to her, I needed to stop. The crowd hollered as Eddie excused himself and went back stage. And it dawned on me, the whole time Eddie was doing his thing; not once did I think about him possibly being my brother nor was there any electrical shock between us.

As I sat there a little embarrassed, a waitress brought over another rum and coke. I gulped that down as Ms. Ineedaman continued to entertain the audience by making jokes about what had just happened between Eddie and me. I'm not much of a drinker but by this time, I was truly feeling those rum and cokes and didn't care what people thought. I was ready to fuck! Eddie had made my dick so hard that I had to re-adjust myself and Ms. Ineedaman noticed and starting making jokes as

131

people began looking at me, smiling and licking their lips. Again, I didn't give a fuck. As I looked about the room, I thought my eyes were deceiving me as I noticed big mouth Jamaal standing in the back near the door. I shook my head and with the lights in my face, I really couldn't make him out definitely but once the lights were off me, he was no longer there but it couldn't be him because he was still in the Stock Aide.

Daymn, these drinks were stronger than I thought, I said to myself.

Again, the lights dimmed and Usher's old jam, "Yeah" blazed through the clubhouse speakers and center stage was Mike wearing the same off-white tuxedo I wore in the Sir Contest.

How did he get that, I thought to myself.

But I had to give Mike credit; he looked good in it and danced his ass off. He definitely would give Usher a run for his money any day of the week. Mike bumped and grinded over to where I sat and the brothas dick was hanging low and all in my face.

"How you doing, Sean, you feel like fucking yet?" Mike whispered as he turned around and sat on my lap while continuing to grind his plump booty against my dick.

"Always," I whispered back.

Mike smiled as he got up and slowly began stripping. As he stood in front of me the whole time, I thought, *what is it about this brotha that makes me feel this way?* Mike was one of those brothas who had a solid build and was packed in the front as well as in the back. Every time I was in his presence, I felt as though there was nothing I wouldn't let this brotha do to me. In the back of my mind, I believed he felt the same way about me. As the music changed with Prince's, "Adore" jam, Mike continued to look directly at me as if I was the only person in the room. He was practically nude at this point with just an off white G-string on.

He approached me and took my hand to follow him up

on stage. Someone placed a chair in the middle of the stage and that's were Mike sat me. The sounds of "Adore" played in my head and all I could think about was sex with Mike in all his glory seducing me, I forgot about the audience and as far as I was concerned, it was just me and Mike. While Mike laid on the floor and squirming his way towards me, out of nowhere Justin and Eddie came out on stage, still in their G-strings and began to tie my hands with rope to the sides of the chair. With Mike in front of me, Eddie on my left and Justin on my right, I noticed people standing up trying to get a better look because with the three of them in front of me, I'm sure it was difficult for them to see what was going on. I guess it was for the best because as Prince continued to sing, the three of them were taking turns in sucking my dick and I was truly in Heaven. The very thought of having all three of these brothas do what they were doing and what I felt for each one of them was incredible.

The only words I could utter from my mouth as I began cumin was, "Wow, fuck, dayum, shit."

Once I finally caught my breath and they cleaned me up, Mike led me back to my seat and I noticed that he didn't wear his Dog Chain with lock and it dawned on me that he really didn't have a "Sir" now because Jamaal was still locked up. So in the back of my mind, I was going to change that tonight. Mike, Eddie and Justin stood center stage as the crowd stood on their feet clapping and shouting, "Encore, encore!"

I sat there watching as the three of them bowed and gave each other love. And seeing how well Eddie seemed to fit right in made me feel good that Mike and Justin welcomed Eddie with open arms. Besides, isn't that what family is all about? They took their final bow and clapped for me and headed back stage. And just when I thought the show was over, Ms. Ineedaman came back on stage. "Oooo child, these mens are all that, whew... Anyway Sean baby, how you doing, you okay?" she asked staring directly at me.

"I'm good," I said nodding my head.

"Humph, I know you're good. I can see that, I just wanted to know if you were okay?" she asked licking her fingers. "Anyway Boo, this next entertainer coming to the stage is a person who has within the last few months have become of very dear friend of mine and from what I gathered, you were his first love." The audience began to "Oooo and aaaah" and in the back of my mind I'm thinking, *who da hell could that be?*

"Anyways, when she heard you were coming home, she wanted to do a special performance just for you. Now, my new daughter has only been performing for a little while but she's good so you muthafuckas act like you got some sense!" she spat looking out into the audience. "But seriously Sean, this one's for you. I bring to you, Ms. Camira Sexton."

The lights dimmed once again and I'm thinking, *who da hell is Ms. Camira Sexton?* But as soon as she stepped out from back stage, I knew it was Cameron. My mouth hung open as I watched him do his lip singing to Beyonce's "Single Ladies." I wasn't sure how to take his performance considering I didn't 'Put a ring on it' as the song suggested. I had to give him credit though because with his mustache shaved off, and all dressed up, he did look a lot like Beyonce.

I also wondered how and why he started performing in drag. Granted, he was only a stick of lip gloss away from being in drag but I wanted to know what was going on with him and Chauntel. Wasn't he still the devoted and loving husband and father? And how did he get to know Ms. Ineedaman and Ms. Amazon? In the past, we really never talked much about drag queens and therefore, I really never knew how he felt about them. But I would have never thought he wanted to be one. As I sat there watching Cam or shall I say, Ms. Camira Sexton, I didn't know whether to stay or leave, I just knew I began to feel a little uncomfortable because he looked at me the whole time. I also saw a few tears escape his eyes and I didn't know if he was trying to tell me something. But just as I was about to get up and leave, Rick took a seat at my table.

"Hey, Sean, long time no see, how you doing?" he asked in a genuine tone.

"I'm good, why do you ask?" I responded with my eyebrow raised.

"I just wanted to know if I could talk to you."

"Shhh, now is not a good time, don't you see there's a show going on," I replied while pointing at Cameron. Once I pointed to Cam, I wondered if Rick remembered who Cam was under the make up and realized that he was the one that messed up his shiny wooden floors a couple years ago. Deep down I hoped he wouldn't because I didn't want to fuck him up in this club considering how security was constantly keeping an eye on me.

"Sorry, my bad," he replied leaning back in his chair and looking around the room as though he was trying to find someone in particular.

Cameron was doing his thing and he was pretty good, I didn't know he had it in him. I guess all those years standing in front of the barracks floor mirror and lip singing to Patti Labelle songs finally paid off. Just as the song had ended, Cameron came over to my table and placed a slight kiss on my right cheek and made his exit without saying a word.

Ms. Ineedaman came back to the stage and announced that Ms. Akasha Casidene was next to perform and for the audience to get their dollars ready cause this bitch worked hard for her money. Well as much as I didn't want to admit it, Ms. Akasha performed her ass off. She did her rendition of Shug Avery from the movie, "The Color Purple."

I hadn't seen too many drag queens perform before, but this Amazon bitch was bad. I had to smile to myself because she had Shug Avery's character down to a "t." Every turn, every movement, every gesture, every look, and every note she had it just like Shug. She even wore the same wig and red sequined dress. I obviously wasn't the only one that felt that way considering all the money she was getting from the audience, even I had to give the Amazon bitch a couple of dollars. But in a sense I'm a voyeur, not just sexually but I enjoy watching people do what they do well and it doesn't matter what it is, if you're good at it, I'mma watch. That's just me and as a result, Ms. Akasha had won me over with her performance.

After Ms. Akasha's performance, Ms. Ineedaman came onto the stage and introduced the next few performers one after the other. There was one that went by the name of Ms. Helena Hollogram who did her soulful rendition of Gospel music and brought down the house. There was a Ms. Sabrina Blue who performed a few slow ballads by Stephanie Mills and Patti Labelle and amazed us all.

Ms. Ineedaman came back to the stage and thanked everyone for coming out and yelled, "So let the party begin." On that note, the DJ cranked up the sound system with Montell Jordan's, "This is how we do it."

"Sir, would you dance with me?" Rick asked.

"Naw, I'm kinda out of it and as soon as the fam comes out, we're going to be leaving," I replied sipping on my fourth rum and coke.

"Well, I know things didn't really start out well between us but I want to take this time to apologize and I wanted to know if I can be one of your "Boys".

"Look, Rick, now is not the time to discuss that, okay? I will be here for a few days and when I get a chance, I'll give you a call and we'll talk about it then. And you know as well as I do, the Boy don't choose the Sir it's the other way around. So, don't piss me off!" I spat as I rose from my seat and greeted Mike, Eddie and Justin as they approached my table.

"Yo man, I missed you," Mike said, greeting me with a hug.

"Ditto," I replied with a broad smile and returning his hug.

"Sir, would you like another drink?" Justin asked.

"No, I'm good but to be honest, I am ready to go," I

stated while yawning.

"So, what did you think of the show?" Eddie asked with his crooked smile.

"You guys impressed me and turned me on all at the same time. Why you think I'm ready to go," I replied smiling from ear to ear and rubbing on my dick.

"Well, I guess we better go," Justin squealed like only he could.

"A'ight, cool, but I wanna say goodbye to Cam first. You guys wait outside and I'll be right out."

"Okay Sir, we'll be waiting," Justin replied as he and the others headed for the door.

I made my way through the crowd towards the back of the stage but Cam was nowhere to be found. "Dayum, where could he have gone that fast," I said to myself.

I shrugged my shoulders and headed out to the front of the club where I saw Rick talking to someone who looked like big mouth Jamaal. I thought I saw his ass earlier and what the fuck is he doing out of prison? But as I tried to catch up with them, they headed out the front door so I ran to catch up, but as soon as I got outside, they were gone.

"Fuck, am I still imagining shit?" I asked no one in particular.

Chapter FIFTEEN

Amtrack Penn Station was crowded as hell; seemed; everyone was going somewhere. I, on the other hand, couldn't wait to get to Brooklyn for Peaches' and Corey's wedding. In all honesty, I couldn't wait to see Peaches. I'd been thinking about her lately and how she fucked my brains out the last time I saw her. Again, her European facial features on such dark skin had me hooked. There was something about a very dark skin sista that I find to be very sexy. Not to mention she was built like a brick shit house.

I gathered my suitcase as I heard the announcement that blurred from the surrounding speakers that Amtrak train 197 going to different cities in New York was boarding on track number six. It was a five hour ride and I could've flown, but the prices of airline tickets with no advance notice was ridiculous, so I decided to catch the train to check out the scenery on the way and catch up on some sleep.

I found my window seat and placed my suitcase in the overhead bin. It was five a.m. and I knew I wasn't going to get there until ten a.m. or so. I didn't get any sleep last night because Justin, Eddie, Mike and I fucked like dogs all night and I was sore as shit. I was so drained that all I wanted to do was sleep and eat as much food with protein in it to restore my swagger so to speak. I must remember to reward Eddie for last night; he handled the situation like a pro. I didn't allow anyone to fuck him but me. Deep down I knew he wanted Mike to fuck him by the way he looked at Mike, but that's against the rules. So, I allowed him to fuck Mike instead since he had already fucked Justin earlier. Yet again, I didn't feel an electrical shock while Eddie and I handled our business, but the sex was still off the chain. God, I hoped that dude wasn't my half brother!

After Mike accepted my offer of being my Boy last night, I thought, *wow, can I really handle all three of them?* And to be honest, as sore as I was, the only answer I could come up with was "no." Fortunately, it would only be for a week or so and then Eddie and I would be headed back to Hawaii anyway. I could hold out until then or die trying but what a way to go. A smile came across my face as I thought of the three of them. Now that Mike is a Boy of mine as well, the only one that can get fucked is Justin. I know he must be in fag Heaven.

******

Amtrak train 197 arrived in Brooklyn, New York at exactly 10 a.m. I didn't realize we had even arrived until one of the Amtrak employees woke me up to let me know. I grabbed my suitcase and exited the train. I'd called Corey the night before things got a little heavy with me and my Boys and informed him what time I would be arriving. I hoped he was in the terminal waiting on me because I really didn't feel like waiting around.

"Yo, Sean, how you doing," Corey asked as he tapped me on the back.

"Man, you betta stop creeping up on a brotha like that," I replied laughing and giving him some dap.

"It's nice to see you again, damn, niggah, look at you all dressed to impress and shit."

"Well, what can I say, I never know who I might meet,"
I replied knowing how good I looked with my light blue Calvin
Klein pant suit and matching Stacy Adams shoes.

"I feel you, bruh. Anyway, let's get the hell out of here.
Peaches is dying to see you as well as some of her family female members. Peaches been talking about yo ass and there's
this one cousin she got named Simone and believe when I tell
you, Halle Berry ain't got shit on her," he rambled on as I followed him to his car.

"Sounds good to me, I look forward to meeting her."

We made it to Corey's car, a 2009 Honda Civic and
drove to the Bronx, where Peaches' family lived and where the
wedding was going to take place at one of the neighborhood
churches.

"So, how was the trip, Sean?"

"It was cool, I slept the whole way here, man. I was tired
as shit, considering I didn't get any sleep last night."

"Why not?" he asked with raised eyebrows.

"I hung out for a few, you know, visiting family and
shit," I replied not wanting to let him know about being a Sir
because that was not his business.

"Yeah, I know how family can be sometimes, wanting to
sit up all night drinking and playing spades, huh?"

"Yeah, something like that. So, tell me more about this
Simone?"

"Man, she is all that. She's twenty two, phyne as shit,
got a nice job, got her own place and an ass that will make you
slap yo momma," Corey replied with laughter.

"So, why ain't she got a man?"

"As far as I know she got one but so what? He in the
military too and stationed in Afghanistan, so fuck him, right?

"Damn, Corey, that's messed up."

"What is?"

"The brother is serving his country and you want me to
fuck his old lady."

"Hell, I'm trying to fuck her myself, what you talking about," he stated while giving me a wink and a smile.

"Excuse me, aren't we here for your wedding?" I asked somewhat confused.

"Yeah, and? Peaches know what the deal is. I didn't tell her I wanted her cousin but she's done girl on girl action while I watched and later participated in.

"Yeah, Corey, but that's her cousin."

"So, shit, she a bitch, ain't she?"

"Damn, man, you cold," I said laughing and giving him some dap.

"That ain't cold, Sean, that's real talk," he said as we pulled into Peaches' family driveway.

We entered into this big Victorian style home and Corey began introducing me to everyone we saw. Deep down inside I wanted to see Peaches again, but Corey stated that she'd left earlier with one of her bridesmaids to pick up her wedding dress. Peaches' family was the typical close knit Jamaican family with heavy accents, dark skinned with the scent of weed almost knocking me down as I entered the house. Of course I wasn't complaining about the weed, the thought of it knocking me down was a good thing.

In the dining room area was a large spread of food consisting of various Jamaican and American dishes. I really couldn't remember the last time I really ate something, so I fixed myself a plate and sat at the dining room table as I watched Corey talk to every honey that was there. What I found to be strange was that even were I sat, it appeared as though he was coming on to every honey he spoke to while Peaches' family didn't seem to notice, especially her six huge, body-building Jamaican brothers.

There was this one honey who Corey was talking to that had to be Simone. I noticed that as he talked with her, he kept looking in my direction smiling from ear to ear. And just as suspected he brought her over to where I sat.

"Hey, Sean, I want you to meet this good looking sista here, Ms. Simone," Corey stated as he looked around at her backside.

"It's nice to meet you, Ms. Simone," I replied while standing up and extending my hand.

"Ms. Simone is not necessary Sean, just call me Simone and the pleasure is all mine," she said extending her hand to shake mine.

"Would you like something to eat or drink, Simone," I asked pointing to the food and drinks.

"No, I'm fine, but I see your still eating so I'll let you finish."

"Would you sit with me while I eat?" I asked pulling out the seat next to me.

"Sure, I would love to," she replied as she took a seat.

"Well damn, two's company and three is a crowd, so I guess I'll let you guys get to know one another while I play host," Corey spat as he walked away.

"So, Sean, Corey has been telling me a lot about you, is it true?"

"Is what true?" I questioned.

"Is it true that you like men and woman?"

"Sometimes."

"Sometimes what?"

"You go straight for the tough questions, huh?" I asked smiling and showing my dimples, hoping it would change the subject. Not that I didn't want her to know because, before I would sleep with any female, she would have to know that I am bisexual. And I definitely had plans of hitting that. But I was hoping that she would at least get to know me a little bit before knowing my sexual preference.

"Why not, it is what it is, right," she replied as she placed her hand on my leg.

"Let me ask you a question?"

"Shoot," she replied as her hand began to stroke my leg

143

under the table.

"Would it make a difference one way or the other?" I asked as my nature began to rise.

"I don't know, to be honest. I've never had the opportunity of knowing up front about a brotha because there are so many DL brothas out here. But with you, I don't know. Also, you would make it hard not to because you don't look gay, you know what I mean, and the fact that you're phyne don't hurt."

"So, because I'm not a finger popping, purse wearing and feminine acting brotha, it would be okay to sleep with me."

"Possibly."

"Okay, that's being honest, I guess," I replied with a full erection at this point while still trying to eat the rest of my food.

"I see you're enjoying your food," she stated as her hand slid up to my thigh and began feeling on my erection.

"It's not just the food I'm enjoying."

"You know, Corey had told me something else."

"Oh yeah, what else did he tell you?"

"He told me that you were his and Peaches lover and that you guys wanted me to join in with y'all tonight," she asked in a more serious tone.

"Are you serious?" I asked with a fake laugh hoping that she wouldn't believe it. Hell, I can't believe Corey actually said that shit to her, Peaches' own cousin. I definitely got to pull his ass up about telling people my sexual preference and I'm their lover. What kinda bullshit is that?

"So, it's not true?" she asked staring me straight in my eyes.

"No, it's not. I mean, I'm not their lover and as far as what they do as a couple is their business, right?" I replied staring back into her eyes. But at this point, I was no longer hungry and wanted to hunt Corey's ass down real quick.

"It doesn't really matter Sean, I was just curious and so I thought I would ask," she replied in a genuine tone.

"Naw, it's cool. I like a woman who's not afraid to speak

what's on her mind. But I have to use the little boys' room if you don't mind, a'ight?" I replied getting up from the table. "Are you going to be here when I get back?"

"Do you want me to?" she asked with a smile.

"Definitely," I responded back with a smile and walked off.

After relieving myself in the bathroom and throwing some cold water on my face, I then searched the entire house looking for Corey but I couldn't find him. I even asked a few people but no one seemed to know where he had gone. As I headed for the front door thinking that there were people out on the front porch, so maybe he had gone out there, coming through the front door was Peaches. I stood there and just watched her and her beauty as she greeted her friends and family.

"If it isn't Mr. Sean Mathews," Peaches stated as she approached me.

"Hey you," I replied as I took her in my arms to give her a hug and of course to feel her body against mine.

"I see you're still sexy," she whispered in my ear as she hugged me back.

"Just trying to be a better man for you or shall I say best man," I whispered back.

"Alright Sean, stop being bad," she responded with a smile as she stepped back from our embrace.

"So there's my wife to be," Corey said as he came up behind Peaches and hugged her around her waist.

"You behaving yourself, my husband to be?"

"Well, you know how I do."

"Yeah, that's what I'm afraid of," Peaches spat.

"Damn, Sean, what am I'm going to do with her? She thinks I'm going to do something stupid around her family. But anyway babe, your Pops wants me to take your Aunt home, so I'll be back in an hour or so okay? You wanna ride with me Sean?"

"Okay babe, and yeah Sean go with this fool to make sure he comes right back. He has a tendency to get lost sometimes."

"Not a problem Peaches, I'll make sure he stays out of trouble and comes right back. Besides, isn't that a part of my job being a best man?" I asked extending my arms out.

Chapter SIXTEEN

I sat in the back seat while Corey drove and Peaches' Aunt sat up front. I was surprised to see that there were so many different Burroughs in New York City. We don't have Burroughs in Baltimore but we do have different name communities. Corey tried to point out things and places of interest as he drove but I had so many other things on my mind that I really wasn't listening. Peaches' Aunt just sat in the front seat not saying anything at all but she didn't come off as being sociable anyway.

Fortunately, we finally made it to Peaches' Aunt's house and Corey was the perfect gentleman and escorted her to her door. I got out of the back seat to sit up front because I couldn't wait to talk to Corey about his big ass mouth.

"So, you ready to have some real fun Sean?" Corey asked as he got back in the car.

"To be honest, I don't know considering how you run yo dayum mouth!" I replied with attitude.

"Whoa Sean, what's wrong, what did I do yo?" he asked looking confused.

"Like I said, running yo dayum mouth! Why did you tell Simone, I was bi? Who gave you the fucking right, dude?" I spat angrily.

"Yo, Sean my bad. I just thought you were cool with your sexuality and you didn't mind who knew," he stated in a genuine tone.

"It's not like that at all, Corey. Personally, I don't think it's anybody's dayum business what I do and if I want them to know, I ... you hear me, I will tell them. Got it?" I spat raising my voice.

"Alright man, dats cool, my bad," he replied softly.

We drove in silence for several minutes and I just assumed that Corey knew his ass was wrong for opening his mouth so therefore, he had nothing else to say. But I had a lot more to say.

"And another thing yo, why did you tell Simone that I was you guy's lover and that we wanted her to join in on our threesome?"

"What's wrong with that man, don't you wanna hit that?"

"Corey, you can't be that muthafuckin stupid. Are you serious?" I replied looking at him as if he bumped his head.

"What?" he asked as if he didn't know better.

"Corey, what we did in Hawaii is our business and that's where it should stay but you don't bring that shit home under Peaches' family home. What if that shit gets back to her father or her brothers and then what? I mean, her father looks like he don't take no bull shit and what he can't fix, I'm sure he would get his huge ass sons' to take care of, know what I mean?"

"I guess you have a point, I really didn't give that much thought," he replied looking pitiful. "But her brothers and I are cool."

"You and Peaches' brothers are cool, Corey, but blood is thicker than water, a'ight? I didn't come up here to get my ass kicked. I thought I was just coming up here to join in on you guys' wedding and have some fun but you gonna get our asses killed if you don't watch your fuckin mouth, dude."

148

Just at that moment, Corey pulled up in front of Peaches'
family's house and maybe I was just being paranoid but the
way some of the family members were looking at us as we got
out of the car, I knew something had to be wrong.

"Yo, Corey, what's up with the family?" I whispered as
we approached the porch.

"It's cool, they always look like that," he whispered back
and laughed as though he just said something funny. "Hey
Cousin Reggie, I see you finally made it, huh?"

"Yeah, man, I got here a little while ago. But check it; I
saw Uncle Charles earlier and he asked me to tell you that he
wanted to see you in the shed. I guess he wants to have that Father and Son-in-law talk before you and his daughter walk
down the aisle," Reggie stated as he looked me up and down.

"Okay, cool, but let me first introduce you to my boy,
Sean. Sean this is my cousin, Reggie."

"Sup," I replied with a nod.

"So, you're Sean, I think Uncle Charles said something
about wanting to talk to you too, if I'm not mistaken," he responded with a smile.

"Alright Cuz, I'll rap with you later. Come on Sean, let's
see what Pops wants," Corey replied as he began to walk away.

"Corey, wait up bruh, where you going?" I asked trying
to catch up with him.

"I'm going around the back of the house to the shed
where Pops is."

"Whoa, and you don't think something is wrong with
this picture?"

"Damn, Sean, you are so paranoid. What you think is
going to happen?"

"I don't know these people like you do. So, as far as I'm
concerned, anything could happen."

"With all these people around?" he questioned as he
pointed to over fifty people in the backyard eating, dancing and
having a good time. "Anyway, Pops probably just wanna have a

father to son-in-law talk, you know like most fathers do."

"I hope you're right," I replied as I followed him to the shed.

As we walked in, Peaches' father who was a big, dark-skinned man with bulging muscles, who reminded me of the actor Ving Rhames, sat at the center of a long table with his sons to the left and right of him. Maybe I was just being paranoid like Corey said but it looked more to me like a firing squad and Corey and I were the targets. In front of this long table were two chairs and Mr. Charles gestured for us both to have a seat.

"Corey, how long have I known you?" Mr. Charles asked.

"Ah, I guess about five years or so but you already know that Pops."

"And when you asked me almost a year ago to marry my daughter, what did I tell you?" Mr. Charles fired back.

"You told me that I had your blessing as long as I never did anything to hurt your daughter, Pops," Corey replied nervously.

I sat there watching the two of them go back and forth as to what was expected of Corey as his son-in-law and it started to make me a little nervous because I had a feeling as to where this was going. And I knew this man had found out that Corey had somehow brainwashed his little girl into having multiple sex partners and living the lifestyle of being swingers. I also knew that it was just a matter of time before he started questioning me as to what my role was in their relationship.

"Young man, what is your name again," Mr. Charles' deep voice asked me.

"My name is Sean Mathews, Sir," I replied as I began thinking about my escape.

"And how do you know my daughter, Mr. Mathews?"

"Well, Sir, I met your daughter and Corey in Hawaii… "

"So, Corey, you like treating my daughter like a whore?"

150

And before I had a chance to digest what Mr. Charles just asked Corey, someone had come up behind Corey and began tying him down to the chair and I jumped up and began running as fast as I could. I didn't know where the hell I was going but I knew I had to get the fuck out of there. I made it out of the shed but before I got to the side of the house, I was caught by two of Peaches' brothers.

"Er, whey tha fuck ya tink ya goin?" One of her brothers spat in a heavy Jamaican accent.

I didn't respond as they wrestled me down to the ground and tried to tie my hands around my back with some rope. All I could think of was that I had no business going in that shed and I should have gotten my shit and left at that moment. Because of my anger and or fear, I managed to get up from the ground and began fighting the both of them. Family members and Peaches' other brothers began to gather around but no one would stop what was happening. Fortunately, I was able to get a good punch at one of the brothers and his ass fell out. That seemed to really piss off the other brother as he stared at me and then pulled out a switch blade while swaying on the balls of his feet from left to right.

"Your ass gonna pay for that, muthafucka," the brother spat angrily while lunging at me with the knife.

I moved out of his way just in time before the knife had a chance to graze any part of my body. I thought I would try to explain the reason why I was even there but I really didn't feel like getting into having a conversation with this brotha, I just wanted to get the hell out of there and no one seemed to care one way or the other as they cheered Peaches' brother on. Just as I began moving backwards to get further out into the street so I could run as fast as my legs would carry me, the brotha lunged at me again.

This time, I tried to grab the knife but instead it punctured my left arm just below my elbow and as I tried to pull away, the knife made a straight line down to my wrist. The blood squirted out of my arm so fast that I was totally in shock and therefore, did not feel any pain. The brotha just stood there looking at the blood as it dripped off his knife while family members began to gasp. I took this moment as my queue and began running as fast as I could. Again, I wasn't sure which direction to go in because this was my first time in New York but at this point, it didn't matter. I just wanted to get to the train station so I could get back to Baltimore.

After ten minutes or so of running and realizing no one was running after me, I ducked into an alley to try to nurse my wound. Blood seemed to be every where as I took my shirt off and wrapped it around my arm to try to stop some of the bleeding and catch my breath. Yet again, I was so angry about how things had gone down that I still didn't feel any of the pain from my wound. However, I was beginning to feel a little light headed. I needed to find a hospital quick to have my arm looked at but I didn't know where one was. I came out of the alley and began walking down a busy street, I don't know the name of it or where I was but there was a police officer on the corner sitting in his vehicle. I don't particularly care for police officers but I needed help badly. The closer I got to the vehicle, the dizzier I became.

"Excuse me officer…I I I…" and before I could finish my statement, I had blacked out.

******

When I finally woke up, I was lying down looking up at a ceiling fan. I tried to clear my vision and realized I was in a hospital with a tube running into my right arm. For a quick moment I couldn't remember what happened until I noticed the bandage on my left arm. I didn't know what time it was or even what day it was, so I rang the button alongside the bed for a nurse. After ringing the button continuously, a nurse finally entered.

"Yes, Mr. Mathews, and how are you feeling today?" she asked sounding a little annoyed.

"How long have I been here?" I asked anxiously.

"One of the police officers brought you in yesterday, don't you remember?" she asked as she began taking my vitals.

"If I could remember, I wouldn't be asking you," I shot back. "So, what day is today?"

"It's Sunday, Mr. Mathews, why?"

"Oh fuck, I gotta get outta here," I responded while trying to get out of the bed

"Oh no, Mr. Mathews, you have lost too much blood. I wouldn't advise you to leave just yet."

"Look Miss, I know you're just tryna do your job but you don't understand. I need to leave now!" I replied raising my voice.

As I finally made it out of the bed and still feeling a little woozy, the nurse ran out of the room. I suspect that she was going to go get the doctor or something but I didn't care. I'mma grown ass man and no one can keep me here if I don't want to be here. I needed to get back to Baltimore so that I could make it to my court appointment by tomorrow afternoon. I slowly took the needle out of my right arm and began looking around for my clothes. Fortunately, my clothes were hanging up in the closet along with my wallet, phone and watch. By the time I got dressed and ready to leave, the nurse had brought back a few doctors, as if they were going to stop me from leaving.

"Mr. Mathews, I am Dr. Ramirez and what seems to be the problem here?"

"There's no problem Doc, I just need to go home," I replied as I walked past him out into the hallway heading for the elevator.

"Ah, Mr. Mathews, I can't stop you from leaving but before you go, would you please sign this release form?" he asked holding out the release form on his clip board. I signed his release form, handed it back to him and got into the elevator. I pressed the bottom button for the lobby area and once there I made my escape outside and flagged down a cab to take me to Amtrak Penn Station in Manhattan.

Chapter SEVENTEEN

I slept the whole way back home and made it just in time to go buy a dress shirt since I left my bloody shirt back at the hospital in New York. My court appointment was at 1:45 p.m. and I walked into the court house at 1:30 p.m. sharp. I emptied my pockets in the small tray at the security desk and made my way through the metal detector. I didn't have my court notice on me and therefore couldn't remember which court room my hearing was in, I checked the board for today's hearings and noticed that my hearing was in court room three.

I opened the door and took a seat towards the back. There were only four other people in the court room so I sat there reading all the rules and regulations of being in a court room. The first one stated that no cell phones are to be on during court sessions. I took my cell phone out and noticed that I had several voice messages but decided to just turn the phone off until my hearing was over. There was a huge banner over the judge's chair with a woman blind-folded and holding a scale that read, *Justice is Blind.*

People slowly but surely began entering the court room as the court room bailiff started reading out court case numbers to check if everyone who had a hearing was there and accounted for. The court room bailiff also warned everyone that cell phones needed to be cut off and if they were to go off during the hearing, they would be confiscated. I noticed all those who hadn't yet read the sign to turn off cell phones going in their pockets to cut them off. I still hadn't seen Mr. Lomax enter the court room, nor had my mom showed up yet.

I still felt a little weak and my arm began to throb. I wish I had at least got a prescription from the doctor before I left. I didn't know what to expect but I just wanted this to be over with so I could go home and be with my family as well as my extended family.

"Here ye here ye, court is now in session with the Honorable Judge Robert M. Chatsworth," announced the court room bailiff.

We all stood up as the judge entered the court room and took his seat. Judge Chatsworth began warning us all of the rules of his court room and how we should conduct ourselves. "Bailiff, will you announce the first case for today," Judge Chatsworth asked his bailiff.

"Case number 100478378 Mathews vs. Lomax," the court room bailiff announced.

Shocked that my case was the first one to be called, I rose from my seat and walked down front and stood before the judge. I thought maybe the case would be dismissed or postponed because I still hadn't seen Mr. Lomax. Just as I was about to be sworn in, Mr. Lomax and, I assumed his attorney, walked up and stood to my right.

"Mr. Mathews, do you swear to tell the truth, the whole truth and nothing but the truth," The court room bailiff asked me.

"I do," I managed to say while holding onto my left arm as it continued to throb.

"And do you Mr. Lomax swear to tell the truth the whole truth and nothing but the truth?"

"I do," Mr. Lomax replied.

"Now that you both have been sworn in, you both may have a seat," Judge Chatsworth ordered.

"Your Honor, I'm the representing attorney for Mr. Lomax. My name is George Rainey, Esquire."

"Mr. Rainey, you will speak when called upon and not before. So, for your clients' sake, I suggest you have a seat as well," Judge Chatsworth ordered while giving Mr. Lomax's attorney the evil eye. "Now, in my court room people will speak when I say so and not before," Judge Chatsworth announced looking out over his glasses into the audience. "This case is about stalking and intent to kill with a deadly weapon brought on by you, is this true Mr. Mathews?"

"Yes, Sir."

"Mr. Mathews, have you ever been in a court room before?" Judge Chatsworth questioned.

"No Sir," I replied wondering why he asked me that.

"Mr. Mathews, I will only say this but one time so listen up. You will address me as Your Honor and not Sir, do I make myself clear?"

"Yes Sir, I mean yes, Your Honor."

"Mr. Mathews, are you being represented by council?" Judge Chatsworth asked me looking over his glasses.

"No Sir, I mean yes, I mean no Your Honor," I responded nervously.

"Well, which is it son, yes or no?"

I turned around in my seat to see if Justin had shown up but he hadn't. However, I did notice my mom who was sitting with, I presumed my father. I was so surprised that I sat there just staring at both of them. He stared directly at me as though he was trying to tell me something. What, I had no idea, but the more I looked at him, the more I realized that I looked a lot like him.

"Excuse me, Mr. Mathews, I asked you a question," Judge Chatsworth stated sounding annoyed.

"I'm sorry, Your Honor, the answer is no," I replied turning back around in my seat.

"And Mr. Lomax, this here is your attorney?" Judge Chatsworth asked pointing his finger at the man sitting next to him.

"Yes, Your Honor."

"And for the record council, what is your name?"

"My name is George Rainey, Esquire, Your Honor."

"Now that we know who we all are, we can get started. Mr. Mathews, you bring these charges against Mr. Lomax, so will you come up to the podium and tell me the reasons for these charges."

I stood up and approached the podium and began my story. "Your Honor, several months ago, I lost my wife in child birth and as I grieved the lost of her, Mr. Lomax found it necessary to send me threatening calls. He also had taken pictures of my wife in her coffin and sent them to me in the mail with a note saying something to the fact that I would be next. And since that time, Mr. Lomax has been threatening my life and on December 1st of last year, I was in the restroom at BWI International Airport and Mr. Lomax came up behind me reciting scripture in the bible with one hand and holding a knife in the other …"

"Objection Your Honor," Mr. Lomax's attorney announced as he stood up.

"What are you objecting to Mr. Rainey?" Judge Chatsworth asked.

"Well, Your Honor, the plaintiff here is rambling on and on about what my client allegedly did to him but my client never did any of those things and what he did do, he did because he was provoked by Mr. Mathews."

"Mr. Rainey, the plaintiff here has a right to say what he feels has caused him to bring this case forward. Now, if you want to cross examine the plaintiff you may do so but let him finish. Now have a seat, Mr. Rainey! Sorry for the interruption Mr. Mathews, please continue."

"Like I said, Your Honor, Mr. Lomax began reciting scriptures from the Bible and lunged at me with a knife. Therefore, I did nothing more than protect myself and in the process I took the knife from him and beat his ass, I'm sorry, Your Honor. I mean, I beat him until he was out cold lying on the bathroom floor and I left to go get airport security and they contacted the police."

I stood there and watched judge Chatsworth go through the file as though he was looking for something in particular, I assumed that the file he was going through was my file and probably looking for the report that the police took while at the scene.

"Are the police present who took this report?"

"Yes, I am, Your Honor," Officer Davidson stated as he came forth and stood next to me.

"Officer Davidson, you heard Mr. Mathews testimony of what happened out at the airport on December 1st, is that how you remember it?"

"Yes, Your Honor."

"Thank you, Officer Davidson, I appreciate you coming today. You may leave."

"You're welcome, Your Honor," Officer Davidson replied as he gathered his things to leave.

"Now, Mr. Mathews this is a very informal hearing and as you can see there is no jury but are you prepared to be cross examined by the defendant's attorney, Mr. Rainey?"

I didn't respond right away because even though I knew I would be asked questions as to what happened, I didn't know if I was really prepared. But something told me to go ahead and get it over with. "Yes, Your Honor, I am."

"Mr. Mathews, will you come up and take the stand please. And remember, you're still under oath," the judge stated. As I did so, I heard the judge say, "Okay Mr. Rainey, your witness."

Once I took the stand, I looked out in the audience and

saw Mr. Lomax looking as though he wouldn't hurt a fly along with his family, including Chauntel. I guess if looks could kill I would be dead by now. I was glad that Cameron wasn't there showing support for them. I glanced over to the other side of the room and again my focus was on my mom and this man she was sitting next to who had to be my father.

"Excuse me, Mr. Mathews are you going to answer my question?" Mr. Rainey spat.

"I'm sorry, I didn't hear you, what was your question?" I replied as though I didn't give a shit.

"Mr. Mathews, are you gay?" he asked approaching me.

"What the fuck... I mean, what kinda question is that?" I asked becoming angry while my arm started to throb once again.

"Mr. Rainey, I don't know where you're going with a question like that but I suggest that you ask another question," Judge Chatsworth stated in a stern tone.

"Your Honor, there is a reason why I asked the question and it does have bearing on this case," Mr. Rainey replied.

"Okay, Mr. Rainey, I will allow it but please get to the point."

"Mr. Mathews, I'll ask the question again. Are you gay?"

"According to Webster's Dictionary, no I'm not," I replied starring at him eye to eye.

"Okay, Mr. Mathews, then are you homosexual?"

"Again, according to Webster's Dictionary, no I am not."

"You know, Mr. Mathews, I'm a little confused. You say you're not gay or homosexual but isn't it a fact that you announced your undying love for the groom at my client's daughter's wedding?"

The people that sat in the court room seemed to have enjoyed what was being played out in front of them as they sat there listening intently. I looked at my mom, and as always, she was there to give me whatever support she could because she gestured with her finger for me to hold my head up high. On the other hand, my father sat there looking as though he was embarrassed or something, which made me even angrier. How dare this muthafucka try to come in my life after all these years and feel embarrassed like he really cared one way or the other.

"Any day, Mr. Mathews," Mr. Rainey spat.

"Yes, that's true," I replied while taking a deep breath. At that moment, people began laughing and talking amongst themselves. I guess it must have been something I said. But again, I didn't care. The only person in that courtroom I cared about was my mom and I knew she had my back.

"Order in my courtroom," Judge Chatsworth demanded as he pounded his gavel. "I will clear this courtroom if there's one more outburst, continue counselor."

"Thank you, Your Honor. Now Mr. Mathews I'm still confused, you say you're not gay or homosexual but you just admitted your undying love for my client's son-in-law."

"It's not confusing; maybe you need to rephrase your questions counselor," I spat sarcastically.

"Okay, Mr. Mathews, I will. Have you ever been married?"

"Yes," I replied without hesitating.

"Then that would make you bisexual?"

"Possibly," I answered fucking with him.

"Possibly, see there Mr. Mathews, there you go confusing me again."

"How so, Mr. Rainey?" I asked, sneering at him.

"Well, you declared your undying love for another man but yet you've been married."

"Yes, Mr. Rainey, I've been married, but I said that earlier if you had been listening." *Muthafucka,* I said to myself.

"Touche, Mr. Mathews, by the way, what do you do for a living?"

This was the one question I hoped I wouldn't have to answer. With the "don't ask don't tell" policy, the repeal has not

SIR, Yes Sir

gone into effect just yet and I could still get a dishonorable dis-
charged if I answered the question truthfully. Besides, what I do
for a living shouldn't have anything to do with this case. I guess
this is the reason why my mom didn't want me to press charges.
This muthafucka was backing me in a corner and I really didn't
know what to do or say. I was beginning to feel nauseous and
weak. I held my head low as the pain in my arm shot through
me.

"Ah, Mr. Mathews, we're waiting for an answer," Mr.
Rainey replied with a smirk on his face knowing full well what
I did for a living.

"Objection, Your Honor." I heard Justin shout. I looked
up and there was Justin in a blue pinstripe suit, crisp white dress
shirt and maroon colored tie with briefcase in hand. He looked
like one of those models for a Calvin Klein ad.

"And who might you be?" Judge Chatsworth asked
Justin as he peered at him over his glasses.

"I'm sorry, Your Honor, but my name is Justin Glover
and I'm Mr. Mathews' attorney," Justin replied as he made his
way up to the podium.

"Is this your attorney, Mr. Mathews?" the judge asked
me.

"Yes, Your Honor," I answered as I looked over at Justin
with a smile on my face. I had never been so happy to see Justin
in my life and there he was coming to my rescue once again.

"Your Honor, first of all let me apologize for coming
into your courtroom late. I was detained in another serious court
case. That being said, I would like to get a continuance so that I
may have time to prep my client," Justin asked the judge sounding so attorney like.

"Okay, Mr. Glover, I don't have a problem with that not
unless Mr. Rainey does?" Judge Chatsworth stated as he turned
and looked at Mr. Rainey.

"Your Honor, I believe that would be unfair to my client
to prolong this case and therefore, I asked the court to dismiss

162

this frivolous law suit."

"And why should I dismiss this case counselor?"

"Insufficient evidence, Your Honor."

"Your Honor, we do have sufficient evidence," Justin chimed in standing up to his opponent.

"Will the two of you approach the bench?" Judge Chatsworth ordered.

I couldn't hear what was being said as they stood in front of the judge but whatever it was, Justin seemed happy about it based on his facial expression. A few minutes had passed and both Justin and Mr. Rainey went back to their designated podiums.

"In light of Mr. Mathews having an attorney, I will grant his counselor a 30 day continuance. At which time we will resume with this case."

"Also Your Honor, I would like the last question that Mr. Rainey asked my client to be stricken from the record."

"Objection, Your Honor," Mr. Rainey blurted out sounding annoyed by Justin's request.

"On what grounds, Mr. Glover?" The judge asked.

"Relevance, Your Honor. What my client does for a living has no bearing on this case whatsoever." After Justin made his request, I looked over at the judge and noticed that he seemed to be taking it into consideration and within a few minutes, Judge Chatsworth had made his decision.

"It is this court's decision to have the last question asked of Mr. Mathews stricken from the record based on relevance. However, everything that was asked and answered up to that point will remain as a part of this case. I'll see you gentlemen thirty days from today. Mr. Mathews, you're excused."

Chapter EIGHTEEN

As Justin and I walked out of the courtroom, I saw my mom standing outside waiting for me. I was feeling so weak that Justin had to help me down the courtroom steps. He kept asking me if I was alright and I just nodded my head. Truth of the matter was I wasn't alright. All I really wanted to do was go to my mom's house and have her nurse me back to health. I know that sounds like I'm a big baby but I think most brothas who face a life and death situation like I had, regardless how old they are, want their mothers. There's no better care in this world than from a mother's love.

"Sean, baby, are you alright," my mom asked as Justin and I approached her.

"No, Ma, I just need to get some rest and eat a decent meal. Can I come and stay at your place for a while?" I asked as I started to become teary eyed.

"Sure you can, baby. You know you don't have to ask me that," my mom replied assuring me that everything would be alright.

"Mrs. Mathews, I'll drive Sir; I mean, Sean to your house," Justin said to my mom as he began to help me to his car. We made it to Justin's car and he was worse than an old mother hen, asking me question after question after question.

"Look, Justin, chill out with all the questions, ok?" I spat, becoming annoyed as the pain in my arm grew worse.

"Sir, at least tell me why didn't you respond to my voicemails. I would have been here on time if you would have told me what time your hearing was."

"I know Justin, my bad but I do thank you for all you did for me today, for real," I responded in a more genuine tone.

"You didn't think I was going to let that asshole make a fool of you, did you?"

"You had my back and I'll never forget that Justin."

"Humph, you better not," Justin replied laughing.

I knew I wasn't feeling well because before Justin and I had made it to my mom's house, I dozed off into a deep sleep and Justin had to try to wake me up. I suspect that he tried his best but I wouldn't and so he decided to slap me in order to wake me up and all I know is that out of reflex, I punched him dead in the mouth. As I realized what I had done, I couldn't help but laugh because poor Justin was knocked the fuck out. He was still sitting in the driver's seat but his face was plastered against the driver's seat window.

I would have carried Justin in my mom's house ordinarily but with my arm in excruciating pain, I decided to make sure the doors where locked as I exited his car and went into my mom's apartment complex. My mom must have been at the window and saw me enter because as soon as I got to her door, she held it open for me.

"Sean, you don't look so good. Go on in to my bedroom, I changed the sheets so you can rest in there and I'll bring you some of my good ole homemade chicken noodle soup and crackers, okay?"

"Thanks Ma," I replied smiling and thinking back to when I was younger and wasn't feeling well. My mom always fixed me her homemade chicken noodle soup as though that would cure whatever sickness I had. And the funny thing is, it always did.

As I undressed and got into my mom's bed, I was beginning to feel better already but I couldn't fall to sleep. I tossed and turned, thinking about all the things that were going on in my life. Seeing Mr. Lomax in the court room today angered me all over again for what he tried to do to me. Also seeing my real father today and how much we looked alike, was kinda eerie. I then started wondering how Eddie was doing and what he was doing. The fact that he could be my own brother was tearing me apart. But I was thankful that Justin was able to get me a continuance, even though I would have to speak to my commander about coming back here in 30 days to show up for a new court hearing. But would Uncle Sam understand and lastly, where was Lil Man and my baby girl? And with all that being on my mind and bothering me, I felt calmness within me and safe just because my mom was nearby.

"What happened to your arm?" my mom asked as she brought me my soup and crackers on a tray and noticed the huge bandage on my left arm.

"Ma, you don't wanna know," I replied softly.

"Yes, I do, what happened to you?" she demanded then sat next to me on the bed.

I had no other choice but to explain to her what had happened on Saturday when I had gone to New York for Corey and Peaches' wedding. She wasn't too happy about that mainly because I hadn't told her that I was going out of town. Needless to say, she loves me and still worries about me.

"What if they had seriously hurt you or kidnapped you and held you hostage and demanded a ransom," she asked upset with me.

"Ma, you watch way too much TV," I responded with a huge smile.

"It's not funny, Sean," she responded still sounding angry.

"I'm sorry, Ma, I don't mean to laugh but it was kinda

funny."

"See that's your problem, you think everything is a joke!"

"Naw, Ma, I don't. I didn't mean to upset you and again, I'm sorry," I replied in a more serious tone. "You forgive me?"

"Yes, don't I always, even though I shouldn't? But anyway, let me take a look at that wound."

My mom began to unwrap the bandage from around my arm and it was the first time I had even looked at it myself. It was still bruised and had over a 100 stitches. I looked at my mom and could see the water well up in her eyes as she sat there and began to slightly run her hand over my new wound.

"It's not as bad as it looks," is all I could really say to soothe her pain.

"You know you going to have this scar for the rest of your life, don't you?"

"Yeah, Ma, I know but its okay because maybe it will be a reminder for me not to do anything stupid again."

"Humph, I hope so. Does it hurt?"

"It did but not now."

"Well, let me go to the store and get you a new dressing for that arm and pick up some Tylenol or something for the pain."

"Wait Ma, before you leave, where are the kids?"

"You remember my friend down the street, Ms. Betty; she kept him for me so I could come to court today. I'm going to stop by there on the way back to pick him up and Lil V are with her grandparents."

"Oh okay. By the way, what happened to my father, I guess he got upset and left?" I asked as I continued to eat my soup.

"Huh, your father, what are you talking about Sean?" she asked looking puzzled.

"Yeah, wasn't that my father with you today in the court room?"

"You sure you feeling okay," she asked as she began feeling my forehead.

"I'm fine now, but who was that man you were with in the court room?"

"Sean, I wasn't with anyone, I came there alone."

"But there was a guy sitting next to you in the court room today wasn't it?"

"No, I don't think so," my mom replied looking at me strangely. "Look Sean, I'll be right back as soon as I can, why don't you try and get some sleep?"

My mom took the empty tray of food that I had eaten and left to go to the store. I laid there thinking I had imagined seeing my father. What the fuck was going on with me? Was I imaging seeing my father because of some kind of traumatic side effect from the ordeal I had suffered? Whatever it was I thought maybe, just maybe, I might be going crazy.

Chapter NINETEEN

When I finally awoke, I wasn't sure what day it was or what time it was but it was dark outside based on the street light that glared into my mom's bedroom window. I also heard voices talking and laughing out in my mom's living room. I looked down at my arm and noticed that she had placed a new bandage around my arm and the pain was gone, thank God. I guess all I really needed was my mom's cooking and some rest. Besides, I knew I was feeling better because when I woke up, my dick was harder than a brick and all I could think about was fucking and getting dicked down by Mike.

"So, you're awake?" my mom asked startling me as she peaked into the bedroom.

"Yeah Ma, I'm awake. Who's that in the living room?" I asked while trying to conceal my boner.

"It's a surprise, come on out and say hello," she smiled while going out into the living room.

As I began to dress I remembered I left Justin out in the car knocked out. I looked out of my mom's bedroom window to see if the car was still there but it wasn't. Obviously he must have awakened and left, at least I hope so considering a white dude in this area by himself would get jumped in a heartbeat. I

SIR, Yes Sir

pulled out my cell to check on him and noticed I had several
missed calls. As I strolled through the missed calls, I saw that
one of them was from Justin.

He must be okay, I thought to myself.

I walked out into the living room and sitting on my
mom's couch was the same man I saw in the court room earlier
that day, my dad and some other Puerto Rican dude.

"There he is, you feeling better, Sean?" my mom asked.

"I'm okay," is all I could really say while standing there
in the doorway and looking at this man who was my father as
he held Lil Man on his lap.

"Sean, let me introduce you to Edward Salgado; Edward
this is Sean, your son," my mom stated proudly.

"Habla espanol?" my father inquired.

"No," I replied coldly.

"Sean, why don't you come and have a seat instead of
standing there?" my mom asked pointing to an empty chair.

"No, I'm a'ight."

"Daddy got a daddy, daddy got a daddy," Lil man began
to sing.

"Yes he does," my father stated in a heavy Spanish accent to Lil Man as he bounced him up and down on his knee.

"Sean, are you hungry, I left a plate for you in the microwave," my mother said.

"No, I'm okay."

"Oh, I'm so sorry, Sean this is your Uncle Sal, your father's brother," my mom stated while looking at this new uncle
of mine.

"Hey, how you doing?" I asked nonchalantly.

My father began laughing based upon something my
Uncle Sal had said to him in Spanish but as I looked at the both
of them, I realized where I got my looks from. I had my father's
face but I got my dimples from Uncle Sal. They both had loud
hearty laughs, well-tone physiques and looked to be in their
early fifties.

"Son, do you mind if I speak to you privately?" my father asked me.

I really didn't know what to say at first, I mean, what this muthafucka wanted from me after all these years? How dare he come into my life and want to speak to me privately. What could he possibly want to say?

"Sean, your father asked you a question," my mom stated interrupting my thoughts. And why was she sounding as though she was on his side all of a sudden?

"Sure, why not," I replied yawning and not giving a shit one way or the other.

"Good, let's go outside in my car. We can talk there," he stated as he lifted Lil Man off his lap and sat him down on the couch.

"Daddy, Daddy can I come," Lil Man squealed as he saw me and his grandfather head for the front door.

"Naw, Lil Man, I'll be right back, okay?

Lil Man began pouting as we headed out the front door. I hated to see him pout like that and he knew it but as far as I was concerned, I wasn't going to be long. My dad unlocked the passenger side door to his old '89 Mazda 626 and I sat there looking out the window thinking how interesting it was that my father and I had the same model type car except mine was newer. My father didn't say anything right away he just took out a pack of Newports and lit himself a cigarette. Bastard didn't even offer me a cigarette, although I don't smoke but he doesn't know that, he could have still offered, right?

"I know you're probably wondering why I'm here, right?" he asked while blowing out a cloud of smoke.

"Yes," I responded without hesitating.

"I just wanted to meet you and find out what kind of man you've become."

"That's it? Well, I guess this conversation is over," I spat while opening the car door.

"Hold on now. I'm not done talking with you, so close

my door," he replied angrily.

I'm not sure why I had obeyed but at that moment, I felt like I was six years old and was doing what my father was telling me to do. So, I closed the door and pouted like Lil Man did a few minutes ago.

"So, your mom was telling me about this court hearing you had this afternoon. You want to tell me what's going on?"

"There's nothing to tell except this muthafucka was threatening my life and when he tried to come at me, I fucked him up and now I'm pressing charges against him," I responded like it was no big deal.

"Do you know who this muthafucka is?"

"Yeah."

"So, why is he threatening you?"

"It don't matter. He's gonna get what's coming to him."

"Well, look Sean, don't tell yo mom but I know some people that can smoke his ass. Just say the word and I'll take care of it for you." My dad replied sounding like an old Gangster.

"Naw, that's cool, I got this," I said smiling.

"I know we just met but I'm still your father so if someone fucks with you, they fuck with me. So, that being said, why is he threatening you?" he asked lighting another Newport.

I wondered if my Dad would still have my back if he knew the truth about his son. He claimed he wanted to see the man I had become but did he really mean it? As I thought about telling him the truth, it dawned on me that it wouldn't matter whether he was in my life or not and therefore, if he didn't like his son being bi-sexual, chances are he wouldn't want to be in my life. So not giving a fuck, I said, "He threatened my life because I tried to take his daughter's husband away from her."

"Say what?" he asked while choking on his cigarette.

"I think you heard me." I looked at him eye to eye.

"What the fuck are you talking about, you saying you're fucking gay?" he asked raising his voice.

174

"Yeah, I am and what?" I spat with bass in my voice.

He began speaking in Spanish and I didn't understand what he was saying but it was obvious he wasn't thrilled to find out that his son was gay. But it really didn't make a difference to me because I've lived my life this long without him and I will continue to do so.

"You mean you're a fucking queer?" he shouted.

"Yo man, don't yell at me. I ain't no fucking queer and I'll kick yo old ass to prove it." I spat staring at him eye to eye.

"Oh, so you want to go up against me. Oh, hell no," my Dad replied as he got out the car and began taking off his jacket and putting up his fists as though he was ready to throw down.

Father or no father, he was not about to disrespect me. I got out the car ready to fuck his old ass up and threw the first punch. Unfortunately, I missed and he threw a counter punch and hit me on the left side of my jaw, I stumbled a little but caught my balance. I felt something running down my chin and as I wiped it, I looked down at my hand and saw it was blood. That made me angry, I mean really angry. My nostrils began to flare and all I wanted to do was kill this muthafucka. I circled him as I held my fists up looking for an opening so that I could knock him the fuck out.

Some of the neighborhood kids began to gather around us and watch as we continued to fight. I found an opening and threw a right upper cut but again I missed as my father lounged forward and punched me dead in my chest, almost knocking the wind out of me as I fell backwards on my ass onto the ground. I looked up at my father and he began laughing at me. I had to admit, my Dad and I were about the same height and weight but why I couldn't seem to hit his old ass is beyond me.

I got to my feet, dusted myself off and suddenly charged his old ass to the ground. He was totally taken off guard and finally I was on top of him throwing punches wherever I could. "Yeah, now what," I yelled looking down at him. As he scrambled to get up, he grabbed my left arm to block a punch I was about to throw and the pain that raced up and down my arm from his hold was excruciating. He then maneuvered himself on top of me and began throwing punches, mostly to my face as I continued to hold onto my arm.

"Edward, what are you doing? Get off of him!" I heard my mom yell. Damn, one of the neighborhood kids must have told my mom I was getting my ass kicked. Talk about embarrassing.

"Aw hell, I wasn't going to hurt him much, he just needs to be brought down a peg or two," my Dad stated as he got off of me.

"Fuck you old man," I spat while trying to get up off the ground.

"Oh yeah, fuck you too, you fucking homo," he replied getting in his car. "Come on Sal, let's get out of here."

My mom and I went into the house and she wanted to know what started the fight. I began explaining to her how it all went down but she didn't understand why I told him about my sexual preference.

"What was I suppose to do, lie to him?" I asked as she began cleaning up my wounds.

"No baby, but what did you expect? You think you can tell your father you're gay and that's that?"

"Yes, that is if he really wants to be a part of my life."

"Sean, it doesn't work like that. Now, that's something that I've accepted because you're my son and I already love you but you hadn't given him a chance to love you like a father. A parent has to love their child first before hearing that their gay. That's all I'm saying."

Thank goodness Lil Man was in his room playing with his Xbox because I didn't know how I could explain why his grandfather and father just got finished fighting. But I listened to what my mom was saying and hey, maybe she was right. But one thing I did know, if I never saw his Spain-u-Rican ass again would be too soon.

My mom finished bandaging me up and made me sit at the dining room table to eat the food she left me in the microwave. After I finished eating, I decided to go and lie down. My stomach was full and the pain in my arm was going away. As I laid there, I couldn't believe that the first time meeting my Dad, he had whipped my ass. It felt strange getting my ass kicked. The last time I actually got beat up, I was in the fifth grade and this dude named Tyrone had beat me up because he wanted my lunch money and I wouldn't give it to him. He succeeded in doing both and I made a vow to myself that that would never happen again and it hadn't, until now.

I tossed and turned as I watched and listened to the clock on my mom's night stand go tic-tock, tic-tock. My mom had one of those old fashioned clocks. She didn't believe in the digital kind that didn't make noise. How she was able to sleep with all that noise was beyond me. I then started thinking about how Justin, Eddie and Mike were getting along. I pulled out my cell to give Justin a call first.

"Well, Sir, how are you?" Justin asked answering the phone on the first ring.

"I'm good Justin, I'm still at my mom's house and you know how mothers can be. But I wanted to make sure you were okay, I didn't mean to hit you man," I said apolitically.

"Hmmm, you sure?" he asked doubting me.

"Of course, what reason would I have to hit you?"

"I don't know, Jamaal would hit me sometimes for no reason at all," he replied sounding sad.

"Well, Justin, I'm not Jamaal and I wouldn't do that to you. And you need to believe that."

"Okay. So, when are you coming over here? Eddie has been asking about you."

"I'll be over there tomorrow, where's Eddie, put him on the phone."

"Alright," Justin replied as I heard him call for him.

"Hey, Sir," Eddie responded.

"You okay, Eddie? How Justin and you getting along? Is he taking care of you?"

"Yeah, he's cool. Although, he does like to fuck a lot," Eddie said laughing.

"Well, I'm sure you can handle it. So, you're alright then?"

"Yeah, I'm good. When are you coming over here?"

"I'll be over there tomorrow. I have a surprise for you."

"Oh yeah, what is it?" he asked sounding excited.

"You'll find out tomorrow. Anyway, is Mike there?"

"Naw, he was here earlier today but I think he went home."

"Oh okay, well I'll see you guys tomorrow and don't tear up Justin's booty too bad," I replied laughing while hanging up the phone.

I then called Mike to see what he was up to and to let him know I needed to see him bad. I didn't know what was going on with me but I needed some comfort and he was the only one that could do that at this point.

"Hey, Sir," Mike stated into the phone.

"What you doing?"

"Just chillin and watching ESPN. What's up?"

"I want to see you."

"When?"

"Now."

"Okay."

"I'll be there in about an hour, cool?"

"See you then."

Chapter TWENTY

After a quick shower and throwing on some clothes, I got to Mike's house in less than an hour. I sat in my car and looked up at Mike's house remembering the first time I came here and how scary it looked. Mike's house was still begging for attention on the outside but on the inside, it was all that. I walked up to the front door and rang the doorbell.

"Perfect timing," Mike replied as he opened the door wearing only a pair of gray sweatpants.

As I entered his house, I stood in the foyer with my back against the wall. Mike was in perfect shape but not like one of those gym rats, you know? I guess what I liked about Mike was that we were built pretty much the same and I didn't live at the gym either, fortunately I had good genes and so did he.

"You look good, yo," I replied while looking him up and down.

"Damn, Sir, I would say the same to you but what happened to your face?" he asked running his hand over my bruised jaw.

"It's a long story and not important," I responded while grabbing him around his waist and pulling him to me.

"Sir, you wanna do this here or you wanna come inside?" he asked smiling at me.

"Okay, Okay. You lead and I'll follow." I followed Mike upstairs to his master bedroom and began undressing.

"Sean, I mean Sir, what happened to your arm?" Mike asked being concerned.

"Another long story," I replied nonchalantly.

"Sir, you come here all fucked up and you not gonna tell me what's going on? Look, you know I have your back, so what's going on?"

I stripped down to my birthday suit and sat in one of the chairs in Mike's bedroom and began to explain all that had been going on within the past couple of days. Mike listened intently and I could see the anger in his eyes as I continued to talk. And for that, I appreciated his concern. Man to man, he made me feel comfortable telling him how I got fucked up while in New York and the ass whipping I got from my Dad earlier. Most times, men really don't discuss an ass whipping they've received because it makes them feel weak. As an example, I wouldn't tell Justin or Eddie that I got my ass kicked because as their "SIR" that would make me look weak and even though Mike is one of my "BOYS", again he didn't make me feel weak or less than. It's kind of hard to explain but I felt he could understand my pain without making me feel less than a man, you know?

Mike got up from his bed and kneeled before me. "It's cool Sir, I still think you're all that and if your Dad don't want to be a part of your life, that's his loss. You know, life can be funny sometimes, when I told my Dad he wasn't happy about it either but it's been four years and now, he's cool with it. Maybe he just needs time to absorb it and who knows, he might accept it one day like my father did," Mike replied trying to soothe my pain. However, as upset as I may have been, the closeness of Mike kneeling before me had my mind thinking and my nature rising. All I could think about was sexing this brotha until whatever pain I may have been feeling, disappeared. I sat there looking down into Mike's eyes as he stared up into mine and

180

suddenly he stood up, took off his sweatpants, held his hand out for mine and led me to his bed.

Mike was a very experienced brotha; he laid me in the center of his bed as he began licking me from head to toe. His tongue and touch had me in a frenzy and even though I wanted to nut and nut hard, receiving a blowjob is not how I wanted to nut. How could I tell this brotha that I wanted him inside of me without coming across as less than a man? Since the time of my initiation in the SBI, all I could think about is Mike and him penetrating me the way I saw him penetrate Justin and even Rick. As a result of not concentrating on what he was doing, I found myself losing my erection.

"Am I not doing something right, Sir?" Mike asked as he looked up at me.

"No yo, you're doing everything right. It's, it's just…" I couldn't even finish my statement.

"It's just what, Sir?" he looked puzzled.

"Wow Mike, I don't even know how to say it, yo," I replied feeling stupid. Not because I wanted to be penetrated but because I can ask for every damn thing else I wanted but I couldn't ask for this.

"Sir, look at me," he asked as he climbed up on the bed and lay next to me.

"What's up," I replied smiling at him and still feeling stupid.

"Sean, and yes I said Sean, talk to me. I'm here for whatever you want. And if I can't give you what you want or need, I can make a phone call and get you what you need or want. Just tell me what it is," he said in a genuine tone.

What seemed funny was that once Mike called me by my name instead of Sir, I found myself becoming aroused again. Was I that insecure with my manhood that I wanted to be penetrated and yet being called Sir caused my erection to disappear?

"Sean, are you here with me?" Mike asked, snapping me

181

out of my thoughts.

"I'm sorry Mike, I'm here yo. Just thinking, that's all."

"I see that, but why won't you talk to me?"

"It's nothing Mike, I'll get over it. Look, it's late, I gotta go," I responded while getting up and putting my clothes on.

The only thing on my mind was to get out of there. There were obviously some issues that I was having and I had to really sort them out because this whole Sir thing and wanting the one person who I actually wanted to be with in a passive role seemed too much for me at this time. And deep down, I knew I was being vulnerable and that's not something I'm used to. I can't be vulnerable, at least not now and not in front of Mike. Before I had a chance to exit Mike's bedroom, he held me from behind and began kissing and licking on my neck. I must have really been in need because my knees began to buckle. I could feel his manhood rising as it pushed up on me.

"Yo Mike, what the fuck you doing?" I asked as if I didn't want him to continue doing what he was doing.

"I'm doing what you want me to do Sean and if you don't want me to do it, then stop me," he whispered in my ear.

For the first time in my life, I actually felt my ass throbbing. And let me say this, "Hot Damn." I used to hear Thomas, Cameron and even Justin say how moist they were or how their ass would throb and I never understood that because the only thing that ever throbbed on me was my fat ten inch dick. So I continued to stand there weak as hell while Mike slowly began taking off my pants, and as I felt them fall to my ankles, I also felt the warmth of Mike's manhood against the crack of my ass. My body reflex automatically leaned forward against the wall as he continued to maneuver himself up and down my crack. The more he held onto his dick and slid it up and down, I actually felt my asshole open and close like a bitch. However, I had no control of my body at that point, it wanted what it wanted. Needless to say, Mike knew this and took full control.

"Spread your legs," he demanded.

I did as I was told and waited with anxious anticipation. I'm not sure what Mike was doing behind me for a minute or so but the next thing I knew was that I felt him lubing me up with one finger, then with two and finally with three. As he inserted his fingers in and out of me I thought, *maybe this wasn't a good idea!* I began to feel some pain and I don't know whether it was his finger nails or what, but that's not what I wanted to feel. Just as I was about to call it quits, he began to enter me, slowly at first but then once he got the head in, he began to slide it in and out. Allowing me time to get use to the feeling but this is not what I wanted to feel either.

It wasn't painful, it was just irritating and as a Top, I now understand what bottom brothas mean by it being irritating. Now, I don't know about most people but the concept for me was like going swimming. The water is cold, so instead of taking your time getting into the water slowly but surely, you dive in all at one time to get the shock of the coldness to the body over with. Therefore, I took it upon myself to push back on Mike so that all of him was inside me. Of course once I did that, the pain was so excruciating that water began to fill my eyes and all the blood in my body felt like it went to my head and I felt like I was about to fall out. So for the next minute or so, I tried to breathe and let the pain subside.

Mike wasn't as big as I was but he was at least all of nine inches or so and thick. Fortunately, the pain did subside and I slowly began to push back and forth against this brotha who I thought was my equal and to let him know that I was cool and ready for him to fuck me silly. With that gesture, Mike took control and made love to my body with such force and such gentleness that I was so turned on that my manhood began to rise on its own. Mike then raised me up from the wall while still inside of me and began licking, kissing and sucking on the nape of my neck. Words really can't express the feeling that shot through my body while this brotha slid in and out of me. And all I could hear him whisper was, "Damn, Sean, I've waited a long time to feel you like this, man." Truth be told, I was so lost and caught up in feeling what I was feeling, I couldn't utter a word; the most I could do was moan like a bitch. I didn't care about anything or anyone other than Mike and pleasing him and being pleased by him. Mike suddenly slid out of me, picked me up and placed me on his bed with a few pillows propped up under me. He then entered me missionary style and for a brief moment I felt the pain again but once he entered the second hole as it's called, and looking into his sexy ass brown eyes, the pleasure returned.

It's funny, because as a Top, missionary position was always considered too personal but now I understand why Bottom brothas enjoy the missionary style and looking into the eyes of the brotha that's entering them. As I felt the sweat of Mike drip down on me, the intensity in his eyes and my manhood pressing against his chest with each down stroke he gave, I felt myself coming to a climax. And this wasn't a climax that I've come to know and know well, it was like cummin for the first time, except I didn't have to play with myself. I felt myself cummin all on its own and to express the feeling of cummin while someone being inside of you is a feeling of true ecstasy, in every sense of the word.

The feeling was so powerful I tried to stop it, but I couldn't because Mike continued to slow stroke and kiss me as though he never wanted to stop. My heart raced, my toes curled and I squirted so hard that it hit Mike dead in the face on his down stroke and it obviously turned Mike on as well because he pulled out of me and began squirting his load on my chest. I don't know what was funny but for the life of me, I couldn't stop laughing. I don't know if that was what they called nervous laughter or what but as much as I enjoyed being in this submissive role with Mike, I knew that this wasn't something I would do on a regular basis. However, when and if the feeling hits, I knew there was only one brotha I could count on so to speak and that would be Mike. Lawd have mercy on my soul…

Chapter *TWENTY-ONE*

I woke up this next morning with Mike in my arms. I looked on his night stand and the clock read 7:45 a.m. I slid out of bed and jumped in Mike's shower real quick so that I could get over to Justin's house and check on Eddie. I didn't realize how hard it was to take a shower and try not to get the bandage on my arm wet. Once I got out of the shower and entered Mike's bedroom, he still appeared to be sleep so without disturbing him, I got dressed and slipped out.

******

As I drove over to Justin's house, I thought about what happened last night between Mike and I the whole way there. I must admit, my ass was sore as shit but bearable. I pulled up to Justin's driveway and noticed his car wasn't there. I thought, *he must have left for work.* I rang his doorbell several times before Eddie came to the door.

"Hey you," I said as Eddie stood before me looking as though he was just waking up.

"It's nice to see you, too," he replied with sleep in his eyes and his crooked smile.

"So, you gonna let me in?"

"My bad," he said as he opened the door to let me in.

"So, how have you been, you missed me?" I asked as I walked into Justin's living room and took a seat on his couch.

"What you think, Sir?" Eddie replied taking a seat on my lap.

Before I had a chance to answer, Eddie had already stuck his tongue in my mouth. As I stated before, I no longer felt the electrical shock when Eddie and I touched but there was still something there between us. And what I felt for him didn't take away from what I felt for Justin or Mike.

"What happened to your face?" Eddie asked as he came up for air and stared me in the face.

"It's a long story. I'll tell you about it as we drive."

"Where're we going?"

"I told you I had a surprise for you, didn't I?" I replied with a wink.

"So, where're we going?" he asked again but this time with excitement in his tone.

"Will you put some clothes on before I change my mind?" I said teasing him. "And hurry up; I'll be outside in the car waiting for you."

I don't think I had ever seen Eddie move so fast. Deep down I couldn't wait to take him to where his brother and sister lived. According to the information I received from Justin, they were living in Philadelphia, Pennsylvania with a single foster mother by the name of Rosario Cortez. She had gotten them from Social Services three years ago and have had them ever since. I too was a little excited considering that these kids may also be my half brother and sister.

I programmed the Philly address into the GPS system and waited for Eddie. As I sat there, I looked out of my side view mirror and saw this car screeching down the street as though it was going over a hundred miles an hour. As it went by, I couldn't believe who was driving. I didn't know whether to just sit there or try to follow the car to see where it was going. I knew that if I took off to follow it, Eddie would be coming out any minute and I didn't want to leave him just hanging. After all, I brought him home so that he could share my world but I've pawned him off on Justin long enough. Besides, what if it wasn't who I thought it was and what if I never caught up with him?

You gonna open the door or what?" Eddie asked tapping on the passenger window and startling me from my thoughts.

"My bad," I replied while unlocking the door for him.

"You seem to always be somewhere else lately, you okay?" he asked getting in the car and putting his seatbelt on.

"Naw, I'm good. Just have some things on my mind, that's all."

"So, where are we going?"

"Didn't I tell you it's a surprise?" Again I said teasing him. Eddie sat there, folded his arms and began to pout. "*Dayum, he is so phyne,*" I said to myself.

******

We made it to Philly within an hour or so and I was just pulling onto the 30th street station exit. Eddie and I had talked the whole way there and I told him about my trip to New York and the long scar on my left arm as well as meeting my father and how that didn't go as well as I would have hoped. Eddie suggested that we go up to New York and get some of his homies so that I could get back at the Jamaicans for what they did to me. Personally, I thought I would leave well enough alone since I had not heard from Peaches or Corey. However, it did bother me that neither one of them took the time out to see if I was okay, considering. The GPS had informed me that we were at our final destination. I parked the car and looked at the cottage style house from the outside that seemed like a warm, inviting home.

"So, who lives there, another one of your Boys? Eddie asked with a little sarcasm in his tone.

"Naw," I replied while looking up and down the neigh-

187

borhood.

"Well, who?" he asked with a puzzled look on his face.

"It's my surprise."

"Okay, so who lives here?"

"Well, Eddie, this is part of your graduation present. You have done everything that I have asked you to. So, as of today, you are a full pledge Boy. Now, remember before we started, you asked me what was in it for you?

"Yeah," he said with a puzzled look on his face.

"And what did you tell me you wanted more than anything?"

"I wanted to see my little brother and sister and have them back in my life, so?" again he asked looking puzzled.

"Well, I was able to get information on your brother and sister and based on my information, this is where they live," I said pointing to the house we were sitting in front of.

"What?"

"You heard me; this is where your little brother and sister live."

"Are you serious?" he asked surprisingly.

"Yeah."

"So, what am I suppose to do, walk up to the door and what?"

"They have a foster mother by the name of Rosario Cortez. She got your brother and sister from Social Services three years ago and she has been raising them ever since. You said you wanted to find them, well I thought I would find them for you."

I guess Eddie was a little taken aback because he just sat there not knowing what to do. He looked over at the house and then looked back at me and back at the house.

"We don't have to go in if you don't want to. I know I might have caught you off guard but at least you know where they are now and maybe we can come back another time?" I replied trying to calm Eddie.

"It looks like a nice house."

"Yeah, it does."

"I guess we can at least meet their new mother, huh?

"Foster mother," I stated feeling the need to reiterate.

"It's been a while, what if they don't recognize me, Sir?" he asked feeling unsure.

"I doubt very seriously that they wouldn't recognize you Eddie, but look, we don't have to do this if you don't want to. I just thought you were serious about wanting to find your family?"

"I'm serious. Do you have any idea how many nights I've sat up and cried about where they were and how they were doing?" he snapped.

"Okay okay, chill. So, let's go," I said opening the car door.

Eddie hesitated a little at first but opened the car door and followed me up to the front door.

"What am I suppose to do?" Eddie asked looking at me nervously.

"You're gonna ring the doorbell and introduce yourself to whomever comes to the door. That's what you're gonna do."

"Here goes nothing," he responded taking a deep breath and ringing the doorbell.

"Wait a minute," we heard a woman's voice say.

We stood on the front door step waiting patiently for a few moments and then the door opened. "Can I help you?" A middle age but fairly good looking Puerto Rican woman asked.

I stood there waiting for Eddie to speak but nothing came out. "Yes, ah good afternoon, my name is Sean Mathews and this is Eddie Salgado," I responded since Eddie just stood there.

"Oh my God, you're Eddie?" she asked looking up and down at Eddie.

"Yes, I am." Eddie replied.

"Y'all come on in and make yourselves at home," she

stated while opening the door so that we could enter.

That took me and Eddie by surprise but I suspected that his siblings must have told their foster mother about Eddie, which is a good thing because obviously, they hadn't forgotten about him. As we entered her home, I noticed that it was well laid out. The living room was on the left and the dining room was on the right.

"You guys can have a seat in here," she stated, pointing into the living room. "Are you guy's hungry? Rico and Lisa are going to be so surprised to see you when they get home from school," she stated as she took a seat in one of the chairs that sat across from us as we sat on the living room couch.

"I am a little hungry," Eddie stated feeling a little more comfortable. "So, you know who I am?"

"Of course, when I first got Rico and Lisa, all they talked about was their big brother Eddie. They would tell me Eddie would do this or Eddie would do that."

Within minutes, Eddie and Ms. Cortez were talking like they were old friends. Ms. Cortez invited us into the kitchen as she fixed us something to eat. Half way through eating, Eddie and her talked and laughed so much that I suspect that she was telling him about his brother and sister. I didn't understand all of what they were saying because they both started speaking in Spanish. Note to self, I must learn Spanish especially since I'm half Puerto Rican.

We finished eating and we were escorted back into the living room. Over the next hour or so, we sat and looked through several photo albums that Ms. Cortez had taken of Eddie's brother and sister for the last three years. I glanced down at my watch and it was almost 4 p.m. and I hoped that they would be on their way home from school soon.

"And this was a picture I took of them a couple of weeks ago when I took them to the Philadelphia zoo," Ms. Cortez boasted proudly.

I could see in Eddie's eyes that he was happy that his

siblings were being raised by a good woman. She seemed to not only care for them but also seemed to love them as well. I could also see that Eddie seemed to be taken by this woman, and who wouldn't be, she had my vote. She was warm, engaging and personable.

"Ma, we're home," we heard what must have been Rico's voice yelling while coming in through the back door.

"Y'all come on in the living room, I have a surprise for you two!" Ms. Cortez yelled back.

Eddie looked over at me and I could see the tears welling up in his eyes. I knew he had probably played this moment over and over in his head many times and it was finally coming true. Rico and Lisa came running through the living room and suddenly stopped when they saw Eddie and me sitting on the couch. I really didn't know what was going through their little heads because at first they just stood there with stunned looks on their face. The next thing I knew was they both just lunged over at Eddie and began hugging him, kissing him and saying something in Spanish. I really got to learn Spanish.

I got up to give them more room and stood over against the wall looking at them express themselves as to how much they had missed their big brother. The tears flowed down their cheeks as they continued to kiss and hug one another. I must admit, it was as they say; *a Kodak moment* and I too became a little choked up watching them together. In a small way, I was a little jealous because if my father was their father as well, that would mean they too were my little brother and sister. I tried to get a good look at both of them to see if there were some similarities and there were. They both had some features of mine but looked more like Lil Man more so than me. I too wanted a big hug and kiss from them but I didn't want to scare them off when Eddie introduced me to them.

"Rico and Lisa, this is a good friend of mine, Sean. Sean, this is Rico and Lisa, my little brother and sister," Eddie said proudly while hugging them both.

"It's nice meeting the both of you," I replied extending my hand. Eddie whispered something in their ear and they both came over and hugged me. And when they did, I got an electrical shock by their touch and I knew then we had to be related. They too felt the electrical shock because it scared them and they backed away from me.

"What's wrong with you two?" Ms. Cortez asked.

"He shocked me," Lisa said while pointing at me.

Eddie looked at me and all we could do was laugh. He was laughing because we used to always shock one another but I was laughing because I knew they were family too, my family.

"Well Lisa, sometimes the static between people can sometimes cause an electric shock. But trust me; Sean is a good guy, alright?" Eddie said hugging and trying to comfort his little sister.

Lisa must have believed her big brother because as we sat around talking and laughing, Lisa came over and sat next to me. I was beginning to love this little girl already. Rico on the other hand was a little more conservative. Ms. Cortez got up and began cooking dinner and we stayed in the living room talking and watching DVD movies. I thought what was interesting was that their favorite movie was, "The Color Purple." It's also one of my favorites and it had been a while since I'd seen it so we all began to imitate the actors on the screen.

"You betta not tell nobody but God, it'll kill your momma," I said being the father.

"All my life I had to fight. I had to fight my brothas," Lisa said trying to sound like Ms. Sophia.

"It's gonna rain on yo head," Rico chimed in.

"My Daddy sho love me, he just don't know it," Eddie confessed sounding like Ms. Shug.

We all roared in laughter as one by one, we all imitated one of "The Color Purple" characters until someone with a key opened the door and ruined everything.

Chapter TWENTY-TWO

"What the hell are y'all doing here?"

"What the hell you doing here?" I replied standing up and not being sure if he was talking to me or Eddie. I also forgot that he obviously belonged here since he had a key and let himself in. "Besides, I thought you were living in Baltimore?"

"So, this is where you live now?" Eddie said sounding sarcastic.

"You can get out of my damn house too. And no, I don't live in Baltimore," he replied raising his voice. "And since when you two started hanging together? I guess it's true, all you faggots know each other, huh?"

The atmosphere in the room had changed and Ms. Cortez came from out of the kitchen and entered the living room, telling Rico and Lisa to go up to their rooms until she called them for dinner.

"Edward, what's the matter with you? This is Eddie, Rico and Lisa's older brother and this is a friend of his, Sean," Ms. Cortez said trying to calm my father down.

"I know who the hell they are. They are my sons and they both are fucking homosexuals and I want them out of my house, now!" he yelled.

There was a moment of silence as the words, "They are my sons and they're both fucking homosexuals" echoed off the walls and floated in the mist amongst us. I looked over at Eddie and he too seemed to be in a state of shock. I guess other than finding his brother and sister and finding out where his father lived, I guess it was a bit much to find out that we are half brothers and have been fucking each other for the past several months.

"So, how did you find your children?" Eddie asked his father.

"His children," Ms. Cortez asked, looking at my father.

"Oh, you didn't know?" Eddie replied.

"I told y'all to get the fuck out of my house," my father yelled.

"Your house, this is my house Edward," Ms. Cortez yelled standing up to my father.

"Oh, so it's like that? You gonna let these faggots come between us Rosario?" he asked trying to hug her.

"I don't know about any homosexuals. All I know is that obviously you are their father and from what I'm hearing, you are also Rico and Lisa's father as well." Ms. Cortez looked into my father's eyes and I could see the hurt and the pain she was feeling due to the fact that she didn't know that my dad was also her foster children's father. She took a deep breath and asked, "Is that why you starting coming around here and show-ing interest in me because you wanted to be near your chil-dren?"

"No, Ma, I love you," my father responded as though he was pleading.

"Answer my question Edward; are Rico and Lisa your children?"

My father just stood there looking like a deer caught in headlights. Eddie and I sat back down on the couch to see how this would play out. My father was being caught in his spider web of lies and Ms. Cortez didn't look like she took shit from anyone, let alone him.

"Answer my question, Edward," Ms. Cortez asked again as she began to cry.

"Okay okay, yes they are my children and the truth is that when I found out that you had become their foster mother, I searched to find you and I did." My father grabbed a hold of Ms. Cortez's shoulders and stated, "When I first started coming around it was to see them but since then I have fallen in love with you. Haven't I proven that to you for the last couple of years?"

Ms. Cortez backed away from my father and took a seat on the chair and cried like a baby with her hands up to her face. I truly felt sorry for her.

"Baby, look at me," my father pleaded as he bent down in front of her on one knee. "Baby, I went searching for my kids. As a father, can you blame me for that? But what I also found was love with a good woman."

"But I don't understand, the kids know that you're their father but they never said anything to me," she stated through sobs.

"Baby, listen to me, their mother was a crack head and I left her years ago. Lisa was too young to remember me but Rico did and I asked him not to tell you because I was afraid you wouldn't want me. Please don't blame Rico for my mistakes. I was happy that I had found them but I also found you and I thought finally, I would have a family again."

As crazy as it seems, I truly started to believe my dad. It was nice to see him so vulnerable and sincere. Of course the ultimate decision to forgive him was not mine and what Ms. Cortez said next kinda blew my mind.

"Okay, Edward, if you want me to forgive you and accept you and your children, I can only do that if you accept your children as well, all of them," she stated looking over at the couch at me and Eddie.

"But baby, they're homosexuals and I don't produce no

faggots," my father boasted as he looked over at Eddie and me with hatred in his eyes.

"Edward, that's my decision, take it or leave it," Ms. Cortez replied while wiping the tears from her eyes.

My father stood up and looked as though he was about to say something but didn't. Instead, he grabbed his keys and walked out. Ms Cortez broke down and started crying again. Eddie got up and went over to where she sat and tried to console her.

"You know Ms. Cortez, my father has a lot of faults but I do believe he loves you," Eddie stated while rubbing her shoulders.

"Thanks Eddie, I really do appreciate that but why does he have to be so damn stubborn?" She asked through sobs.

"Well, don't blame him for that. I think that's just a family trait for all the Salgado men," Eddie replied trying to lighten the mood.

"Ms. Cortez, do you have any idea where he might have gone?" I asked.

"Look, I think you young men can stop calling me Ms. Cortez and just call me Rosa if you don't mind?" she stated while trying to pull herself together.

"Okay Rosa, do you know where he might have gone?" I asked again.

"Yeah, he went to some strip joint called Jake's Bar over on Spruce Street. He always go there when we have a disagreement."

"Okay good, I'll go after him and don't worry, everything will be alright," I said trying to make her feel better.

"You want me to go with you," Eddie asked.

"Naw, stay here with Ms... I mean Rosa. I'll find him and bring him back with me," I replied walking out the front door.

******

I had to park a few blocks from the club because there were no parking spaces available that were closer. It also appeared as though the bar was packed because there was a long ass line outside. I got out of my car and made my way down to Spruce Street and walked straight up to the door and handed the security guy a twenty dollar bill. I was let in without any questions. I stood in the back of the bar searching for this so called man who was my father and truth be told, if it were not for Ms. Rosé I wouldn't even be here. I think my father made it very clear that he didn't want to have anything to do with me or my kind and that was cool with me but for whatever reason, Ms. Rosé loves this man and it was not my intent to cause any problems in bringing Eddie and his family together.

It was rather dark inside and made it difficult for me to find my father. Most of the lighting came from one spot light that shined on center stage. There was this big booty dark skinned sista doing her thang as she spun around on the dance pole. There wasn't much to be said for the decor of the club but those that were present seemed to be enjoying the show for what it was worth. The big booty sista only wore a gold colored G-string and within seconds, she had come out of that as the male audience clapped, whistled, grunted and held dollar bills in their hand, waiting for their turn to stick the bill on various parts of her body. As the stripper strolled over to the left side of the stage and the spot light followed her, I noticed my father sitting down front at a table by himself, drinking a beer and holding a few dollar bills in his hand.

Old ass man couldn't handle that if he tried, I thought to myself as I approached his table and took a seat.

"What da fuck you want?" he growled at me.

"Nothing," I replied while putting in my order for a Heineken from a waitress walking by.

"She sent you down here, didn't she?"

"No, I asked her where you were and she told me. I

came here on my own."

"For what?" he asked sarcastically.

"Look dude, I'm only here because of your woman. For whatever reason she loves you and she's a good woman and I wouldn't want to be the reason for coming between you two. Now I know you don't give a shit about me and trust and believe, the feeling is mutual but I do like Ms. Rosa and I wouldn't want to be the cause of her pain. So, why don't you be a man and go home to your woman?" I replied looking at him eye to eye.

"Be a man? What do you know about being a man? Get the fuck outta here!" he said waving his hand at me.

"A man is someone who takes care of his family and handles his business. Being a man is not based upon who or what you sleep with, you ignorant muthafucka!"

I started to get up and leave but I noticed that most of the audience was looking in my direction and I thought they obviously overheard my conversation but as I focused my attention on stage, there was a phyne ass red hair white chick doing her strip tease and trying to get my attention. I turned to my father and said, "Look man, I'll make a deal with you."

"Deal, what kinda deal?"

"You seem like you're a gambling man, so I'll tell you what, if I can get this white chick on stage to kiss me and give me her number without me giving her any money, we both leave and go home. If I can't, I'll get up and leave and you will never have to see me again!"

"Oh, so I see you're stupid too, huh? Go ahead player and get your feelings hurt. These bitches in here are about their money, so go ahead." My father said laughing out loud.

"So, we got a deal?" I asked holding out my hand to shake his.

"Yeah player, I'll take that bet," he said shaking my hand.

I was going to get up and go on stage but I thought it

would be best if she came to me, that way, it would be more up front and personal and my father could get a better look. I turned my chair facing the stage and sat back, got comfortable and waved shawty over to where I was. Just as if it was planned, she came right over to me and straddled herself on my lap.

"What's yo name shawty?" I asked while smiling ear to ear at her.

"My name is Catherine but my friends call me Cat," she replied while smiling just as hard back at me while grinding on me.

"Well Cat, I'm here with my dad but we are about to bounce and I just wanted to get yo number before I left."

"Is that right?" she asked while looking over at my dad.

"Yeah, that's right."

"215-555-6776, you gonna call me tonight Sir?"

"For sure, Cat. Now before I go, I want you to plant one right here," I said while placing my finger to my lips. Without question, Cat lean down and kissed me like I was her one and only man. As she got up to go back on stage, I thought I would freak my dad out even more, so I slapped Cat on her ass as she sashayed away. I then looked over at my dad and his mouth was wide open with a dumbfounded look on his face.

"So, was that man enough for you?" I asked sarcastically.

"Whatever man," he said waving his hand at me once again.

"Well, we better get going," I snapped while getting up. I know that was a dirty tricked that I played on my dad, not letting him know that Cat and I had met before during my training as a Boy and once when I had become a Sir, so fuck him. My dad followed me but I could see that he was really loss for words as well as I knew he really wasn't ready to leave at that point but a bet is a bet, right?

******

We returned back to my dad's house and as we entered, everyone was at the dining room table eating their dinner. Both Ms. Rosa and Eddie looked shocked that I was able to bring my dad back with me. Fortunately, there was no arguing or confrontations from anyone. Ms. Rosa carried on as though nothing ever happened by saying, "Well, you guys sit on down so I can fix y'all a plate."

"That's okay, Rosa, Eddie and I have to head on back but thank you for everything," I said while giving her a good-bye hug.

"Okay, baby, but you boys stay in touch and feel free to come by anytime," she said hugging me back.

"We will," Eddie replied getting up from the table.

Before leaving, Eddie hugged and kissed Rico and Lisa and promised them both that he would be back to visit them again soon. I could see the sadness on their faces as we were walking out the door. My dad didn't say shit as we left and we didn't say shit to him either.

******

The drive back down on 95 South heading for Baltimore was kinda strange and awkward between Eddie and me. He was very quiet at first but I knew he had a thousand questions about our new relationship as brothers.

"So, how did you get him to come home with you?"

"It's a long story," I said with a smile.

"So, what happens now?"

"About what?"

"About us, my brotha," Eddie spat putting emphasis on the word brotha.

I really couldn't respond to his question, I just didn't know what to say. I just kept driving hoping that the words would come but they wouldn't.

"Fuck," Eddie snapped.

"What, what's wrong?" I asked being startled.

"I was going to make you my boyfriend," he replied in a whisper.

"Wow, why is it that when shit happens in relationships, you don't get a forewarning that this might be your last time sexing that person?"

"I know, right?" Eddie replied in agreement. "You know, I'm glad you were able to find my little brother and sister, thank you for that and I do mean that in all seriousness but you also took you away from me."

"I know, I guess it was cool since we didn't know but now that we know, that makes all the difference in the world."

"Damn, Poppy."

"Damn, I don't get "Sir" no more?" I asked jokingly.

"Not now. Just my luck I would start to fall in love with my own damn brother, ain't that a bitch?"

Chapter TWENTY-THREE

Eddie and I made it back to Baltimore in record time and I decided to stop by Justin's house because both Justin and my mom had been blowing up my cell phone. I knew Justin was probably wondering what was going on since I hadn't really spent too much time with him since I'd been back. And I knew he probably wanted to discuss my new court hearing date for which he was granted a contingency. That was the cool thing about Justin, he took his position as an attorney very seriously but he also knew how to have fun and 'kee-kee' as he would say.

I parked in Justin's driveway and both Eddie and I approached the front door and before we had a chance to ring the door bell, the door swung open with Justin standing there looking as though he was upset about something.

"Where have y'all been?" he questioned us as though we were children.

"It's nice to see you too, thanks for the love," I said as we entered.

"Sir, I've been calling you since this morning, why hadn't you called me back?"

"Don't blame Sean. Justin, it's my fault," Eddie replied as we took a seat in his living room.

"Wait a minute; you ain't got to take blame for shit Eddie. I had some business to take care of and that's all you need to know Justin. So what's with all the attitude?" I questioned him while becoming angry.

"Look Sir, I don't mean to come off that way but I found out some information today that you need to know," Justin replied in a serious tone.

"Okay, so what's going on? What's so important that got you all upset?" I inquired.

"I got a call this morning while I was at work from another attorney friend of mine that works in the Appeal Office on base," Justin stated sounding nervous.

"And?" I replied.

Justin took a deep breath before saying, "He told me that Jamaal appealed his conviction and won and was released from the Stock Aid a few weeks ago."

"What the fuck you talking about, he killed his own damn cousin Thomas and that shit was on video. So, what do you mean he won his appeal?" I asked furiously.

"Well, according to the transcripts, his new attorney won his appeal based on self defense," Justin replied sounding apologetic.

"Self defense, that's some bullshit. What do you mean self defense?" I spat as I stood up with my fists balled up.

"Calm down Sean, let Justin finish," Eddie stated while trying to get me to sit back down. "So, how is that possible if it's on video tape, Justin?"

"Sir, do you remember that on the tape, Thomas went upstairs to his bedroom and took out his gun from the closet?"

"Yeah and?" I spat clenching my jaws.

"Jamaal followed him and they both began to wrestle over the gun and the gun eventually went off in the process. Therefore, Jamaal's new attorney argued that his client was in fear of his life. Hence, his self defense claim."

I was so pissed off that I couldn't think straight. How in the hell could he get away with killing Thomas? Self defense my ass, that was some more military bullshit. I just sat there almost in shock trying to get some kind of understanding as to what Justin had just told me. I felt as though justice was not served and therefore, I had let Thomas down. For a quick moment, I thought about finding out where Jamaal was and kill him myself.

"Where is Jamaal now?" I asked Justin while cracking my knuckles.

"I don't know, Sir. I asked my friend, but he didn't know whether Jamaal was still on base or whether he was transferred to another base or not."

"But he's still technically serving in active duty?"

"Yes," Justin replied in almost a whisper.

"Come on Eddie, let's go," I stated while getting up off the couch.

"Wait Sir, where are you going?" Justin questioned sounding concerned.

"I don't know," I replied feeling angry and frustrated.

"Sir please, just stay here. Don't go out there and do something you're going to regret," Justin stated sounding like a mother hen.

"It's cool, Justin; I'll keep an eye on him, a'ight?" Eddie said trying to assure Justin.

******

Not really having a destination in mind, I found myself subconsciously heading towards base. I wasn't sure what I would do if I saw Jamaal but I do know that I had to see for myself if he was really out of prison. And if he wanted to throw down, I was more than prepared. Eddie tried to make conversation with me to see where my head was but I gave no response; I was on a mission. Unfortunately, we drove around on base for over an hour but didn't see Jamaal or his car. I guess it was for the best because I don't know what I might have done if I had spotted him.

"Sean, why don't we just go? Besides, we don't know if he is still on base. Like Justin said, he might have been transferred to another base," Eddie said with a worried look on his face.

"Yeah okay, I wanna stop by my mom's anyway. I think she might get a kick out of meeting my brother," I replied, smiling at Eddie.

"That's funny; you never said much about your mom. You did mention that she was raising your son and your in-laws were raising your daughter but that's about it. So, what do I call her?"

"Ma."

"She wouldn't think I was being presumptuous if I called her Ma?"

"No, everybody calls her that. She would be insulted if you didn't."

We pulled up in front of my mom's place at 10:30 p.m. As we climbed the stairs to her apartment, I hoped she was still awake because I had so much to talk to her about and since I've been home, I hadn't spent much time with her. I must admit, I was feeling a little guilty. I opened the door with my key and all lights were out. There was a glimmer of light coming from down the hall leading into my mom's bedroom. I suspected that she was lying in bed watching television. I turned on one of the lamps in the living room that sat on a side table and invited Eddie to have a seat. I tiptoed down the hallway to my mom's bedroom and looked inside. The television was on but I wasn't sure if she was awake or not, so I whispered, "Ma, are you still awake?"

"Yeah, baby, where have you been all day?" My mom asked yawning.

"I had to take care of some business, no big deal. Hey, I

have someone out in the living room I want you to meet, is that cool?"

"Who is it?" She asked not sounding too happy about me bringing someone over her house this time of night.

"It's a surprise, so throw something on right quick and come on out, okay?" I replied, then turned around to head back out into the living room.

Once I got back out into the living room, Eddie had stood up to look at some family pictures my mom had on the walls and on the mantle piece.

"That's a picture of me and Venus on our wedding day," I stated then stood next to Eddie.

"Hmmm, I see. Who's that?"

"That's Lil Man, the fruit of my loins," I said proudly while laughing.

"You so silly. Who is that?"

"Who does it look like?"

"I don't know but it kinda looks like you."

"And you would be right. I think I was about sixteen in that picture," I replied, thinking back to when my mom took the picture. "Oh I'm sorry, would you like something to drink?"

"No, I'm good, maybe later."

"Hi, how are you? I'm Sean's mother and you are?"

"Oh Ma, I didn't hear you come in. This is Eddie, Eddie this is my mom."

"Nice to meet you, Mrs. Mathews," Eddie replied.

"Didn't I tell you to just call her Ma?"

"You might as well Eddie, everyone else does," she stated, while taking a seat on the couch.

"So, Ma, who does Eddie look like?"

"What do you mean, who he look like? I don't know, Sean. It's a little too late to be playing games and you got me out of my bed. So why don't you just tell me," my mom stated sounding frustrated.

"A'ight Ma, I'm sorry, I don't mean to play games," I

stated taking a seat next to her. "Well, I guess the only way to say it is to just come out and say it...Ma, Eddie is my brother."

"Your brother, Sean what are you talking about?" My mom asked looking and sounding confused.

I began to tell my mom how I met Eddie in Hawaii and how we became good friends. I didn't mention to her that we had been fucking. After all, the less people who knew that we've been fucking, the better. People seemed to understand most things in life when it came to sex but not when it came to incest, which is still very much a taboo in today's society. Anyway, I informed my mom that because of the friendship Eddie and I had, I wanted to help him find his little brother and sister that had been adopted several years ago. Long story short, I had found them and took Eddie to Philly to see them and the woman who had adopted them and even though it was a happy reunion, my father lived there with this woman. And in the process of an argument, he admitted that both I and Eddie were his sons and because we were faggots he didn't ever want anything to do with us.

I stopped at that point and looked at my mom and tried to figure out what she was thinking but she didn't seem happy or sad. I continued with the rest of my story and waited to hear what my mom had to say. But she said nothing.

"Ma, you okay?"

"Yes baby, I'm fine," she stated in almost a whisper.

"You sure, Ma," I asked while giving her a hug.

"Of course, I'm sure. What do you expect me to say or do, Sean? You think I should be mad because your father is in love and living with another woman?"

"Naw Ma, I'm just...,"

"You just what," she said cutting me off. "Eddie, was your mother's name Sonya?"

"Yes Madame, I mean yes, Ma," Eddie replied. "Did you know my mother?"

"I really didn't know her, but I met her once when I went

208

to New York one weekend to spend time with your dad. How is she?"

"I don't know, she left home one day and never came back."

"Awe, you poor thang, that must have been very difficult for you. What did you do?" my mom asked getting nosey.

Eddie began telling my mom his life story as I sat there listening to the both of them talk to each other as though they were old friends. I must confess, I enjoyed watching them get along together so well. Eddie had also discovered her weakness the same as Cameron and Gabe had and that was to make her laugh. Eddie had her cracking up over the smallest things.

I got up to go and check on Lil Man to see how he was doing. He was still asleep but I guess I just wanted to go in his room just to look at him, the same way most parents who love and missed their children sometimes do. And just as I expected, Lil Man was still fast asleep and like most proud parents, I wanted to wake him and take him in the living room so Eddie could see him as well, but as a parent I know not to wake a child up in the middle of the night because they will be up until sunrise. He is such a wild sleeper that I pulled the covers back up on him and tucked him in and kissed him on the forehead before I went back out to the semi-family reunion.

"Everything okay, Sean," my mom asked.

"Yeah, just wanted to check on Lil Man," I replied taking my seat in the empty chair.

"Oh, I was just wondering. Eddie and I have been talking most of the time and you've been kinda quiet."

"Naw, it's cool. But I do have to tell you something," I replied in a serious tone.

"Oh Lawd, what's wrong now?"

"I just found out today from Justin that Jamaal, remember Thomas's cousin Jamaal?"

"Yes, he's the one that got locked up for killing his own cousin. What about him?"

"Justin told me that his sentence was overturned by his appeal and he was released from the Stock Aid," I replied still feeling angry.

"How could that be, wasn't it all recorded," she asked with a puzzled look on her face.

"Yeah, Ma, but his new attorney appealed his case based on self defense. Thomas went for the gun and Jamaal followed him and there was a struggle and Jamaal took the gun and fired it at Thomas for fear of his own life, hence his self defense plea."

"I'm so sorry to hear that baby, but you know the good Lawd knows what happened and he definitely will be judged by the King Himself," she replied hugging and trying to comfort me.

"Yeah, I know, Ma," I said in a whisper.

"Well, with that being said, it's late and I'm going to bed. Are you boys staying here tonight or over one of your friend's place?" my mom asked getting up.

"We were going back over to Justin's but it's almost two in the morning, so I guess we might as well crash here," I replied looking at Eddie to see if it was ok with him.

"Someone can sleep on the couch and Sean if you move the coffee table out of the way, I can make a make shift bed here on the floor and someone can sleep there," my mom replied while getting pillows and blankets out of the hallway closet.

"Since you're guest, I'll let you sleep on the couch," I gestured to Eddie as I began to move the coffee table out of the way.

I helped my mom with the make shift bed and couldn't wait to get in it. I took everything off except for my pants. I threw my Timbs on one side and my shirt on the other side. I was so tired that I felt myself dreaming before my head even hit the pillow. I'm not sure how long I had been asleep when I felt Eddie spooning up against me as he put my arm around him.

Needless to say, my mind began to race and it didn't take long for my dick to catch up.

Even though my nature tool wanted to squirt over his entire body; my concerns where like anybody else's in a situation like this. First of all, this is my mom's place; I've never had sex in my mom's place before. Secondly, my son lay no more then 30 feet away fast asleep, what if he wakes up and catches me? And lastly, this is still incest and even though I know its incest, and as I lay here with Eddie in my arms and trying to get my dick to go down, my dick didn't seem to care or was just not listening, one way or the other.

One fact about Eddie is that he sleeps in the nude and the second is that he doesn't like sleeping alone. So, I can't say Eddie made the first move just because he was naked, because he laid there as though he was sleeping like a baby. There was no grinding on the lower part of his body nor was there any touchy feely. I, on the other hand, was faced with temptation and lust. I tried to reason with myself that this wasn't incest because incest is nasty, ugly and the very thought of relatives fucking one another makes me want to throw up. However, this brotha and I have had sex several times before not knowing we were even related, and it was off the chain.

Besides, this is the first time Eddie and I had been this close and alone since being in Baltimore. Earlier, Eddie and I had a brief conversation about the fact that we are brothers, but he nor I gave a definite "no" to our sexual desire for one another. I felt I was at a cross road because as much as I wanted to continue our Sir and Boy relationship, I didn't want people to gag at the fact that I enjoyed having sex with my own brother, correction, half-brother.

And beyond the aforementioned, who has to really know that Eddie and I are brothers? Maybe I'm making a mountain out of a mole hill or maybe I'm grabbing at straws to justify my strong sexual desire. I believe my thoughts were so loud that Eddie began to squirm in my arms as though he was waking up and wanted to make my decision for me.

"I thought you were so sleepy." Eddie whispered as he turned around to face me.

"I was until…"

"Until what?"

"Until you brought your beautiful self down here and laid in my arms."

"My bad, I can get back up on the couch if you want me to."

"Naw, you don't have to," I replied before I had a chance to take it back.

"So, what was this you were saying earlier about relationships going bad and having that one last time to be with that person, sexually?" Eddie reminded me as he climbed on top of me.

"Wow shawty, why you making this so hard for me?" I asked as I palmed and squeezed his ass cheeks.

"Am I not my brother's keeper?" he asked with his signature crooked smile.

"Ha ha, very funny."

Eddie leaned down and gently placed his lips onto mine and from that point, it was on. As before, there was no electrical shock but the chemistry between us was just as electrifying. With every excuse I came up with, for what we were doing was wrong, I kept telling myself that he was no ordinary brother. I didn't grow up with him, we had no sibling rivalries, and we didn't share clothes or a bedroom together. However, the thought of him being my brother in partial DNA only, made it a little freakier. Which caused one to think, if you were gay, would you have sex with yourself?

After minutes of kissing and licking every pore of Eddie's body, he rose up off me and began pulling down my pants. I was so stimulated that I was afraid that once he would take me in his mouth, I would bust right then and there. Fortunately, the thought of being caught in the act kept my juices on

stand by so to speak and allowed me to continue in such ecstasy. Eddie took all of me in his warm, wet and velvet-like
mouth with such hunger. I then forgot all about being caught or
him being my brother. With each stroke, my muscles flexed as
my body jerked all at the same time.

All I could think of is being inside of him and pounding
his hot ass. I didn't have any lube on me and I knew Eddie did-
n't either, so I rolled over and propped Eddie in the doggy style
position and went to work eating out his ass like it was butter
pecan ice cream. It didn't hurt that like a few other bottom
brothas, Eddie's ass made its own juices. After being able to
stick in three of my fingers, I was more than anxious to dive in
and feel Eddie, especially if this was going to be my last time.
And my younger brother was throwing his ass back at me as
though he didn't want me to forget how good he really was.
And how could I, this was the first dude that brought tears to
my eyes the first time we had sex. Needless to say, I couldn't
hold it any longer and tried to pull out but Eddie continued to
back up on me and I realized why, he too was coming.

"Sean, what in the hell are you doing?" my mom asked
with anger and a shocked expression on her face.

Chapter TWENTY-FOUR

At that moment, I wished that I had had the power to disappear. I felt as though I had totally disrespected my mom to the highest level. I couldn't believe this was really happening. I immediately threw the covers back on Eddie and me as my mom continued to stand there looking for an answer. How could I respond? What could I say? I know her question was *what was I doing?* But the real question was, *how could you do this to me and in my own house?* Eddie stayed hidden under the covers as I searched my mind looking for a descent response.

"Sean, I asked you a question," my mom reiterated while standing in the doorway tapping her foot. "Look, why don't you put some clothes on and come in my room. I want to talk to you," she said as she turned around heading back to her bedroom.

"Yes, Madame," I replied sounding like a child knowing that I was about to be scolded.

I stood up and began putting my clothes on as Eddie laid there looking sexy and sad for me all at the same time.

"I'm sorry, Sean. I didn't mean to get you in trouble."

"It's not your fault, Eddie. I didn't do anything I didn't

feel like doing."

"I don't know your mom that well but she seems really upset."

"She is but its okay," I said trying to reassure Eddie and me that everything would be ok.

I finished dressing and went into my mom's bedroom as she sat on her bed waiting for me. I knew she was upset and I wasn't sure how I was going to get out of this. I didn't know whether she was going to knock me upside my head or what so I stood in the doorway of her bedroom.

"Yes, Madame?" I stated feeling guilty.

"Sean, have you lost your mind?" she asked angrily while facing me.

"No."

"Then why would you bring that mess in my home?"

"Ma, I'm sorry and I promise that will never happen again," I said as sorry as I could.

"You're sorry? Do you realize what you just did?"

"Yes," I replied while changing the weight of my body from one leg to the other.

"No, I don't think you do, Sean. You are what you are and you're my son and I'm going to always love you but I don't want that mess in my home. Do you understand?"

I shook my head.

"No, I don't think you do. And on top of that, you just introduced me to him as your brother. You mean to tell me that being gay doesn't give you a conscience as to who you sleep with?"

"No, Ma, it's not like that. I do have a conscience."

"Really, how so, explain to me how you can come in my home and have sex with your own brother?"

I had to admit that it did sound kinda crazy, especially the way my mom had put it so the only thing I could do was explain to her how Eddie and I really met. Even after explaining the whole story, she just looked at me and replied, "So, what would you have done if it was your son that had come out there and saw you doing what you were doing, then what?"

"I don't know," I replied in a whisper.

"You don't know? Look Sean, I know you're a grown man but you really need to be more responsible with this lifestyle of yours. If you're not gonna have more respect for yourself or me, at least have some for your son. He don't need to be involved in any of that. Now, even though he is your son, I took on the responsibility of raising him, so with that being said, I want you and Eddie to leave my house, now!"

"But Ma…"

"Don't 'but Ma me' Sean, just leave," she said, looking at me disapprovingly.

I can't begin to explain how hurt I felt. I'd never done anything to my mom for her to be that upset with me and yes, being a Momma's boy I never thought I could do anything to her that would cause her so much pain. I turned around heading into the living room and as I went by my son's room, I tiptoed in and sat on his bed, just to look at him once again. I felt my eyes watering as I touched his face with my hand.

"Is it time to get up Dad?" he asked still half asleep.

"Naw Lil Man, go on back to sleep," I responded as I leaned down and kissed him on the forehead and went back into the living room to get Eddie so we could leave.

******

The sun was about to come up as we headed back over to Justin's house. I explained to Eddie my mom was upset with me and not him but Eddie still apologized. Truth be told, it wasn't his fault. As I said before, I didn't do anything that I didn't want to do. However, I wished it had not happened because I never wanted to hurt my mom in any way. She was the one person in this world I could always count on and with her being upset with me, I truly felt lost.

This lifestyle has brought me some fun overall but it has

also brought about a lot of pain. People have always argued about this lifestyle being a choice or whether one is born that way. And why would anyone in their right mind choose this lifestyle? It didn't make much sense to me but the ironic thing is that I was one of those individuals who had chosen this lifestyle. Therefore, I began thinking, *what would my life be like if I had remained straight?*

Eddie tried to have a conversation with me the whole way to Justin's, but I really wasn't in the mood to talk. It's funny; I wasn't in the mood to do anything. I was tired but I knew I wouldn't be able to sleep because my brain wouldn't stop thinking. I didn't feel like talking, what was there to talk about? I eventually came to the conclusion that I just wanted to be alone so that I could sort out my own thoughts but where could I go to be alone?

"I see Justin is still home," Eddie said as we pulled into his driveway.

"Hmmm, it's almost eight in the morning. He should be at work by now," I replied getting out of the car, wondering if there was something wrong.

Eddie opened the door with the key that Justin had given him and we saw Justin out in the kitchen cooking breakfast.

"Bout time you guys showed up," Justin said sounding happy to see us.

"Why aren't you at work?" I asked.

"Wow, no 'good morning'?"

"Good morning, Justin," Eddie and I replied in unison as we both gave him a hug.

"That's better. Are you guy's hungry?" Justin asked.

"I am," Eddie replied taking a seat at the kitchen table.

"What about you, Sir?" Justin inquired.

"Naw, not really."

"Well, I took the day off and besides, I have some good news for you that might give you an appetite," Justin teased.

"I'm listening," I replied taking a seat at the kitchen

table.

"I spoke to Captain Randall, your old CO and informed him about your court hearing and that I was able to get a 30 day contingency."

"And? What did you tell him for?" I asked becoming angry.

"Calm down, Sir. I told him because I knew you had to go back to Hawaii this Sunday. So, I figured as opposed to you having to leave and come back in a few weeks, I would ask Captain Randall if he would just allow you to stay here at Fort Meade under a Temporary Duty assignment."

"What did he say?" I asked feeling a little better bout having time to spend at home and get my mom to hopefully forgive me.

"He said he would consider it but wanted to meet with you first," Justin said shrugging his shoulders.

"Sounds like a good idea, Sean. I would meet with him if I was you," Eddie stated while grubbing down his food.

"When does he wanna meet?" I asked.

"This Friday at noon."

"Did he say why he wanted to meet with me?"

"No."

"Hmmm, I wonder what he's up to?" I said nibbling on some bacon Justin had just placed on the table.

"Why you say that," Eddie asked.

"What you don't know Eddie is that Captain Randall and Jamaal were the main ones trying to get my ass out of the military because of my sexual preference."

"Oh, I see, so why would he try to help you now?" Eddie asked looking at me.

"Exactly. Look, I have some business to take care of. I'm going upstairs, taking a quick shower and heading out. You guys have fun, a'ight?" I hugged them both and whispered in Eddie's ear, "Don't tell anyone we are related." He nodded.

******

After a quick shower and changing clothes, I jumped in the car and headed back towards Baltimore. Not sure where I was going to wind up but I did want to stop by my in-law's so I could spend some time with my baby girl. Fortunately, Venus' father's car was parked out front so I knew they were home. I parked behind my father-in-law's car and proceeded to the front door to ring the bell.

"Hey, Sean, I heard you were home," my mother-in-law stated as she opened the door for me.

"Yeah, Ma, I had some unfinished business I had to take care of, so I had to come back. Ah, is Lil V here?" I asked standing in the hallway.

"Hold on, let me get your dad," she replied walking out into the kitchen.

Go get dad, I thought to myself. I didn't ask for him, I just wanted to see my baby girl.

"Hey, Sean, how you doing?" my father-in-law asked.

"I'm good, is Lil V here?"

"Why don't we go into the living room and have a talk," he stated as though he was giving me an order.

"Okay," I replied trying to keep my cool.

"Well son, there's been a lot of talk since you've been gone and I don't like any of it," he replied sitting down on his favorite lazy boy chair.

"And what's that, Sir?" I responded taking a seat on his couch.

"Sean, I have always treated you like a son, haven't I?
"Yes Sir."

"There's no easy way for me to say this so I'm just going to say it. There's been a lot of talk about your sexuality around the church and this court hearing you filed against Mr. Lomax. Do you know he is one of the head Deacons at our church, son?"

"Yes, I do know that. How could I not? I've been a

member of that church for the past five years or so," I replied becoming angry.

"Well, Sean it's like this, your mother-in-law and I don't want you here. We are a very religious family and we don't go for that homosexual lifestyle that you lead."

"Excuse me? I personally don't care what you go for; I'm just here to see my baby girl."

"I'm sorry son, I can't let that happen. I don't want my granddaughter growing up around a father that's gay."

"So, you think you can just take my daughter away from me?" I asked angrily as I stood up with my fists balled and nostrils flaring.

"Honey, should I call the police?" my so-called mother-in-law asked as she peeked into the living room.

"The police? Yeah, call the muthafuckin police. Y'all have my daughter here and won't let me see her. Yes, call the dayum police," I yelled.

"No honey, there will be no need for that. Now will it, Sean?" my father-in-law asked while showing a glock tucked into the front of his pants.

"So, you gonna shoot me now?" I asked not believing what I was seeing and hearing from these church people who welcomed me into their home and treated me like a son.

"No son, I don't want to but I will defend my family against anyone who wants to harm them, including you."

"I'm not trying to do anything but see my daughter. Where is my daughter?" I yelled while standing over top of him.

"Ah son, I think you better leave now. Don't make me do anything you will regret!" He cautioned while aiming his glock right at my forehead.

The anger in me was so strong that I could barely breathe. How dare these people think they could just take my daughter from me, let alone think that I would be an unfit father based on my sexuality? I calmed down and decided to leave because I was definitely going to have Justin file papers to get my daughter back. And to think I was trying to do the right thing and let them raise her based on the fact that they lost their own daughter. They wanted to play hard ball, fine with me. So, as I left I replied, "I will be back to get my daughter for good."

I jumped in the car and began driving with no destination in sight; just drove until I was too tired to drive any longer. In all honesty, I felt like my world was crashing down on me and the weight of it was too much for me to bear and at that moment I just wanted to die.

Chapter TWENTY-FIVE

I found myself out on Route 40 West driving in circles and I suddenly remembered a high school friend of mine named Scooter who used to sell whatever kinda drugs an addict would want in this area. My plan was to cop some meth, coke, and weed, get a fifth of Gin and find a seedy motel and end my life.

Route 40 West is basically a county area of Baltimore but there was more drug trafficking out here than it was in the inner city. As a result, most of your middle class whites who moved out into the county to get away from the drug wars were beginning to move back into the city. I turned down on Rolling Road and as luck would have it, there was Scooter on the corner, doing his thing.

"Hey, Scooter, w'sup?" I asked as I pulled alongside the curb.

"Yo, Sean my niggah, how's Uncle Sam treating you?" Scooter asked while giving me some dap.

"He acting like a bitch," I responded.

"Yeah man, I feel you. Oh, I heard about your wife, sorry to hear that, bruh," he stated sincerely.

"Thanks man, I appreciate it."

"So, what brings you in my neck of the woods?"

"Just tryna cop some of that good stuff I hear you got."

"Well, my man, you came to the right place," he responded while looking around as though he was paranoid.

"I need to get some meth, coke and some weed, cool?"

"Damn, Sean, all that, didn't know you got down like that, bruh," he replied, giving me all that I asked for with a total price of a buck fifty.

I gave Scooter his money and placed the drugs he had given me in the glove compartment. I gave Scooter some dap and pulled away looking for the first liquor store I could find to get my fifth of Gin. As I continued to drive, I decided to get a room downtown at the Belvedere Hotel where Gabe used to stay and where I found out about Gabe and Venus' private affair. After all, I think that's where all my troubles began so it seemed so right to have it end there. Lawd knows, I just didn't care anymore.

I picked up my fifth of Gin at one of the many liquor stores that lined every corner of the city and parked outside of the Belvedere Hotel. I grabbed the drugs from the glove compartment and placed them in my pocket as I made my way to my death.

"Welcome to the Belvedere Hotel, how may I help you?" the bubbly female clerk asked.

"Yeah, can I get a room for the night?"

"Sure can, let me check the system right quick. Ah, would you like a double or single?"

"Single would be fine."

"Okay Sir, I have one available on the 6th floor and that's $89.99 per night plus tax and that comes to $101.76. How would you like to pay for that?"

I didn't want to pay by credit card because it left a paper trail. I'm not sure why I didn't want a paper trail but watching TV and movies, you learned that whenever you knew you were doing something wrong, you never leave a paper trail. However, after checking my pockets, I didn't have enough cash on me because of the money I gave to Scooter for the drugs he sold me, so I had no choice but to use my Visa credit card.

"Charge, please," I responded while handing my credit card and driver's license to the bubbly hotel clerk.

After checking in and signing a couple of forms and receiving my key, I caught the elevator to my room which was 666, surely a bad sign. I opened the door to my room and stood in the doorway thinking, *this is where it all ends.*

I walked in and locked the door behind me. I turned on the TV set and began taking all of my clothes off. I don't know whether it was the coldness of the room or because I was becoming a little nervous as the chill bumps crept upon my skin. The first thing I decided to do was take a nice hot shower because I didn't want to be found stinking up the place.

After my shower, I draped the white terry cloth towel around my waist, kneeled in front of the bed and began to pray for my soul.

"Dear God, I know it has been a while since I've called upon your name but life has been unbearable for me. I come to you and ask you for forgiveness in taking my own life. I know that taking one's life is the ultimate sin but I just don't know what else to do. Forgive me for my lifestyle and loving another man and if I am wrong for doing so, I pray that you have mercy on my soul. Father, I pray that you continue to bless my Mom and my children and I also pray that one day they will forgive me." I began to feel the tears well up in my eyes as I kneeled there feeling sorry for myself and my family.

"I've let my family down. My mom is my world and I have caused her to be against me as I feel the whole world has turned their back on me. I know I have made a lot of wrong decisions in life and at this point, I'm just tired…I am soooo tired, Father. Is this a test of my conviction or is this your will? Lord Jesus, as strong as I've been, right now I feel so alone and weak and need your guidance. I've never been one that could pray a prayer that most Christians can pray but Father I do pray from

225

the heart and with sincerity. Lord, if you can hear me, would you send me a sign to let me know you're there?" I waited a minute to see if there would be a sign of some kind but there wasn't one.

"Heavenly Father, regardless as to what happens to me, I just want to say thank you. Thank you for all the blessings and happiness that you have put in my life and those individuals you have put in my life as Guardian Angels. I know that if it hadn't been for you and your Son I wouldn't have made it this far. You have protected me since birth and I say thank you. Thank you for your love, your patience and most of all, thank you for your Mercy. Amen."

I wiped the tears from my eyes, stood up and gathered the drugs out of my pants pocket along with my cell phone. I took a seat at the dinette table and placed the drugs on top, listening to my cell phone buzzing the whole time. I didn't check to see who it was because at this point, it didn't matter. I grabbed one of the glasses from the bathroom and poured my Gin and began rolling me a thick blunt. The Gin burned my throat as it went down but it felt good. I hadn't slept what felt like for days so I couldn't wait to close my eyes for good. I had become tired with life and all of its hurdles and obstacles.

I'd finished rolling the blunt and I couldn't help but laugh considering I had not rolled a blunt before so the blunt itself was kinda fucked up but I was going to smoke it nonetheless. I took my first hit and after choking and gagging for a minute or so, I got used to the smoke as it filled my lungs. I took another shot of Gin and it felt good, real good as it made its way to my liver. After drinking three or four Gins straight and smoking a couple of blunts, all I could feel was my dick getting hard. I sat there with my head hung low looking at my dick and laughing as though someone had just told a joke. Here I wanted to commit suicide and all I could think about was busting a nut.

I leaned back in the chair, pulled the terry cloth towel

from around my waist and closed my eyes. My nature stood up straight looking and wanting attention. I began to caress myself as the thoughts of Eddie giving me head entered my mind.

"Suck that shit boy, do that shit," I said out loud over and over. My body began to tighten as my muscles began to flex and I knew it was just a matter of time. "Right there Eddie, yeah bruh, feels so good, dayum niggah." And just like that, my nut shot out of me with a vengeance.

Maybe it knew it was going to be my last but whatever the reason, it shot up and landed a huge puddle on my chest. I stood up to go into the bathroom to clean myself off but suddenly I began to laugh hysterically about Eddie being my brother. I laughed so hard that my sides began to hurt as I tried to crawl my way into the bathroom. I finally made it to the bathroom and as I stood there trying to wash the nut off my chest, I began thinking about my son and daughter and I then started to cry.

Methodically, I returned to the dinette table and poured another shot of Gin as my tears continued to flow. Through watery eyes I prepared my meth and coke, for I needed something stronger because the pain I felt was literally killing me and I just wanted it to be over. I gulped down my glass of Gin and began slicing up my coke. As I've seen on TV, I lined up the coke on the table and rolled up a dollar bill and began snorting line after line. I've never snorted coke before but it was so strong that not only did it burn my nose but also caused me to fall off the chair. The crazy thing was I felt no pain and if I hadn't noticed that I was on the floor, I wouldn't have known that I had fallen.

The buzzing of my cell phone kept going off and it was driving me crazy, "Would someone answer that dayum phone?" I yelled out loud as I struggled to get off the floor as it continued to spin beneath me.

"Dag Sean, get it together, bruh." I heard someone say. The voice startled me that I found myself crawling into bathroom to hide from it. "Yo Sean, what you doing, bruh?" The more I heard the voice, the more it began to sound like Thomas.

"Yo, Thomas, whey you at?" I asked then peeked out of the bathroom.

"Over here Sean, why you hiding and shit?"

I stumbled out of the bathroom and looked around the room but no one was there. My body felt cold and I began to shiver as I walked over to the dinette table and took my seat so that I could try out this thing called meth, better known as crank, tweak or ice. I tried pouring another glass of Gin but the glass on the table wouldn't stop going in circles so I held the bottle up to my mouth and downed as much as I could in one big swallow. "Sean, you need to pray, man." I heard another voice say.

"I already prayed and you see where it got me, I'm tired of praying. Hell, why don't you pray," I spat as I looked around the room.

I didn't have a pipe to put the meth in so I crushed it up as fine as I could and began snorting it through the rolled up dollar bill and waited for it to take over my body with its affect.

"Will someone answer that Goddam phone!" I yelled.

"Sean, wake up!" I heard someone say.

Within minutes of taking the meth, I found myself on the floor sprawled out as my eyes kept rolling to the back of my head. "Sean, wake up!" I heard the voice say again. "No, I don't wanna wake up, leave me alone. This is where it all began so it might as well end here," I mumbled as I felt my body go limp and begin to drift away. I felt no pain and all I could remember is seeing a bright light ahead of me and I knew I was finally going home.

Chapter TWENTY-SIX

When I opened my eyes I expected to see and hear angels singing and giving praise to our Heavenly Father but that's not what I saw. I was lying in someone's bed and as I looked around the room, the surroundings were familiar but I couldn't place them. My head was pounding so hard that I couldn't think straight. I tried to sit up but couldn't. I laid there looking up at the ceiling wondering where I was and how I got there. I'm not sure how long I had been out but it was still light outside so I couldn't have been out long.

"Hello," I said out loud hoping to get someone's attention.

"Well, sleepy head, you finally woke up, huh?"

I tried to raise myself from the bed but the pain in my head was throbbing so bad that all I could do was lower my head back on the pillows. "Whose there?" I asked holding my head.

"Sean, what do you mean whose there?"

"Gabe, what are you doing here?" I asked as he leaned over me.

"This is where I live Sean. Now, how are you?" Gabe

asked as he placed a cold pack on my forehead.

"How did I get here?" I asked sounding confused.

"I brought you here because from what I could see, you were trying to kill yourself," he replied sounding a little upset.

"But how did you know where I was?"

"I have been calling you all day and when you finally answered the phone, I couldn't make out what you were saying. You kept saying something about answering the dayum phone. So I knew something was wrong and I asked where you were and you said something about being at the Belvedere Hotel and wanting to end it where it all began. I then checked down at the front desk and saw you had gotten a room there on Wednesday afternoon."

"What day is today?" I asked groggily.

"Friday morning, why?"

"What time is it?"

"7:35."

"Oh shit, I gotta go," I said trying to get up from the bed.

"No, Sean, I don't think that's a good idea," Gabe replied while holding me down on the bed.

"You don't understand, Gabe; I have to meet with CO Randall at noon today so that I can be granted a TDY assignment until my court hearing later this month."

"Well, look, you still have a few hours so why don't you take a hot shower and I'll make you some breakfast."

"I don't have time to do all that, I still have to go and get my uniform on before I meet with Captain Randall."

"Can I call someone that can bring your uniform here?"

"Hmmm, where's my phone, I'll call Justin," I replied looking around for my phone.

"I put it in your pants pocket, I'll get it for you," Gabe replied as he found my phone and handed it to me.

I searched through my phone looking for Justin's number but my sight was so blurry that I could hardly see. I handed the phone back to Gabe and asked him to dial Justin's number for me. Justin answered on the 2nd ring.

"Sir, where are you?" Justin asked screaming into the phone.

"Yo Justin, stop screaming man, I'm right here," I responded while holding my head.

"Where is here, Sir?"

"I'm at Gabe's."

"Do you know what today is?" Justin asked as if I didn't know.

"Yeah Justin, I know today is Friday. That's why I'm calling; I need you to bring me my uniform so that I can meet with Captain Randall at noontime."

"Well, I'm glad you hadn't forgotten. What's his address?"

I gave Justin Gabe's address and decided to take a long hot shower knowing that it would take Justin at least an hour to get here since it was morning rush hour traffic. After my shower, I threw on one of Gabe's robes and walked into the kitchen and took a seat and watched as he fixed me breakfast.

"So, I've been here for the last day and a half, huh?"

"Yes and I was a perfect gentleman as I nursed you back to health," Gabe replied with a chuckle.

"I guess I should be grateful, huh?" I responded while swallowing some orange juice Gabe had poured in a glass for me.

"Yes, you should be and contrary to what you believe or think, there are people here that still love you."

At that moment I realized that Gabe was one of those guardian angels that I had thanked God for putting in my life and once again, he had used Gabe to come to my rescue and allowed me another day to live. And as unhappy as I felt, God had blessed me with another day just to find a way to be happy. A true sign...

"Thank you Gabe, thank you for saving my life and I understand why you left Hawaii," I replied while hugging him.

"A'ight a'ight, cut out all the drama," Gabe stated while slapping me on the back of my head as he walked away and began putting food on the table.

For a brief moment we sat at the table eating in silence. I couldn't believe how hungry I was because I was eating everything in sight. Gabe just looked at me from time to time and laughed. The saying must be true that once you come from an inch of death, everything is better. Food tastes better, the sun shines better and hopefully sex will feel better. I also began to realize how blessed I am and how thankful I am just to be alive. How can I possibly make a change in my life to be happy if I'm not here? All the thoughts that came into my head seemed so much clearer than before.

My thoughts were interrupted by a knock at the door. I knew that must have been Justin. Gabe got up to answer the door.

"Hey, Gabe, I would appreciate it if you didn't mention any of this," I asked as he walked by me.

"And why would I wanna do that, Sean?" he asked as though he was surprised that I asked him that.

I suddenly realized that I should go to the door as well since Justin and Gabe never really met. Of course they know each other based upon what I have told them about each other but never truly met in person.

"Hello, you must be Justin," Gabe asked as he opened the door.

"Yes I am, is Sean here?"

"Hey, Justin, thanks for bringing my uniform. Hey, Eddie, I didn't know you were coming with Justin," I replied as both Justin and Eddie walked in.

"And why would I not Sean, we were worried about you. Why didn't you call?" Eddie asked sounding upset.

"Awe, y'all worry too much. Gabe, this is Justin and Eddie. Justin and Eddie, this is Gabriel, Gabe for short," I replied introducing one another.

232

"Nice to finally meet you guys, are y'all hungry? I can make some breakfast if you like," Gabe responded trying to be cordial.

"No thanks," both Justin and Eddie said in unison.

"Well, Sir, it's almost 10 a.m., don't you think you should be getting dressed?" Justin asked as he looked at his watch.

"Yeah, you're right. Why don't you guys have a seat and get acquainted and I'll be right out."

As I began to put my uniform on, I felt good. I had a new outlook on life. Today was going to be a good day. I was going to get my TDY assignment, I was going to make amends with my mom, spend more time with Lil Man and have Justin file papers to get my lil girl back. As the saying goes, a problem is only a problem until there's a solution and I had many solutions to make.

After dressing, I took one last look in Gabe's full length mirror and I couldn't help but laugh at a saying Cameron used to say, "I am too phyne to be dead."

******

Since my vision was still a little blurred, Justin volunteered to drive me to the base to meet with Captain Randall and Eddie came along for the ride. And not a moment too soon, because I walked in the room as Justin was asking Gabe, which Boy was he? Gabe just looked at him like he was crazy. One day I will have to tell Gabe about myself.

"Sir, so are you going to tell us what you've been up to for the last couple of days?" Justin asked while trying to start conversation.

"Had to take care of some business, that's all," I responded.

"Isn't Gabe the guy who went to Hawaii with you?" Justin inquired.

"Yes, what about it?"

"Wow, Poppy, I didn't know you brought someone to Hawaii with you," Eddie stated.

"Oh, you didn't know Eddie? Mr. Gabe is the minister that's so in love with Sir," Justin replied being catty.

Justin could be such a bitch sometimes but he's valuable to have around. He's good looking, good in bed, and he's a superb lawyer. I realized that you have to take the good with the bad when dealing with friends as well as with sex partners. I also realized that in his own way, Justin was insecure. I guess being the only white Boy out of the bunch would cause that but truth be told, I wouldn't change a thing about him. He means well and he makes me laugh.

"Earth to Sean, Earth to Sean," Eddie stated trying to get my attention.

"Yeah what?"

"Are you with us?" Justin asked.

"Yeah, I'm here, just thinking, that's all," I replied looking out the window as we pulled into base.

"Have you thought what you were going to say to Captain Randall?" Justin asked.

"Not really, what's there to think about? I don't know what he wants or what his questions are going to be, so the only thing that I can do is respond honestly, right?"

"Oh Lawd," Eddie chuckled.

As we were about to make a right onto Llwelyn Avenue, this car came out of nowhere and stopped in front of us.

"What the hell is his problem?" Justin snapped.

"Fuck him, pull around him Justin, that asshole," Eddie responded.

"Oh fuck, that ain't who I think it is; is it?" Justin asked trying to get a better look.

"Who you talking about?" Eddie asked.

"A'ight, Sir, just be cool. Don't do anything we'll regret," Justin replied as I already started getting out of the car.

"Looks like someone need some driving instructions," I

spat as I walked over to the stranger's car.

"Well, well, well, if it isn't Mr. Sean Mathews. How are you enjoying living my life?"

"Excuse you, your life?" I asked as I stood next to the driver side window with my fists balled, waiting for him to make one false move.

"Ah, come on Sean, you know what I mean. Don't you, Sir?" he replied with a huge laugh.

"Shouldn't you be in prison?" I asked sarcastically.

"I've committed no crime, why would I be there?"

"Murder, asshole," I spat.

"Wow, Sean, haven't you ever heard of the term, self-defense?"

"Yo, muthafucka, why don't you move this piece of shit out the way?" Eddie yelled while walking up to the car.

"Damn, Sean, I see you gotta phyne little pitbull here. Where did you get him from?"

"Don't worry about where he got me from. You need to go fuck off somewhere." Eddie was pissed.

"Yo Sean, get yo Boy man, I really can't take him too serious because his lips making my dick hard," Jamaal spat while laughing.

Before I had a chance to realize what was going on, Eddie had grabbed Jamaal out of the car by his collar and had him down on the ground punching him in the face.

"I suggest the next time you talk to someone whose lips make your dick hard, you make sure you're man enough to back it up. Punk bitch," Eddie shot back.

I was so stunned that I just stood there and laughed hysterically. I couldn't believe what Eddie had done. I looked over at Justin in the car and his mouth was wide open as though he couldn't believe what Eddie had done either. I grabbed Eddie off of Jamaal because people were driving by and began to stop. I didn't want a scene nor did I want any of the MP's to drive by and write out a report. I got Eddie back in the car and we drove off and as I looked back, I noticed Jamaal's license plate that read, *Milbru4u.* And it all began to make sense.

We pulled up in front of Captain Randall's building just a few minutes before noontime. I hopped out of the car while Justin and Eddie waited in the car for me.

"Good afternoon, I'm here to see Captain Randall," I stated talking to the desk clerk.

"Is he expecting you," the desk clerk asked.

"Yes he is, my name is Specialist Mathews."

"Okay, why don't you have a seat and I'll let him know you're here."

I took a seat and waited nervously for Captain Randall as I looked around the office, remembering the times I'd sat in this very chair waiting on my fate, so to speak. The only difference this time is that I really didn't care what Captain Randall thought or did. Either he was going to let me stay or he wasn't and it's not like I didn't have the money to buy another ticket to fly back here anyway. Although, I was hoping to stay so that I could spend time with those who really cared and loved me, not to mention make amends with my mom.

"Specialist Mathews, Captain Randall will see you now," the clerk stated while interrupting my thoughts.

"Thank you," I replied as I entered Captain Randall's office and stood at attention.

"At ease, Specialist Mathews," Captain Randall stated as he looked at me over his glasses.

"Good afternoon, Sir," I replied standing at ease.

"Sean Mathews, it's been a minute. How have you been?"

"I'm good, Sir, and yourself?"

"Same ole, same ole, but what's this I hear about you and a civilian court hearing?" he asked as he took his glasses off and leaned back in his chair while placing his hands behind his head.

"Sir, Yes Sir," I replied nervously.

"Well, Specialist Mathews, don't have me guessing. What is it all about?"

"Well, Sir, it's not that big of a deal. I filed charges against someone who was stalking me, that's all," I responded not wanting to go into details.

"Specialist Mathews, I don't know if you realize it or not but you belong to Uncle Sam. You don't have any business in filing a civilian law suit."

"I understand that Sir, but I felt as though my life was in danger and therefore, I did what anyone in my shoes would have done. Besides, the person that was threatening my life was a civilian."

"Would it have anything to do with this," he responded as he opened his top desk drawer and threw my handbook, "Sir, yes Sir" on his desk in front of me.

"No Sir," I replied somewhat angrily. I knew at that point Captain Randall knew all he wanted to know and this meeting was for his benefit and not mine. I tried my best not to show my anger because I'm sure that's what he wanted so that he could kick me out of the Army for good. I racked my brain wondering how he got my handbook because I had it in my luggage the whole time at Justin's house.

"You know, Specialist Mathews, I read your book and this is some sick shit."

"That's a matter of opinion, Sir," I replied trying to keep my cool and wondering how the hell he got my handbook.

"So, you don't think it's anything wrong with being gay, is that what you're saying?"

"Wrong, according to whom, Sir?"

"Are you gay, Specialist Mathews?"

"I'm sorry, Sir, I'm not able to answer that under the 'Don't Ask Don't Tell' policy."

"Oh, cut the crap Specialist Mathews, you know as well as I do Obama had that whole 'Don't Ask Don't Tell' policy repealed. So spit it out, you're as gay as they come, you and your boy Cameron. And speaking of PFC Jenkins, I guess you going to be walking around in drag pretty soon like he is, huh?"

I knew Captain Randall was just trying to get me angry and the sad thing is that it was working too. The gay community and certain other political groups had given President Obama praise for signing the bill to Repeal the "Don't Ask Don't Tell policy but it had not gone into effect yet. But the so-called heterosexual community was split in their opinion of the new bill and I knew Captain Randall was totally against it and was trying to set my ass up. Therefore, I thought the best thing for me to do was just stand there and take it like a man until he was finished. But the blood in my veins began to boil and I began to perspire profusely as I clenched my fists together.

"Hmmm, that's it, isn't it. You never had a father so I guess you would love just any man that comes along, huh Specialist?"

"Sir, no Sir." I replied angrily.

"Yes, it is, Sean, so why not confess, you're gay, aren't you? How you going to stand in front of me and deny what you are. Isn't that some kind of gay sin?" Captain asked as he stood up and began circling me. "Hmmm Sean, I know you're gay cause you smell gay," he laughed while he continued to antagonize me. "Oh, I know what it is; you're gay because your mom didn't know how to teach you to be a man, that's what it is. Damn it, Sean, just admit it so we can get out of here, if you're gay, you're gay, what's the big deal? Are you gay?" he yelled in my face.

This muthafucka here was really pissing me the fuck off and I had had enough of his high and mighty military bullshit. So, I clicked my heels together, came to attention as my nostrils flared and the sweat poured from my face and eyeballed him the way he had eyeballed me and shouted, "Sir, Yes Sir!"

Also By Mike Warren

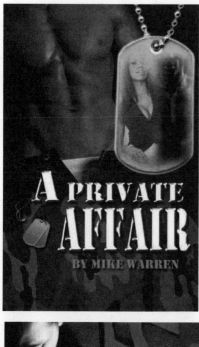

PART 1

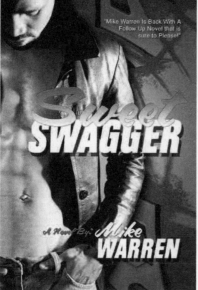

PART 2

LCB BOOK TITLES

See More Titles At
www.lifechangingbooks.net

ORDER FORM

MAIL TO:
PO Box 423
Brandywine, MD 20613
301-362-6508

FAX TO:
301-579-9913

Ship to:	
Address:	
Date:	Phone:
Email:	
City & State:	Zip:

Make all money orders and cashiers checks payable to: **Life Changing Books**

Qty.	ISBN	Title	Release Date	Price
	0-9741394-2-4	Bruised by Azarel	Jul-05	$ 15.00
	0-9741394-7-5	Bruised 2: The Ultimate Revenge by Azarel	Oct-06	$ 15.00
	0-9741394-3-2	Secrets of a Housewife by J. Tremble	Feb-06	$ 15.00
	0-9741394-6-7	The Millionaire Mistress by Tiphani	Nov-06	$ 15.00
	1-934230-99-5	More Secrets More Lies by J. Tremble	Feb-07	$ 15.00
	1-934230-98-7	Young Assassin by Mike G.	Mar-07	$ 15.00
	1-934230-95-2	A Private Affair by Mike Warren	May-07	$ 15.00
	1-934230-94-4	All That Glitters by Ericka M. Williams	Jul-07	$ 15.00
	1-934230-93-6	Deep by Danette Majette	Jul-07	$ 15.00
	1-934230-96-0	Flexin & Sexin Volume 1	Jun-07	$ 15.00
	1-934230-92-8	Talk of the Town by Tonya Ridley	Jul-07	$ 15.00
	1-934230-89-8	Still a Mistress by Tiphani	Nov-07	$ 15.00
	1-934230-91-X	Daddy's House by Azarel	Nov-07	$ 15.00
	1-934230-88-X	Naughty Little Angel by J. Tremble	Feb-08	$ 15.00
	1-934230847	In Those Jeans by Chantel Jolie	Jun-08	$ 15.00
	1-934230855	Marked by Capone	Jul-08	$ 15.00
	1-934230820	Rich Girls by Kendall Banks	Oct-08	$ 15.00
	1-934230839	Expensive Taste by Tiphani	Nov-08	$ 15.00
	1-934230782	Brooklyn Brothel by C. Stecko	Jan-09	$ 15.00
	1-934230669	Good Girl Gone bad by Danette Majette	Mar-09	$ 15.00
	1-934230804	From Hood to Hollywood by Sasha Raye	Mar-09	$ 15.00
	1-934230707	Sweet Swagger by Mike Warren	Jun-09	$ 15.00
	1-934230677	Carbon Copy by Azarel	Jul-09	$ 15.00
	1-934230723	Millionaire Mistress 3 by Tiphani	Nov-09	$ 15.00
	1-934230715	A Woman Scorned by Ericka Williams	Nov-09	$ 15.00
	1-934230685	My Man Her Son by J. Tremble	Feb-10	$ 15.00
	1-924230731	Love Heist by Jackie D.	Mar-10	$ 15.00
	1-934230812	Flexin & Sexin Volume 2	Apr-10	$ 15.00
	1-934230748	The Dirty Divorce by Miss KP	May-10	$ 15.00
	1-934230758	Chedda Boyz by CJ Hudson	Jul-10	$ 15.00
	1-934230766	Snitch by VegasClarke	Oct-10	$ 15.00
	1-934230693	Money Maker by Tonya Ridley	Oct-10	$ 15.00
	1-934230774	The Dirty Divorce Part 2 by Miss KP	Nov-10	$ 15.00
	1-934230170	The Available Wife by Carla Pennington	Jan-11	$ 15.00
	1-934230774	One Night Stand by Kendall Banks	Feb-11	$ 15.00
	1-934230278	Bitter by Danette Majette	Feb-11	$ 15.00
	1-934230299	Married to a Balla by Jackie Davis	Mar-11	$ 15.00
		Total for Books		$

Shipping Charges (add $4.95 for 1-4 books*) $

Total Enclosed (add lines) $

* Prison Orders- Please allow up to three (3) weeks for delivery.

Please Note: We are not held responsible for returned prison orders. Make sure the facility will receive books before ordering.

*Shipping and Handling of 5-10 books is $6.95, please contact us if your order is more than 10 books. (301)362-6508